What do you see?

THE LIBRARY OF PAMAT

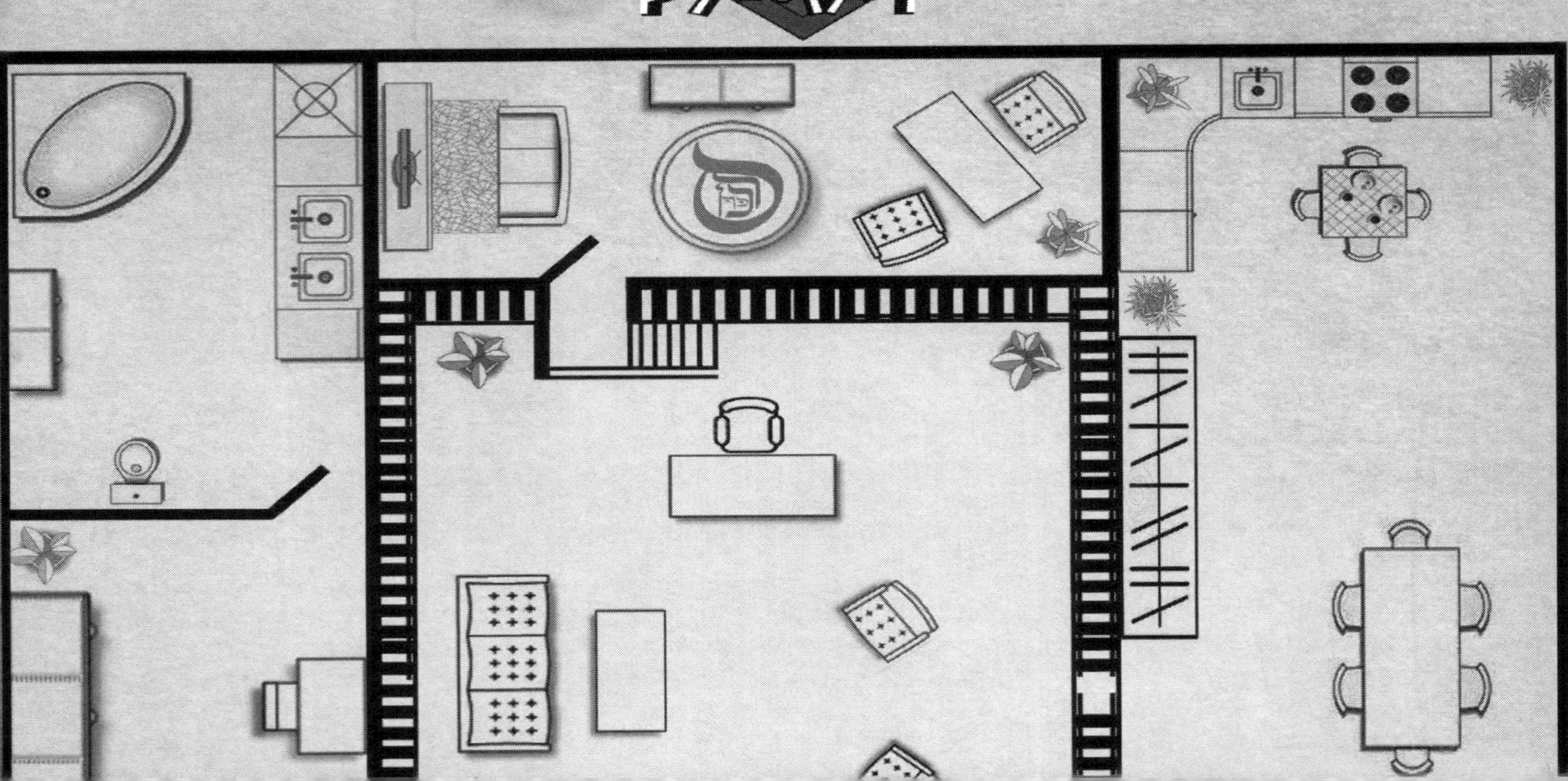

{A reader can never be a thief}

Author's contact

notgraytruman@gmail.com

First and foremost, All gratitude to God for giving me the will and power to follow my passion

All Thanks to my beloved parents and family

A special thank you to all my beta readers: Gabbey, Rayenne, Zoe, Nadia, Salma, Chelsea and Ruth

Last but not least, all thanks to everyone who believed in me

Content

Hello curious felines;

We are uncertainly certain that all of you humans know the story of Icarus; how he was stupid enough to approach the sun and got his waxen wings melt by its apricity - bla bla bla. But, what if that featherless chicken survived?

Before you start reading to snoop on what really happened, we want to offer you a challenge. Agreed? You continued reading so obviously you do.

We left a handful of puzzles inside this book; riddles, codes and hidden messages. Your task is to find and solve them all to reveal this book's secrets. You will find untold information about some of the characters, future events in the book and real life, other things too. It all depends on how sharp you are.

7.15.15.4 – 12.21.3.11

CHAPTER ONE
CHOOSE OR DIE

1326 BC – Somewhere above the gray leaden skies of Crete, a m**a**n with wings of wax plummeted unwillingly, piercing through the dense clouds to create a wide r**i**ng of clarity, followed by burning pebbles like lava, as the wind molted his melted feathers to s**m**ithereens of dusty ashes, leaving a feeble trail of black.

Drowsy, he used his injured arm to cover his face before slamming into the **s**urface of the sea. He tensed, bracing for impact - - But he felt nothing! Perplexed, he opened his eyes to see his carcass floating one foot above his wavy reflection.

A melted piece of wax slid down over his damaged wing and splashed into the water.

CHAPTER ONE

"Sheesh!"

The water beneath him wobbled. **S**oon after, slime-like, it rose, forming a bubble of foam, one that coiled the wounded man, to eventually absorb him down to an unknown fate.

The man couldn't perceive the weight of his cadaver nor the motion of his limbs, only a mixture of warmth and chill wrapping his skin. **H**is mind bared one baffled thought:

'*Am I drowning?*'

He curved into a foetal position while **s**pinning slowly down into darkness. He surrendered to a **d**arker thought:

'*Is this death? This must be it*'

Moments after, he sensed his weak body squeezing out of a liquid embrace and gently landing on a solid ground.

Freed from the slimy bubble, his face fell on a round, bl**a**ck and white carpet; an artistic piece that had a beautiful mermaid with white hair embroidered on its midst. That was before he barfed on it and painted it gr**e**en.

"Cough!"

Bug-eyed, he took a deep and long breath, careless of the reeking smell of puke. The torn angel rested his ri**g**ht cheek on the stained carpet. Faint, he cleared his throat with a series of sour and harsh coughs, while rolling his eyeballs up with his dazed vision.

All he could see was that the ceiling of this place was too distant from the floor, and to his knowledge, a ceiling that high could only exist in a castle or something as such; however, that only gave him an idea, and not an answer. Also, he couldn't flee the doubts that he might have met his doom, and this was probably the afterlife, or one of its unknown stages.

He placed both palms on the floor beneath his shoulders, enjoying the soft fibre tickling his fingers, a satisfying sensation that gave him a boost to hardly push his body up after a croaky sigh.

Several bones cracked low while he rose. He squeezed his lips shut to suppress an agonizing groan but didn**’t** pause.

“Umm!”

He panted pai**n**fully when taking a kneeling posture, easing down his pain through a few heavy breaths. Glazed, the winged man dropped his exha**u**sted hands palms up, thus rested his chin on his chest, **c**oughing spits of blood on his naked skin.

Even with his terrible condition, his instinct drove him to inspect before he could lower his guard. He rotated his head slightly to the right, peeking through his wet and lazy eyelashes, but his vision was still foggy. Therefore, he forced his hand up to rub his eyes, pushing the water out of the wa**y**. Not the best sight, but clear enough to observe his surroundings.

The afterlife as he thought was a vast room with a wooden dark floor, many rounded carpets of unique designs, outspread all over the place, nine if he could count them. On his left, two chairs of polished red-wood and matte-black leather. On the right, an **a**zure door centred with a golden dragon emblem, one that thr**o**bbed with a motion of brightness that came from within. While the strings of its wraith-beam flashed yellow lights on colourful lines on both sides. When the man focused his vision for a better look, he saw that the blurry lines were scrolls and books of various colours and sizes; the wall itself was a bookshelf, and so were the others. The ceiling too; it was a horizontal bookshelf.

‘*But how come the books in it aren’t falling on my head,*’ the man thought

While looking up, he crossed fourteen moon-shaped lanterns, floating haphazardly around the book room to illume the entire place.

His tiring panting calmed down as he regained some of his stamina. He looked down to his clutching fists, thus pressed the dripping quiffs off his face to see a long corridor in front of him, one wasn’t there moments ago. It was bright, with endless bookshelves on both sides, topped by an arcade-roof of bricks.

“Could it be the way out of this book room?” Baffled, he mused low

“A library,” corrected a man behind him with a deep voice

Alarmed, the injured man made a sharp turn whilst quickly reaching for his sword, but ended up clutching thin air! The scabbard was there, but not the

(6-8) (14-17) (4-3) (2-4) * (10-9) (15-10) (5-10)

sabre. He locked his scowling **e**y**e**s on a stealthy man; on a far vintage desk, sitting inside a body of black smoke. He was wearing black from the neck down. Also, a black mask that covered his upper face, one with nine **t**humping eyes, six glowing-white, two dark-**red** on the sides of his forehead and a big cri**m**son one on the centre.

All nine ey**e**s kept moving in different directions except for the crimson one. It was fixed on his guest.

"It is a library - - young Icarus," the man in black stated with a soft tone, hinting that he knew his guest's name, while tapping his fingers on the emerged edge of the desk. The low drumming tune was slow and somehow irritating.

"Is this what you're missing?" he asked calmly with a smile, holding Icarus's **s**word from the end of its pommel with two fingers, as if it were displeasing to be held properly. **H**e swung the sword left and right like **a** c**l**ock's pendulum.

"No violence please, let us not be - - uncivilized," he added, elongating the nail of his middle finger into a sharp claw. He used it to gently clank the sword, turning the weapon into a fading mist.

Icarus's hands squeezed into fists, raising them to his jaw level, **m**entally ready to receive any attack, but his quiv**e**ring body showed otherwise.

"Who are **y**ou - - Gois?" Asked Icarus, cautiously sliding his knees back while his eyes fixed on the p**o**tential threat, the one he assumed was a Gois. That was what his people called mages; humans who can use magic naturally. The reason behind him acting warily was that many were classified as non-human, placed side by side with d**e**mon**s** and fiends.

"I'm not afraid of you," said Icarus in a defiant tone, creasing his forehead. Not out of anger, but a way to intimidate his opponent.

The **m**age smiled, surprised. He used his pointy claw to gently scratch his chin whilst processing Icarus's words.

"Mm! Gois!" he hissed, shrinking his claw back to a **r**egular nail, if you can call his scarlet sharp nails regular.

"Not being afraid of a Gois is quiet logical. After all, the likes of **y**ou are immune to magic," he stated in a pensive tone, thrusting both hands inside his trousers' pockets. He spoke in a way as if he wanted Icarus to know he was **f**amiliar with his nature.

_ (10-2) (14-15) * (2-7) (3-3) (7-4) * (17-1) (12-11) (4-6) (1-12)

CHAPTER ONE

"Well, Gois - - have a delightful tune when spoken, but we prefer to be called Gray - - Gray Trueman," the man introduced himself with a slight grin, standing straight, displaying no hostility, at least according to him.

"The man who saved your l**i**fe," he claimed, widening his smile, as if he were waiting for a '*thank you,*' only to be ignored by Icarus, for he was too concentrated on finding a way to flee.

First, he glanced at that azu**r**e door on his left, but quickly switched to the other direction, for he was ignorant of what's hidden behind the golden dragon, and he wasn't ready to ris**k** going deeper into the rabbit's hole. Nothing on his right but more bookshelves, and as he turned back round Gra**y**, he glimpsed a black door behind him; however, he knew he **c**ouldn't run past the man in black in his bilious state. Even with his immunity to magic, fighting a mage was a d**e**ath sentence without the necessary measures.

Gray was following Icarus's trail of sight, looking left when he did, and right. He then gave him a blunt look.

"Are you looking for something? Gratitude perhaps!" A sarcastic Gray jested, showing no expression of sardonicus.

Icarus's glares became more aggressive after that provocative comment.

A disappointed Gray shook his head no, locking all nine eyes on Icarus.

"A '*Thank you*' will do," he grumbled, cross**ing** his legs while resting his back on the desk behind him.

"Or how about - - I will serve you for the rest of my **l**ife," he added in a flat and mocking tone.

"Saved me you say!" Icarus jeered, trying to stand, careless of all the pain he endured. Like a fierce wolf. '*Survive first, and leave licking your wounds for later,*' that was the idea.

Icarus spat on the floor while untying the scabbard off his belt.

"So why do you reek of killing intent?" He fumed, gathering every ounce of strength with long breaths, and without warning, he threw the scabbard at Gray. Only to see it dissolve into ashes halfway, but there was no time to be startled. He bolted into the long corridor behind him. It seemed like the right

and safer path to go for, but the moment he stepped in, the corridor **n**arrowed as if the passage itself elongated.

"Poof!"

A body of heavy dark fog exploded underneath his foot like a land mine, filling his surroundings. Still, he ignored the confusion and the pain and continued ahead.

With one arm guarding his face, and the other swinging upfront to clear his way, Icarus kept pushing forward through the fume until he grasped a lig**h**t. And when he reached the bright window, Icarus plunged through with no procrastination, fleeing the prison of smoke.

Icarus got his weak body off ground. Canine-like, he settled on his elbows and knees, coughing drops of blood on a black and white carpet with a white hair mermaid co**ve**red in vomit. However, he didn't notice that, for he could barely keep his eyes open.

He stoo**d** on his shivering legs and staggered for a few steps before falling on his knees again. You guessed right, he found himself back in front of Gray.

Opening the right side of his mouth wider than the other, Gray clanged his right fangs against each other in a d**r**amatic tempo while imitating a Be**e**tho**ve**n piece.

"Why? You're damaging that poor body of yours," a confounded Gray hinted, motioning to the burns Icarus had on his sides and back.

"Shut up," a dizzy Icarus grunted

"You shut up. We don't want these wounds to rot and reek all over the place," a tranquil Gray said, taking his hands out of his pocket. He looked up to a bronze holed box hanged on the ceiling.

"Kara, come here," he called loudly

"Eek eek!" sharp chatters came from the box as it moved.

Icarus looked up to glimpse a movement through a hole in the cube's base, and as one lantern floated closer, he glanced at big black eyes staring back at him, glowing in reaction to the moon lantern.

In a moment, something teal rapidly leaped out of that hole onto Gray's shoulder, then behind his back.

Seconds after, a small hand rested on Gray's **sh**oulder, followed by a shy teal monkey-like creature peeking from behind.

"Don't be afraid dear, go treat his wounds," said Gray, patting Kara's head, not noticing the aghast look on Icarus's face when he saw Kara.

"A Kirada!" Icarus sneered aggressively, tightening a fist in Kara's direction as a threat.

He was familiar with her kind. Kiradas are one of the smartest dark fiends; they're also known of imitating h**u**mans, especially in combat, and unlike other fiends, Kiradas are social creatures the same as human. They have organiz**ed** communities and even a task structure, which makes them more dangerous as a group. Therefore, Kara's lovable and fluffy appearance wasn't enough for Icarus to let his guard down.

"If that thing approaches me - - **I** will end its life, then yours," glowering, he snarled, scaring Kara away. She jumped off Gray's back and ran behind the desk.

"Enough," yelled an upset Gray with a thick and **p**enetrating voice; a shout that stupefied Icarus and made the vellus hair on his nape and shoulders tingle. It was more like a wave of rage than words, one coming from a powerful being.

Gray's white eyes narrowed for seconds. But after seeing the effects of his rage on his guest, he sighed audibly, taking deep breaths to calm down. The man in black moved his hands casually as he spoke in a calm tone:

"You are a Mingan, and your kind can sense hostility - - right?" Gray stepped back closer to Kara, who ran behind his leg and embraced it tightly before she peeked at the Mingan with a scared eye.

Gray's words were correct. Mingans can detect hostility among other things. They are the natural enemy of all fiends - - or any magical creature; with their immunity to magic, overwhelming strength and unique hunting skills, as if the creator himself gave the humans a chance to fight back.

"Do you sense any hostility coming from us__" asked Gray with a croaky voice, patting **Ka**ra's head,

"__or Ka**ra**?"

Icarus opened h**is** eyes wide, thus narrowed them again, **p**e**er**ing hardly to scrutinize them both. **T**he Mingan penetrated the two with his vision. He flinched, confused. Thus did the same thing over a**n**d **o**ver, as if he were loo**ki**ng for something but failed to g**ra**sp it.

"But - - but the killing intent__" a puzzle**d** Ic**a**rus stuttered loud then low, rubbing his bleeding nose,

"__It was there - - moments ago"

Gray clapped his hands twice to steer Icarus's attention his way, keeping his palms joined while sp**ea**king.

"That was yours," a serious Gray clarified, separating his hands to manifest a sphere of concentrated black smoke in between.

T**he** two-hand sized ball of darkness arrowed towards Icarus's wary face. Even with that excessive speed, his reflexes forced his arms up to build a wall between his face and the sphe**r**e, thinking it was an assault, but the black spherule stopped one foot away.

Icarus peeked through a window between his lifted arms to see a **s**word's pommel emerging out of the smoke, a familiar one.

"Clearly - - not ours," Gray added, addressing the sword and the killing intent Icarus claimed he sensed.

The Mingan recognized the grip of his blade. He stared at Gray first, cautiously placing his quivering finger on its end. He tapped it twice before sliding his hand down to grab it.

"Sigh!" Icarus unsheathed his sword out of the sphere with one pull then held the blade vertically, looking at his aggressive features on the perfectly polished steel like a mirror. He then stared at Gray briefly.

"Apologies," said Icarus with a calm tone, putting his sword back into the torn scabbard. It took another moment of silence before he continued with an admission of gratitude:

"And - - thank you for saving my life"

(5-4) (15-1) * (17-5) (12-4) (4-10) (19-13)

Icarus is genuinely a kind person, but the trauma he went through forced him to be hostile and over protective. He also had an awful experience with a Gois before, still, he wasn't the kind that judges the whole based on an individual. Not to forget the tolerance he found from Gray, but that bids the question, why was he helping the Mingan?

Gray's mouth curved into a **s**mile.

"You are very welcome," he said with a silvery tone, thus nodded his head to Kara, who ran hesitantly to one of the wing-chairs, keeping her cautious eyes on Icarus. She pushed the chair hardly closer to Icarus.

"Eek eek!" Kara panted heavily, thus noticed she was too close to the man who threatened her life minutes ago. A spooked Kara squeaked, running back to Gr**a**y.

Gra**y** chuckled from Kara's behaviour, walking to the other wing-chair. He sat down, placing one leg over the other, one Ka**r**a used to jump onto his lap.

"Have a seat," he said

Icarus kept his eyes on Kara. His fixed eyes displayed his disapproval on the **way** Gray was tr**ea**ting a fiend. To a Mingan, fiends are only there to be hunted, not taken as pets. But Gray is no Mingan. He scratched Kara's belly with one hand while using the other to pat her head.

"Beautiful creatures__" Gray said, admiring his furry companion,

"__and brilliant, aren't they?" He added, trying to loosen Icarus's tension, for he didn't need a Mingan instinct to see that his guest was having malicious thoughts about his Kara.

"Not the ones I encountered," Icarus cringed, placing a stained hand on the chair offered to him. Numb enough to not discern the pain his torn carcass was bearing, he stood up on quivering legs, then dropped on the chair.

"Ah!" he leaned back, resting his head on the soft cushion. At that moment he wished he could simply close his eyes and sleep, but he couldn't risk lowering his guard in the presence of a stranger, let alone a Gois. He took a while to answer.

"Brilliant, yes - - I agree, they are indeed brilliant, in how to kill," said Icarus acerbically, justifying his intimidation by Kara.

"One bite with **the**ir venomous saliva can put down a horse in minutes," said Icarus hoarsely, lookin**g** at Kara whil**e** she tried to **n**o**t** make eye contact out of fear.

"Ven**om**ous saliva you say!" rep**l**i**e**d Gray with an uncertain tone, while faking a blunt expression.

He grabbed Kara's **f**ace gently, fixing it on Icarus's direction, and even with her being o**b**edient, she still didn't want to look at Icarus. Instead, she **r**olled her eyes all the way left.

"You see, young Mingan, there is a needle - - inside the end of their fangs," said Gray, forcing his finger inside Kara's **m**outh but she didn't w**an**t to open it.

"Don't be shy dear," he insisted until she did.

Her teeth and fangs **w**ere surpr**i**sing**l**y big in comparison to how sma**l**l her h**e**a**d** was. They were white with a hint **o**f yellow, and unlike humans, **s**h**e** had two uvulas instead of one.

Gray pushed one of **h**er fangs down. It cl**i**cked, revealing a **s**harp needle out of its tip.

"See this! All you need is a slight pressure," said Gray

Icarus flinched, crinkling his nose.

"I don't think it is wise for you to expose yo**ur** skin to that froth," he rasped wit**h** **a** disgusted expression, at the same **t**ime worried.

When Gray saw Icarus's concern for someone, who as far as he knew might be a threat, he grinned, taking his finger out, then thrust it inside his chest pocket, pulling out a silky napkin.

"If what you said was true, we would have been down by now; however, fortunately for us - - **yo**u're not. But in fact, their saliva has healing properties," Gray stated confidently, wiggling his wet finger before using the napkin to wipe it clean.

When done, he pushed the cloth inside his closed fist, and like a cheap magician, he opened his hand and the cloth vanished. It was a weak move to impress a Mingan.

"That was unnecessary," Gray admitted dully. Soon after, he continued after faking several short coughs:

(5-4) (6-13) (3-1) * (24-4) (18-11) * (6-2) (11-14)

"Anyway, let us put it this way. The needle inside is venomous, while the saliva of Kir**a**das is more effective than Blood Roots. We believe you're familiar with those?"

Icarus's eyes jumped when he heard Gray's words, but he chose **to** hide his interest by slowly shutting his eyes halfway.

The blood roots Gray mentioned were not the bloodroots you know. The kind-**lo**oking white petals flowers you buy to someone as an apology, no. These blood roots are nearly the opposite. Hideous plants, similar to a Venus flytrap but twice as big, and their exterior is darker than black. It feeds on insects or even small ferrets if one falls inside its thorn cage. But what makes it a nearly impossible herb to find was its whereabouts. It only blooms near the nest of an Amaranth Peacock, also known as the Blaze Phoenix.

"The Amaran**th** Peacock for healing - - the White Swan for stamina and the Blu"

"**I** know - - I'm not an amateur," Icarus interjected Gray who tried to an uncalled for lesson; however, the Mingan couldn't deny the fact that Gray did give him a valuable information, one a Mingan could kill for.

Mingans would spend a fortune to get a small phial of Blood Roots, when they could easily find a Kirada and extract their

saliva. Icarus knew that knowledge is power, and that was a start of him acknowledging Gray's mastery.

"Thank you for the lecture," he replied reluctantly whilst looking at the black door behind Gray's desk, then turned to the azure door on his left.

"Now, can you tell me how to leave this place?" he asked

Gray stared at him silently for moments, thus smiled, turning his attention to Kara.

"Mm! We can't let you out," he replied casually, tickling Kara's neck, who tried to stop him with her small hands.

Icarus tried to lean forward but couldn't. So he creased his forehead to not show weakness, looking at Gray with glowing eyes while slowly placing his hand on his scabbard.

"Showing your true colours? Gois," he said with tensed brows.

"Ind**ee**d, a concerned colour," a relaxed Gray answered without making eye contact, then stated apathetically:

"For if we do, you die"

Threatened, Icarus clutched the **p**ommel of his sword stealthily whilst keeping his eyes on the man in black.

"What do you mean?" Snobbish, he as**k**ed, sliding the sword out slowly, without making a sound.

"Is that a threat - - Gois?!" Icarus kept calling Gray by 'Gois' **as** if it were an insult.

Without looking, Gra**y** snapped his finger, and the pommel heated instantly, searing Icarus's hand.

"Ouch!" he shook his hand, giving Gra**y** an annoyed glare, realizing that there was no way over this man's head.

"Are y**ou** stupid? Why would we save you - - if we want you dead?!" A chagrined Gray argued, looking at Icarus with his side red-eye. He tapped Kara's back, indicating her to go back to her box.

"What we meant was, if we let you go, Apollo will finish the job," Gray declared Icarus's aggressor. He pointed to Icarus's burns with a lazy finger.

"And as you can clearly see, if it weren't for us - - she would've been successful," he stated

Gray didn't know that the **M**ingan wasn't listening to a word he said after mentioning Apollo. Her name echoed inside Icarus's head, driving his carcass to quiver. Something clicked inside him, something he couldn't control.

"Ap - - Apollo!" shaking and puzzled, Icarus stuttered, battering his teeth. The one who fearlessly hunted numerous monsters trembled over a mere name. But that was no fear; there was no word for it.

"That was Apollo? But - - why? Wait - - what is happening to me?" Bug-eyed, he quizzed, turning pale whilst trying to move one of his frozen muscles.

"Tsk!" Squeezing his hands into fists, an angry Gray gnashed his teeth discreetly, looking at Icarus shivering.

"Who would've thought, the great Icarus falling for that whore's spell," he whispered low, thus calmed and relaxed his fists.

He waited for Icarus to overcome his ambiguous feelings.

"**The** why - - we might have an idea, but no certainty yet. **B**ut, at l**ea**st now you know why you can't leave, **and** given your condition, she clearly did something to you. That, we can help you with," G**r**ay explained quietly, reassuring that his guest's safety was guaranteed inside the library.

Mean**w**h**il**e, a **l**eather hand sprouted out of the cushion behind Icarus, gent**l**y pressing a point somewhere **b**etween h**i**s neck and shoulder, a poke he didn't sense giving his sta**te**.

"Not to mention that you will faint any moment now," Gray hinted to Icarus to check his bleeding nose with a simple hand gesture.

B**l**ank, Icarus rubbed two fingers through the bottom of his nose, while tasting his own blood with his lower lip. He thou**ght** his dizziness was from losing too much blood, not knowing that the hand that sunk back inside **the** chair was the reason.

His hea**d** moved in ci**r**cles until he gave it a quick sh**a**ke to sober. The faint M**i**ngan looked at the blood on his fingers, rubbing it lingeringly. He shift**ed** his vision towards Gray, who lowered his leg and stood up. But his sight was foggy, seeing **G**ray's body w**o**bbli**n**g as he stepped closer to him.

"Easy big boy!" said a worried Gray, not knowing that his voice was already fading.

He approached Icarus, who left his chair to fall on his knees, coughing more blood on the floor.

"Damn it - - I ruined your place," faint, Icarus murmured, as his vision started to faze, while his eyelids got heavier, until he crushed on his chest then face like a broken puppet.

First, all he saw was pitch black darkness, sensing a burning chill spreading from his shoulders to the rest of his somnolent body. Then, he saw a blue flash behind him, followed by a grievous throb inside his heart.

"Groan!" Icarus screamed in agony, starting to receive sharp stabs and slashes all over his carcass. Flashes of coquelicot kept showing him images of himself crucified, getting tortured by flying whips and swords of fire, thus burned in an inferno that blazed his flesh, leaving only a screaming skeleton. Just to be w**r**app**ed** in a rejuvenating flesh and skin seconds after, and the moment his full body was completed, the same happened over and over.

After a timeless hell, everything stopped, except for a phlox and blue light passing by every few seconds, like a lighthouse torch. I**ca**rus thought his arms were melting again. But when he looked to the side, he saw his wings who he thought they were burned to ashes were back, good as new, but turning to liquid; like je**ll**y snakes, they slithered from his arms to his nape, then down to his shoulder blades. Icarus cri**ed** so loud as the wax infiltrated him, cutting his flesh before fusing with his muscles and bones. The pain grew greater, forcing out a loud echoic shriek.

A great beam of yellow appeared above him like a small sun, followed by a beautiful female echo, penetrating his five senses and somehow making the pain fade slowly:

"**I**carus, come back to me"

The golden light enlarged, filling the space Icarus was trapped in, until it blinded his vision.

"Who are **you**?!" Bilious, Icarus shouted, opening his eyes whilst panting heavily, spooked.

The first thing he saw was **G**ray staring right at him from above, wearing a wide smile. He had both thumbs up while taking a silly posture. Icarus **no**ticed it was only a painting, hanged on the ceiling.

'What is wrong with this man?'

Icarus thought before realising he was lying flat on a comfy bed.

The M**i**ngan took a deep breath, followed by small coughs while touching the bed's soft mattress.

"Was it a nightmare?" He said faintly, trying to move his head up; however, Icarus couldn't shake the feeling that it was more than a realistic nightmare.

"Ugh! My head," wan, he complained groggily, using his right hand to put some pressure on his forehead. While doing so, he noticed that his hand and fingers were wrapped in bandages, and so was his head. He raised the other hand to sense his wounds, but ended up experiencing a sharp pain on his back.

_ (13-1) * (4-10) (6-16) (8-2) * (16-3) * (23-2) (18-7) (19-13) (1-1)

CHAPTER ONE

"**O**uch! What the - -" a baffled Icarus said with a sour voice. He cleared his throat while using his elbow to push his upper body up.

After sitting straight, he tri**ed** touching his back by stretching his arm over his shoulder. After a lousy try, he saw a dark-gray majestic closet, covering most of the white wall on his side, and on one of its doors, a tall-mirror with a curved frame.

A weak Icarus rubbed the bottom of his feet before placing them on the fuzzy gray carpet underneath. He couldn't deny himself the pleasure of rubbing his toes against its satisfying softness.

Slouchy, the Mingan stood thus staggered ponderously to the mirror, while checking the rest of the bandages on his arms, chest and waist.

Rigid, he ro**t**ated his shoulder and t**i**lted his **he**ad left and right, slowly, trying to loosen his muscles.

"My head - - my back! Why is it heavy!?" agonized, he whispered low, then stopped before the mirror, facing it with his back to get a better view.

"Damn it!" **Sho**cked, Icarus gasped, grasping small bat-wings hanging on his shoulder blades. They were pure white on the edges and slightly transparent in the middle.

Conf**u**sed, he twisted his left arm, stooping his head and body whilst reaching for the left-wing's tip with his fingers.

"Slither!"

His wings reacted to his motion and spouted out slowly. Icarus started sensing his new wings as if they were numb limbs, like a fresh pair of hands emerging from his back.

A pained Icarus squeezed his lips shut while crinkling his eyes and forehead, observing the wings grew taller. His cringed expression switched from pain to disgust. For the pain he had was easy for him to endure. Or maybe it had something with what he experienced in that terrible vision.

Icarus moved his shoulders up and down carefully, revealing some veins throbbing at the muscled beginning of both wings. Suddenly, he felt a sharp sting when his wings emerged completely. They were taller than the Mingan himself.

"Ugh!" **He** groaned, tightening his muscles and acc**id**entally spread his left wing to its limit, cracking the mirror.

"Shit!" Icarus cursed before he glimpsed the **s**plit **r**eflection of Kara at the door behind him.

The small Kirada ran away the moment their eyes met.

Icarus turned around sharply, recklessly clawing the closet with his wing,

"Shiit!"

The annoyed M**in**gan stopped moving to avoid damaging anything else. He tried folding his stretched wing like the other one, using his back muscles and hand. But befor**e** he could reach it, they were both sucked back inside his shoulder blade, leaving no deformities.

Confounded, Icarus nuzzled the spot with the tip of his fingers, and found no distortions. He sighed audibly, not knowing what happened; however, the things he witnessed during his lifetime saved him from an unnecessary panic attack or trauma. He simpl**y** thought of these wings as something he could treat later. This is how bizarre the world of Mingans.

"Mingan - - Hey Kid!" he heard Gray's voice calling on him from outside.

He looked at the open door of the room. It was the azure door with the dragon emblem. Now he knew that wasn't his way **ou**t.

He inspected the room briefly. Simple white walls and ceiling, except for the Gray poster above the bed, the closet he damaged, a small wooden desk and chair, on it a black shirt, and finally, another black door facing the entrance, and down on the side corner, his sword was leaning straight against the wall.

Icarus took a step towards his blade, thus stopped, looking at the bandages and clean clothes. It was obvious that someone had taken care of him. He breathed out, thus grabbed the black shirt.

Before wearing it, Icarus noticed it had two long slots on the back, and according to his measurements, it matched perfectly with where his wings are.

"This man h**ad** everything ready," he whispered, acknowledging Gray's competence with a slight of perplexity.

Icarus wore the shirt that had a graffiti written on it, one that said '*I have a Gray-t Daddy'* but the poor man couldn't read English yet.

(8-3) (3-8) (1-8) (10-1) * (15-3) (19-9) (3-9) * (1-2) (29-3)

He sauntered out of the room to see Gray sitting casually on his chair, wearing a coy and disturbing smile. While Kara stood behind him, holding two rolls of bandages. **Icarus** looked do**w**n to see a thi**r**d ro**ll** at **h**is feet. It must of been one that K**a**ra dropped while fleeing. He gently tapped the bandages on his arm while gi**v**ing Kara a faint smil**e** as a '*thank you*'

"She **t**ook good care of **y**ou during these days," said Gray, pointing his **h**and at the couch on Ica**r**us's side as an invitation.

"We b**e**liev**e** y**o**u have a few que**s**ti**ons**"

"I do! Wait - - days!" Icarus replied and baffled right after, while sauntering towards the couch. He sat down, keeping his upper body leaning forward, in case his wings chose to pop out on their own.

"First - - we want to know if you're feeling better?" A mild Gray asked.

Icarus was wondering why was Gray using we instead of I, he was curious if it was an accent or of megalomania. **But** chose not to ask nor highlight it. He slid his thumb on his crannied lips, showing thirst.

"Pain, in every muscle from head to toe, but nothing I can't bear," he said, while slowly clutching both of his grips repeatedly.

"However, I have this strange - - that this body isn't mine!" He added in an uncertain tone.

Icarus rested his elbows on his thighs, locking his eyes on Gray.

"Since yo**u** claimed you know not the reason behind this assault," he said dejectedly, trying to not look doleful.

"Do you at least have an idea of what she did to me?" A concerned Icarus interrogated, but his voice turned croaky before he finished his question.

"Ahem!" he cleared his throat thus swallowed the little spittle he had.

"Kara, can you please get our guest a drink?" Gr**ay** ordered Kara, who rushed to the bookshelf behind Gray. She climbed up to the second line. After counting six books to her left, she pulled a thick f**e**ldgrau book halfway out.

"Click!"

A part of the bookshel**f** was a hidden door. She ran inside the secret room then out in less than a minute, holding a fat bottle with a raffia basket **w**oven around its base, long neck centred by a bulb. In the other hand, two wooden cups paled inside with t**a**r.

Kara placed the bottle and cups on the table before Icarus, thus took two steps back, standing straight with both hands on her belly while switching her vision between Icarus and the bottle.

"Drink, it wi**ll** help," Gray said

"Sweet date-palms rum from the southern desert, the best drink we can offer," he added, turning his right palm up and towards the rum as an invitation,

"And can you please serve one for us as well?"

Icarus grabbed the bottle by its neck. He pulled the cork-closure out, thus gave it a dog-sniff.

"This smells good," delightfully, he said, grabbing his cup. He poured one for himself and one for Gray.

Kara grabbed Gray's cup and ran to back to him while cautiously keeping her eyes on the drink. Icarus took a sip, shifting a surprised stare towards Gray.

"Hold on. This is not rum!" He perplexed

Gray chuckled, taking the cup from Kara's hands

"You mean not intoxicating. A wise man would never take something to weaken his mind," he replied in a poetic tone, thus drank the cup in one sip.

Gray rested his back while releasing an audible and refreshing sigh. His hand freed the cup, dropping it on the floor, and unexpectedly, the wooden cup crushed like glass. Icarus looked at it, turning to smoke. At the same time, a new one appeared on the table next to the bottle.

"How do you find it?" said Gray

Icarus gave him a weird look for the constant use of magic. Thus, like Gray, he finished his cup with one go, just to pour another right after.

"**Re**freshing, and the sweetest drink I ever tasted," he answered pleasantly, taking no time to drink the second one and pour a third. Icarus smiled, realizing the drink was but a simple way to ease down his tension.

"I think I'm prepared now," he said, putting the cup d**o**wn

"Very well," Gray smiled thus switched to a more serious face, thrusting a hand in his pocket, and took it **out** closed in a second.

"We want to highlight something first. The wax Daedalus used to build both of your wings__" Gray stated, then opened his hand wide, revealing a small piece of a shiny white wax. He used his forefinger to propel it to Icarus,

"__is not of his making nor his property"

Icarus snatched the piece in midair with his right, then shook it on his palm and watched it changing forms. But that was not the first time he had seen it. After all, he helped Daed**a**lus build their artificial wings.

"Are you accusing my father of theft?" replied Icarus in a de**f**ensive tone

"On the contrary," Gray interjected

"It is impossible for him to do so, but - - we reckon one of the two__" he said, raising two of his fingers, to put one down with ea**ch** word spoken,

"__Found or given"

Icarus narrowed his eyes with heightened qualms. Where would you find such a unique matter? Or who would be willing to give you a priceless thing like this?

"Wait, why Impossible?" A curious Mingan asked. After a brief moment of thinking, he widened his eyes, surprised,

"Do you mean__" he mused with his eyes fixed on Gray, who nodded his head yes with a grin,

"__another realm," Icarus answered his question

Gray freed a short impressed whistle, thus clapped his left palm half-curved on two of his right fingers, applauding Icarus whilst giving him a compliment, pressing on the first half of each word.

"You are frighteningly observant!" he wowed

"Correct - - Olympus to be exact," stated Gray, confirming Icarus's assumption.

"What lies in your h**an**d, is called Ruu. Only Zeus - - knows of its substance," he explained more, pointing at the flexible piece of wax Icarus had on his palm.

"Ruu!" said a curious Icarus, dropping the wax from one hand to the other.

Gray pressed each finger together, forming a steeple. **H**e looked at Icarus with a hesitant stare. But he couldn't withhold this kind of information to himself.

"Yes, and one of its intrinsic properties, is when exposed to a human soul, it causes it to exp**and** enormously," explained Gray with a serious tone, thus used his black smoke to sway the small piece from Icarus's hand to his. He clasped it inside his grip.

"But only a few survived the transformation," he clarified, opening his hand to show that the piece was slithering under his skin like a worm before it vanishe**d**.

Stupefied, Icarus had his mouth agape for seconds. He didn't know if Gray's words were a amiable way to tell him he was dying or a congratulation that he was one of the lucky ones.

The Mingan sighed and tried to remain calm. It was the time to know more, not to panic.

"How many?" Asked Icarus, trying to measure and comprehend his current situation,

"And - - am I one of them?"

Gray scratched his chin, thinking, acting like he was counting when he already had the answer ready.

"Four, according to our knowledge__" Gray asserted, then pointed his finger at Icarus and said in a straight tone,

"__And you, the fifth"

Icarus swallowed his own saliva, thus puffed all the air out of his lungs, realizing he'd survived a rendezvous with his reaper. But he couldn't take Gray's words as insurance, not yet.

"But how can I be sure - - this transformation was a success?" Uncertain and stressed, Icarus hypothesize**d** pessimistically.

"Or if this is temporary. Is there a chance that maybe my body will reject it and perish later on__" Icarus kept announcing his cynical ideas out loud, while Gray crossed his arms, and watched him blabber **in** silence,

"__I also bear in mind having an unusual nose bleed when I came here. I never had one in my life," he added, only **to** get interrupted by a chuckle from Gray.

"A nose bleed you say!" Gray giggled

He repeated himself then laughed, shaking his head no while laughing louder. He then paused to give Icarus a scary glare, with all nine eyes narr**ow**ed and locked on the Mingan.

"Your mind bears **n**othing. In these three days, you went through hell and back," Gray claimed, painting a bewildered expression on the Mingan's face as he listened quietly.

Gray sighed, relaxing his face and eyes, for he noticed the unnecessary ire.

"We - - had to use a very complicated spell only to lock your conscious," he informed

Then, using his forefinger, he rapidly drew a human-brain of smoke in midair. He waved his hand, turning the drawing into a three-dimensional figure, like an advanced hologram of black mist instead of light.

"Only to prevent you from losing your sanity, or worst - - your humanity," Gray added, drawing a bright circle inside the lower back of the brain.

Icarus looked at the circle turning into a dark sphere, and inside it a thicker blackness; one that was pushing its way out.

"The nightmare I had!" said a confused Icarus, switching his vision to his wounds. He looked back at Gray with a mistrustful look.

"Wait - - You tempered with my mind?" startled, he inquired.

"We had to," deadpanned Gray, giving him a lazy shrug.

"You see - - your mind was not the only thing we were protecting, but the library as well."

"The library!" perplexed, Icarus said, adjusting his body an inch forward.

G**r**ay nodded his head slowly while calling for Kara with two taps on his thigh.

"Apollo used your weakened state **to** control you," disenchanted, Gray stated, placing Kara on his lap.

"She even forced you to attack our friend," said Gray, curving an unpleasant side smile.

"**K**ara!" Icarus gasped low with a concerned look

"No," Gray replied with a higher-pitch than usual, thus modulated his voice back.

"Of course not, not my dear Kara. If that was the case, you would've been - - dead," he emphasized in a very cold manner.

Icarus sensed that he really meant every word he said, that Gray was really willing to kill him for a Kira**da**; however, the Mingan was relieved. He couldn't bear the idea of hurting the creature that treated him when he was knocking on death's door. Good d**e**eds are truly impactful on one's heart, to change a killing intent to a feeling of concern.

"What matters, is that we are all safe, and you - - survived the transformation," Gray said, joining his palms together.

"Adding to that, the spell we used is preventing Apollo from taking control - - Again," he rea**ss**ured, highlighting the last word.

"And didn't you **n**otice that your body isn't quivering at the mentioning of her name."

Suddenly percipient, Icarus forced an obviously fake smile with his brows knitted. He did miss that.

"Ahem! Thank you," he said in a formal tone, straightening his posture.

"You're welcome," replied a stolid Gray

Icarus massaged his creased forehead, using his thumb and forefinger, freeing a long sigh while thinking. It was one of those times when you have so many questions but lose track of what to ask.

"So, from what you told me, if Apollo came after me, doesn't that revoke the possibility that Zeus gave the Ruu to my father?" Icarus concluded, scratching his short stubble beard, thus he stared at Gray as his eyes widened.

"My father! What happened to my father? " Aghast, he fretted grimly

"Safe - - and well. You were the only one **t**argeted," a relaxed Gray answered, putting Icarus**'s** heart at ease, then curved a half grin.

"For a **s**harp person, you were rather slow there," Gray commented in a sardonic tone, highlighting **the** fact that Icarus left the safety of his father unnoticed for that long.

Icarus cleared his throat, forcing a cough out.

"He's a big man, he can take care of himself," deadpanned Icarus, faking an impassive expression. That changed Gray's mood in an instant. One of things the man in blac**k** hates is a liar, especially one whom lies to himself. How i**r**on**ic** coming from the man who takes joy in manipulating others with bending the truth.

"Lying about your feelings is pathetic. So would you please - - deny yourself the pleasure of doing so with us," bit**ter**ly, Gray scolded Icarus in a relaxed and soft tone.

"Oll wright, Oll wright, let's fold this page now? Since you said he's safe, I'll take your word for it," a disturbed Icarus replied fitfully.

"Very well," Gray accepted

"Good," Icarus said, resting his back on the couch. Left with no ideas, he looked at Gray, waiting for some, or at least one.

"Now, what do you suggest I do?" puzzled Icarus, relaxing his hands on his knees.

Gray grinned slyly, as if he were waiting for the Mingan to speak those exact words.

He swayed both hands up thus reeled and rotated them closer to one another while releasing thick smoke meddled with black fire from his palms to form a hand-size dark ball in between. Then, he rapidly clapped his hands and separated them slowly, creating a scroll of dry yellow paper.

"A contract," Gray smirked, using his bare hands to put down the black flames that were eating the scroll's edges.

"A contract!" repeated a perplexed Icarus, furrowing his forehead.

"Yes," Gray confirmed simply

"You - - go"

He dropped the scroll. The roll formed paper-legs before landing on the floor. It ran towards Icarus like a professional jogger, then climbed on the table and jumped onto Icarus's lap.

Kara applauded the scroll's efforts with a wide grin.

"I knew saving my life was not an act of ki**nd**ness," cold, Icarus huffed low, while opening the con**t**ract.

He scrutinized it, sliding the tip of his thumb on its sharp edges. After two gentle flicks on the bottom of the **s**croll, he sniffed it and even gave it a quick lick.

"This is a real Binding-Scroll," affirmed Icarus, admiring the rare piece **in** his **ha**nds, a powerful item that you can't find in the magic store next door.

"I see you're a man of rich resources."

"Thank you, and now - - care to hear our offer?" Beatifically, Gray asked, resting his hands on his knees.

"Care to tell me your actual name?" Icarus replied with a question, to show Gray that he knows his host was hiding his true identity, but why? That question remains answerless.

"Not now," Gray answered simply, what made Icarus roll his eyes thus back to Gray.

"It seems we have no choice," a snide Icarus replied, forcing a smile as he surrendered to Gray's suggestion

"Go ah**ead**, name your conditions," said a lazy Icarus and Gray took no time to state his offer,

"First, you accept us as your mentor. Second, you can't leave this place until we say so, and that is when you finish your training__" Gray stated with a clear voice and a quick tone, and while speaking, his words were inked onto the empty scroll as if an invisible quill was writing on his behalf,

"__Third, you will do as we instruct and not to disobey. Fourth, and most important," said Gray with a wicked smile.

"When you finish your training," he said, raising two fingers as options.

"You will have **to** choose between two. Join us on a mission that we can't reveal until you agree__" Gra**y** lowered his index, leaving his middle finger up while giving Icarus a provocative smile,

"__or leave free and you will never see or remember us," he grinned

"Eek eek!" Kara looked at his middle finger up on Icarus's face then lau**gh**ed, but Icarus was ignorant of **the** meaning behind it. So he started at Kara bluntly, then looked at Gray with his brows up.

"That's all!" said Icarus, surprised and re**li**eved at the same time. He saw Gray's conditions as simple, not the usual conditions you waste a binding scroll on.

"I really went far with my thoughts"

"Why, what did you think?" asked Gray, blunt and curious.

"Never mind," replied a smiley Icarus, looking at the contract in his hands.

He cleared his throat, thus said with a clear voice:

"I Icarus, son of Daedalus, agree on the terms of this sacred scroll. Kä **T**äm"

The moment Icarus breathed the last word, **b**l**a**ck **fl**ames started eating the scroll from the bottom up. When the contract turned to smithereens, Icarus thrust his finger inside his shirt's ne**ck**, pulling it down to see a small glaucous circle tattooed on the midst of his chest. The Mingan is now marked by a promise he can't break.

A cheerful Gray clapped, leaving his chair. He walked towards Icarus and made a simple dancing spin before he reaches him.

"All done, you are now our first apprentice, and us your first mentor," Gray gloated, leaning forward to shake Icarus's hand, who shook his hand but also shook his head no.

Gray narrowed his white eyes, confused and disappointed at the same time.

"Your - - second!" Hesitant, said Gray slowly, but Icarus shook his head no again.

"Your third?!" He bleated with a hint of disappointment.

Icarus nodded his head yes, while Gray freed Icarus's hand aggressively.

_ (15-9) (2-5) * (15-8) (17-5) * (1-4) * (6-6) * (8-7) (5-14) (14-15)

“Dear friend, you are - - a slut of a disciple! Very well, third it is,” half-hearted, Gray said tightly, turning around hastily.

He headed to the bookshelf **be**hind his chair, thus slid his forefinger through the books. It seemed more as if he were choosing a book and not looking for one.

“We may not be your first, but - - we sure will be your favourite. All **yo**u need to do is think **of** our training as a - - journey,” he said louder than necessary, picking up a small book with a vermillion hard cover.

Gray turned to Icarus with a confident smile, thus promised:

“One that will forge yo**u** to be the finest warrior ever existed”

“Not intere**st**ed,” a clod Icarus gave a quick reply with one eyebrow up.

“**I** only wish to survive this, go out, and live my remaining years in peace,” said Icarus simply

“Years!” said **G**ray, filled with confusion thus asked with his head slightly tilted to the left

“Don’t you mean Millenniums? Wait, did we miss mentioning that?”

“Huh!” A vacant Icarus gasped, tilting his head in the **op**posite direction. Both looked at each other for several awkward moments. Icarus eyes started to slowly widen before he blurted.

“When you said ‘*soul expanding*’ you meant I’m immortal?” He dropped a jaw.

“No! No - - No,” Gray demurred the Mingan’s wild thoughts

“No one, and we mean no one - - is immortal,” he stated with a serious tone, walking slowly closer to Icarus to explain:

“We thought you understood. Listen, your lifespan - - expanded enormously”

“So - - nothing has changed but the years I can possible live?” asked Icarus pensively, lowering his voice to a whisper for no reason

“Yes, exactly,” replied Gray, giving Icarus a faint applaud.

“Ow! Still, that’s so much! Look at how my hand is shivering!” Icarus wowed, observing his unstable lifted hand.

"Easy, kid. You never know. You can go for a pizza and get hit by a bus. End of story"

"What's a Pizza, and bus?" Clueless, Icarus asked with a strange look, as if the poor man didn't alr**e**ad**y** have enough on his mind.

"Ah true, this reminds us," Gray said

He showed the claw of his **f**o**r**efinger, then casually cut a lock of hair. He placed the cords on his palm thus rolled them into a large ring. Adding a soft blow of air, he converted the fibrous hair to a solid bracelet.

"What is that?" asked a curious Icarus

Gray approached the M**ing**an, thus asked for his wrist while placing the ve**r**millio**n** book under his armpit.

He explained, while thrusting Icarus's hand inside the magical bangle.

"We will be visiting different places and times"

"Times - - Are you a time traveller now!" surprised, Icarus interjected, pulling his head back away fr**om** Gray's creepy ey**es** peering at him.

"Yes times, and no not really, you will get that question answered with my name - - or **m**a**y**be before that. Anyway, you will be needing this," replied Gray, having a hard time putting the bracelet on Icarus's tense fist. He con**t**in**u**ed in a tight tone:

"This allows us to share our memories with you, of course, not everything," Gray smiled thus sighed relieved when he finally managed to put the bracelet on.

"We can't have you asking us '*what is this and that?*' when we're inside"

"Inside what?" A concerned Icarus asked, stepping back away from Gray's bizarre mask.

"You'll see," Gray grinned dementedly

The man in black grabbed the book with one hand while adjusting his coat with the other, then the neck of his shirt.

"You look ready as well," he said, sizing Icarus up, thus took a few steps back.

"Come and stand here," he beckoned Icarus with a tap of his foot

Icarus did as orde**red**. He stood straight, facing Gray, who gave him a crafty grin while resting the book on his chest.

"What now?" Icarus asked bluntly. And before saying another word, he got sucked into the book in a flash, followed by Gray,

"Swish!"

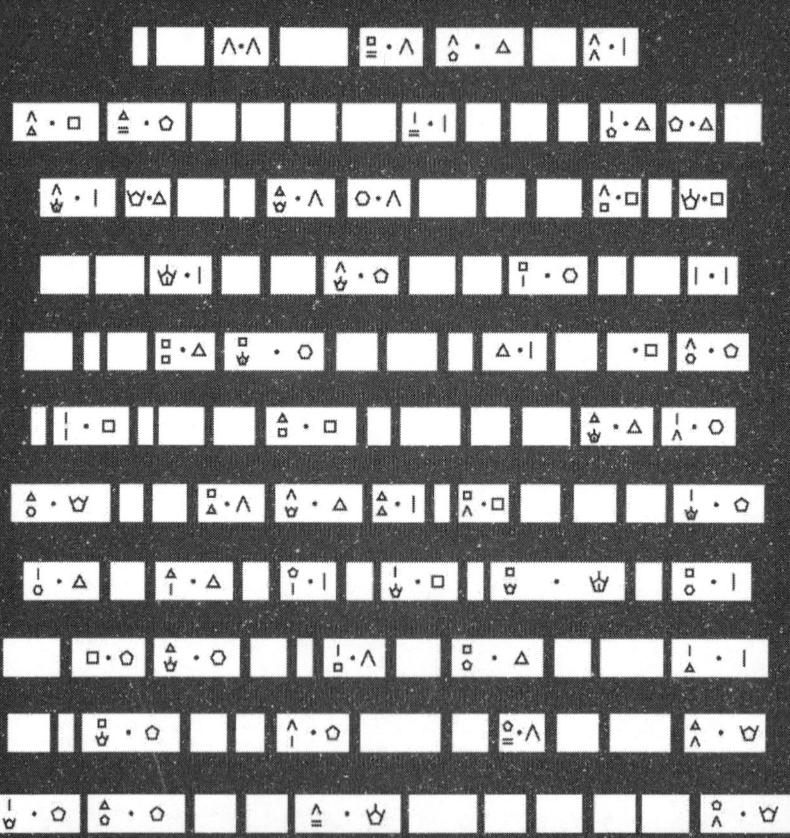

CHAPTER TWO
WHAT CAN A TWIG DO!

1921 - Dallas, Texas, in a dreary land, covered by a vast plain of fluorescent-hued rocks, **i**nterspersed with mountains of various heights and sizes, covering the humble and distant clouds in the horizon, above cr**a**c**k**ed and arid grounds that sours your throat just by staring at them, inhabited by dry lifeless trees, standing as **wa**rning **s**igns at every deep clef.

A hickory cockroach s**we**pt out of a sage bush, followed by a gam**bo**ge scorpion. After a rapid chase, the sharp pedipalps clutched its prey. The scorpion stung his victim repeatedly until it stopped trembling, and right before the eight-legged creature feasted on its crispy meal, Gray's vermillion book fell off from the sky, heavily stomping the two crustaceans and the ground unde**rn**eath it.

"Squash!"

The book opened, and out of it emerged two arms, palms on the ground, the two limbs pushed the cleft ground and Gray's head sprouted out of the slender gap between his shoulders like a squeezed balloon. Elongated through the cramped space, thus popped into its original form, and so did the rest of his body.

_ (2-3) * (5-1) (5-2) * (6-13) (10-9) * (6-4) (3-9)

CHAPTER TWO

"Good," he said, str**ai**ghtenin**g** his coat. He gave his shirt an abrupt shake before he leaned down, grabbing the book.

"Eas**t**," he whispered, glancing at the sun while placing both his hands and the book on his forehead to **sh**ade his three upper eyes and closing the other six. Gray took three full steps, then stood straight and locked his e**y**es on the crooked ground,

"Here!"

"Boom!" a heavy blow came from underground, followed by several more. Gray stepped back hurriedly. After a few min**or** earthquakes, the ground cracked, **and** out of the fissure burst a dusty fist, then another. Like a mole, Icarus dug his way out of the unmarked grave he found himself cornered in.

Gray approached him and folded his body down, standing on the tips of his feet.

"It took you longer than we anticipated, but well done," Gray said **sc**o**r**nfully, which was a lie. Icarus came out faster than he expected, but Gray wasn't one to miss irritating Icarus, who was panting rapidly, with his lower body still buried.

The Mingan glared at Gray with his sandy face, blowing dirt off his lips. After a stomach groan, Icarus puffed his cheeks and opened his eyes large. Some**thin**g unpleasant was coming out.

Gray stood straight rapidly, washing the smile off his face.

"Please don't," he begged frowningly, sweeping his feet back. Another thing the man in black didn't foresee.

"Barf!" a nauseous Icarus blew a massive load of vomit, and strangely, the smell took no time to reek. A Disgusted mentor placed the back of his fist against his nose as a failed attempt to block the rankness.

"We did not see that coming! Damn it, why does it smell like an ogre's swamp!" Gray groused, looking the other way while kicking some dirt above the vomit. But the acidulant smell penetrated his nostrils anyway

"You know what, take your time," he said low with a revolted down-smile then walked away, putting a distance between him and his wan partner.

Drunken and drowsy, Icarus squeezed one eye shut; he hadn't yet comprehended anything of what was happening, and who would've.

"What was - - where? Barf!" baffled, Icarus stuttered before he puked again. He spoke as if his tongue was numb.

"Next time - - tell me be**for**e you," Icarus blabbered while giving his head a slight shake as a sob**er**ing boost, **th**en puzzled:

"Wait, you can teleport!"

Gra**y** furrowed from far, tapping one foot. He was ignoring his apprentice's commentary and rethinking his decisions instead.

"Did we - - make a mistake!" Disillusion**ed**, said Gray vexingly, questioning if he chose the right person.

The man in black freed a deep huff and walked back to Icarus, who pulled the rest of his body out; however, he preferred resting on his hands and knees like a scraggy coyote in case he needed to throw up once **mo**re. Gray circled around, avoiding the vomit, then stood behind his pallid companion. He thrust his arm into thin air.

"Woof!"

Half of his limb vanished, as if it were inside an invisible pocket, one he extracted a small flacon from. Using two fingers to block his nostrils, a careful Gray leaned down closer to Icarus as if the Mingan had some contagious disease.

"Smell this - - it will help," a disgusted Gray said, putting the bottle down while trying not to look at the scrambled puke. He then noticed the end of his coat gliding on the dirt.

"Shit!" he grunted

Icarus grabbed the bottle, des**pera**te for anything that could help. The moment he opened it, a pleasant strawberry redolence filled the entire place. A blinking Icarus took a long sniff, sobering up instantly. He stood up straight and walked backwards, stepping away from the mess he made to end up bumping into Gray.

"You, you caught me off guard," ambivalent, he argued with his finger at Gray's face.

Gray gave him a sharp stare as he complained in an aggrieved tone, exaggerating the movements of his hands. The Mingan didn't know his mentor was disappointed to a point **wh**ere he seriously thought of slapping him dead on **the** spot.

"Make sure to warn me the next time you try something mad. Ah yes, and I'm keeping this," Icarus kept whining, then referred to the flacon in his raised hand, but Gray snatched it aggressively.

"Give me that. Are you a baby?" Gray grunted, crashing the bottle into a fading smoke. He then poked Icarus's dusty chest while talking.

"We are not gadabouts, we're here - - to train you, not to take you on a damn picnic," Gray scolded Icarus, who squeezed his mouth shut, embarrassed and perturbed. He knew he wasn't **one** to complain or argue training. So why did he?

The Mingan shook some of the dirt off his shirt then **said** respectfully:

"Oll wright. Apologies. You are correct, this is no picnic"

He narro**we**d his eyes, and kept quiet for moments, then asked bluntly:

"How d**o** I know what a picnic is?"

Gray tilted his head forward, pointing at his bracelet.

"Ah true, this!" Icarus said with a discomforted smile, shaking the bracelet, then the dirt off his clothes. Gray snapped his finger and a dense body of water dropped on Icarus, washing him clean.

"This is much better. Now let the sun do the drying," grinned Gray, thrusting his hands into his pockets. They both saw what he did as a discreet punishment, or a way to loosen his frustration, but none cared to comment.

Icarus took off his shirt to squeeze the water down, while Gray already walked south. He looked back at Icarus to rush him, and the Mingan did, he followed with a slow run. Gray leaned down and grabbed a paltry stone while moving.

"Take your wings out," Gray ordered with a precise tone, tossing the stone up and down casually, then added, looking at Icarus with a side eye:

"We want you to get used to them"

Icarus moved his shoulders back whilst tightening his muscles. He gave Gray a look of uncertainty, then asked:

"But what if someone see me?"

"See you! We are inside a memory," **a**nswe**re**d Gray, turning round the Mingan.

Icarus finally knew where he was. He wouldn't have guessed if not told, for everything looks and feels real. Gray looked heave**n**ward, pointing his finger at a rough-legged hawk flying above them. Icarus observed the flying bird just to see it freeze in mid-air. He squinted, focu**sin**g his vision, for he was dubious of what he saw. The hawk flew backwards for seconds, then reversed to normal. It seemed to Icarus as a glitch you see on an old video-record.

"All you see here is under our control," a confident Gray said, putting his arm down,

"Therefore, you're not to be seen or interact **wi**th anything unless we **all**ow it"

Icarus paused, observing the hawk as he screeched while flying towards the nearest mountains. He then followed Gray to land a weary question.

"You can manipulate memories?" Icarus asked discreetly, hiding his doubts.

"We can," Gray replied in a deadpan tone, thus back to tossing the stone up and down.

A tense Icarus walked in silence for a few steps, biting his **th**umb-nail until he gathered the courage to ask:

"Have you manipulated mine?"

Concerned, he swallowed the little saliva he had in his dry mouth.

Gray stopped, tapping a foot **b**ef**or**e he turned to Icarus, who likewise paused, looking at Gray warily. The man in black crossed his arms, squeezing his lips shut while drawing an impassive expression.

"Mm!" Gray started making weird drumming noises with his lips whilst thinking of an answer. While Icarus looked at him with an accusatory look, bracing to reject any lie Gray spits out.

"Not so quick now!" gibed Icarus, crossing his arms and accidentally spreading his wings. He spooked, ruining his stolid state, but rapidly shifted his focus back to Gray, giving him a serious stare, hinting that what happened won't shake him from getting his answer.

CHAPTER TWO

G**r**ay sighed as his nine eyes closed briefly, then opened partly.

"We don't believe a simple denial will convince you! Will it," he **said** in a soft tone, **the**n added loud with a slight hiss:

"Ah, yes,"

He raised his hand, placing the small s**to**ne between his forefinger and middle finger while Icarus ti**l**te**d** his head to the side, clueless. Gray gave his hand a rapid shake, and the one stone became two.

"What's that - -"

"Shush," Gra**y** denied Icarus the right to comment. He looked at a dead tree on his left, and **w**ith**o**ut warning, he flicked one of the stones with his thumb like a bullet, piercing the hard trunk as if it were made of a flimsy paper.

"Plok!"

Gray grinned, looking at Icarus, who kept his eyes on him without blinking.

The man in black pointed his next shot at Icarus, who maintained his tranquillity, giving Gray a de**fia**nt glare. His mentor, on the other hand, seemed serious about taking the shot. He stiffened his hand to the extent that his muscles became audible, aiming for his apprentice's forehead.

Gray's thumb snapped as he propelled the gravel! The shot was as fast as light; however, the pair of wings was **not** the only gift Icarus gained from his transformation. His rapid eyes observed the stone in slow-motion; streams of wind rounded the stone like small turbans, exfoliating micro-pieces off its shell. With his cu**rr**ent speed and agility, it was easy for him to dodge, but why didn't he? He didn't move or even flinch. Icarus allowed the pebble to go through his forehead as if he were a nonphysical ghost.

Gray curved a surprised smile thus **ch**uckled, for he didn't expect such level of bravery, one he considered as madness rather than being fearless, and that moment of admiration reminded him of the real Icarus.

"Mm! Clearly you trust us, then why the dull question?" pleasant, Gray asked, loosing up his hands with gentle shakes and clutches.

Icarus threaded a hand through his hair, pressing it back.

"You're mistaken," he sighed, sliding his hand down to his nape,

"First, I trust you don't want me dead," he crossed his arms and continued with a fixed tone:

_ (15-4) (3-3) (1-1) * (2-13) * (19-7) * (5-8) * (10-5) (22-1) (9-2) * (25-7) (6-4)

"S**e**cond, you confirmed it with this frivolous show just now. There was no kil**li**ng intent when you shot that stone." Icarus approached Gray, leaving only a little **sp**ace **in** between and stated:

"But, I don't trust you with my mind - - nor with my memories, I only trust me"

Icarus leaned closer to Gray's face, sharing his breath. He then grunted slowly whilst magnifying every word spoken:

"And I - - Have - - **a** good reason"

"And what would that be?" Gray asked lucidly

"Isn't obvious? You - - don't trust me either," answered Icarus, poking Gray's chest.

Answerless, Gray stared at him silently, looking at Icarus's half-opened mouth, inappropriately close to his face. Without warnings, Gray sprayed Icarus's mouth with a breath-spray.

"Cough!" the Mingan backed away, **wi**ping his tongues and lips as his face crinkled from the sour taste.

"What - - enough with the stupid tricks, can you maintain a serious conversation for five minutes," Icarus snarled loudly, while spitting the taste out of his mouth.

Gray pushed the small bottle inside his chest-pocket, while waving the air farther from his nose with the other.

"We are serious, but so is **your** breath," Gray huf**fe**d lightly, disparaging Icarus's accusation.

"Oh shut it," be**ll**igerent, Icarus fumed, placing his slightly curved index against his mouth then pointed it at Gray's face.

"You really think I don't know what that grimy mask of yours is; an Ennkapros boar, known as the nine realms boar," a fed-up Mingan asserted, confident, folding his wings as his muscles tightened out of irritation, then continued spitefully whilst lowering the volume of his angry voice:

"I know an Ennkapros can form a cloak to hide its presence. Keeping it as a pet is enough to grant you a life of privacy. So **tak**ing it as far as to transform it into a vizard without killing it, which I'm certain, it wasn't easy, even for a mage like yourself, can only mean one thing - - what you're hiding is much - - much greater." Icarus ended his conclusion with a strong sigh.

Gray stood there silent, curving a faint smile on his face, then deadpanned with an indifferent **to**ne:

"So!"

Icarus closed his eyes slowly, **bi**tin**g** the interior of his bottom-lip just vigorous eno**ugh** to hurt but not injure, he then exhaled shakily.

"So?" he asked calmly

"Let us be clear," Gray replied, squinting his eyes, upset. His moody personality switched in seconds, as always.

"It is not about '*not trusting us*' as **you** say, but rather, us kn**ow**ing more than you do. You're used to being the smartest person inside every bevy," he chided with a silvery tone yet acerbic.

"What's that supo - -"

"Shut - - up. You're the apprentice here. We talk - - you listen," Gray prevented Icarus from interrupting then continued his scolding:

"First, you say '*you don't trust us with your mind,*' to the same person who saved that mind from insanity. Second, the things we plan to do - - are gravely dangerous, more than your current self can bear. We **will** need a partner, not a bloody doll__"

And as Gray was still speaking, Icarus was bold enough to interrupt again with an unconvinced tone,

"Why not a doll?" he asked, making Gray reply with an angry shriek:

"__Because DOLLS break," a lightning fell behind him as he spoke the last word.

A livid Gray noticed a dark cloud forming above his head, so he closed his eyes for several seconds, calming himself with a long sigh, and the cloud faded, clearing the sky and putting Icarus's throbbing heart at ease.

"A partner would willingly give his life to save yours. However, a doll will always wait for a command," Gray added calmly.

Icarus sensed that Gray's words were an outcome of a previous experience.

'*Did he lose a partner? Or did he try to control someone but it didn't work well for him?*'

The Mingan had many questions but didn't dare to ask, especially after uncovering a tension between him and his new mentor. Also, he can't apologize because he didn't consider himself entirely at fault, so he lowered his head to massage his nape, as a way to avoid eye-contact.

_ (9-9) * (17-10) * (1-1) (9-14) * (4-6) * (19-1) * (2-3) (5-1)

WHAT CAN A TWIG DO !

Gray breathed **in** and out, then started walking on his way. The two understood one another. Best to do was to give Icarus the time he needed before he can trust the man in black. **Like**wise, give Gray the time to **p**rov**e** himself. After all, they were literally stuck together now.

"Let bygones be bygones. Trust but don't forget to distrust," said Gray casually with a flat tone, while beckoning Icarus to follow. **The** Mingan sighed faintly while his wings flapped, reacting to the wind, thus a**sk**ed as he slowly ran after Gray:

"Where are we anyway?"

"Look there," Gray replied, pointing his finger to a faraway object, which Icarus stared at confused. Gray used his finger to tap Icarus's wrist.

"**Le**ave the reading for this," he said

Icarus used both hands to adjust his wings, while twitching his eyelids half shut to see what Gray was pointing at.

"Where?"

He squinted at the pointed direction to see a wooden sign **of** a dark-brown frame, standing on the side of a sandy and crooked road, and inside the sign's board, two white words written with long and italic letters. Icarus read the words slowly:

"Dallas, Texas!"

He furrowed while receiving information from the bracelet. He felt it filling his memories like a Deja-vu, but that fascinating ability made him miss the fact that he could heighten his vision.

"Wait! My vision!" dumbfounded, he gasped, looking at Gray, who smirked.

"Yes, y**our** carcass is improving to synchronize the growth of your soul. And now, how about we test your speed," Gray explained, tapping Icarus's shoulder before bolting ahead at an excessive speed.

The Mingan flabbergasted for a moment, then smiled and dashed to the chase. Icarus was known as the fastest man in Athens, but the super speed he was experiencing was beyond his wildest imagination. It made everything around him freeze, even the surrounding air turned to a transparent and soothing liquid.

The Mingan took no time to catch up with Gray, and as they ran alongside the road, they passed by a big truck filled with ch**op**ped trees.

(3-5) * (6-11) * (3-11) (32-10) (12-1) * (16-12) * (24-2) * (7-11) (1-3)

CHAPTER TWO

"**I**'m more surprised that these things are familiar to me," he said with a pleasant smile. He then looked round at Gray, who kept widening the gap between them in a slow ratio.

"I thought Goises are supposed to have weak bodies!" he commented with an unsure tone, thus remembered that all this was inside Gray's mind, which meant he could do whatever he wanted.

Several minutes after, Gray stopped easily in the spot like an Olympics spear that pierced the furthest point in the field. However, it wasn't that easy for his apprentice. Icarus sled past **Gr**ay, leaving a l**ong** cloud of dust behind, and because his feet weren't enough to be used as breaks, he begged his wings to spread so he could use them as support. After a decent amount of tries, he was finally successful.

Icarus cleared the body of dust around to find himself in the middle of n**ow**here.

"Damn it!" a **di**sappointe**d** Icarus grunted, aggressively stomping his foot on the ground, a childish act to blame the ground for his failure. He used his heightened vision to look around, but nothing was to be seen except for bleak plains of rocks **and** dead trees. Icarus followed his trails back, but this time with a careful and slow run.

Finally, he reached Gray, who stood und**er** the faint shade of a lonely Palo-verde tree, standing tall on the pinnacle of a hunched steep slope. The man in black waited for Icarus to get closer.

"We're here," Gray said, then trudged to the edge, overlooking a one-**st**o**r**ey house with a torn wooden facade, and a small barn on the back, inhabited by three piglets, and further behind the long road on the side, the low city of Dallas.

Icarus looked at the house, then the town from one side to the other. Bracelet or not, the memory he received didn't keep him from gazing on what he saw.

"Where is '*here*' exactly!" he said, looking back at the house to see two boys dashing out of the front door, followed by a third.

"I have a feeling we're not here for aviation lessons"

Gray kept observing the youngest boy chasing after the other two, getting pushed down every time he catches up with them. You could tell they were brother from the same repeated features they had, the olive skin and dark eyes, likewise, their similar haircuts.

_ (17-4) * (1-1) * (14-4) * (9-5) (13-15) * (22-13) (9-8) (19-7)

"As we said before, your body is improving on its own. What we need now is to focus on training your **mi**nd," clarified Gray, shaking some dust off his sleeves.

"Do you see that kid, the skinny **on**e," said Gray pointing his clawed finger at the boy who was being bullied by his older siblings.

"The one getting roughed?" a snide Icarus asked to be sure. Concurrently shrugging, hoping to lift his w**in**gs up from the hot ground.

Gray asked Icarus to turn around with a simple reel of his finger, and when the Mingan did, Gray started poking Icarus's pressure points whilst talking.

"Yes, the one getting roughed," he mimicked Icarus's tone

"We want you to think of him - - as your teacher in this trip," he added, then gave his apprentice a gentle back-slap,

"All done"

A confused Icarus orbited, facing Gray with a puckered forehead a**nd** a blunt look. He did hear what he said, **but** he wasn't willing to simply swallow it.

"Did you say my teacher? That twig?" he asked boastful**ly**

"Yes," Gray answered simply, walking back to the tree whilst taking off his jacket. He folded it tall then hung it on a low branch.

"Don't complicate it. All you need to do - - is follow him around," an easy-going Gray added, swaying his hand slowly to create a mattress of a velvet cloud, floating a hand-span above the ground.

"Is there a hidden message behind this?" Asked Icarus, while observing his wings as he moved them at will, gratitude to Gray's unusual massage.

Gray didn't respond. He reclined, enjoying the slight breeze under the tree shade; above his head, dangled a broken dry branch, hung on a thicker one by a thread, so he pulled it and tossed it towards Icarus before placing both hands under his head as a pillow.

When the Mingan intended to protest for an answer, Gray replied:

CHAPTER TWO

"This stick under your feet," said Gray, rubbing the back of his head on his palm, then asked **with** a sleepy tone:

"Do you think you can use it in a fight instead of that sword you're so proud of?"

Icarus looked down at the twig, breaking a long l**in**e of silver ants. **He** searched for any means to this question but found none.

"Even a fragile stick can blind an eye," he answered, leaning down to grab the stick, but his h**and** went through instead. He tried again and again but nothing.

"Always a pleasure to hear your bright answers," replied a praising Gray, turning on his side whilst yawning and stretching his legs.

"Now, go keep an eye on the boy"

"Tsk!" Ic**ar**us gave Gray an annoyed glare, then walked to the edge. He spread his wings and back several times to confirm that he had control over them, then decided it was time to try them.

The winged-man jumped, swaying down whilst hardly trying to maintain a straight line; however, landing was the easy part.

Icarus folded his wings, sauntering towards the boys, and as he approached the **t**hree, a thick woman stepped out of the house; she had her fists resting on the sides of her hips, while holding a wooden spoon that spilled some tomato sauce on her stripped kitchen apron dress instead of her pistachio smock.

"Flaco!" glowering, she called with a hoarse shout.

"What do you think you're doing, wallowing your culo on the ground?" she scolded the skinny kid for ruining his clothes, tapping the spoon on her large thigh, she tilted her head left while opening her eyes broadly like a jumbled owl, rushing him to stand up and shake the dirt off.

"But Mama!" crestfallen, Flaco sniffled, looking at his two brothers mocking him.

His mother used the wooden spoon to beckon him, stomping her foot harder as she replied with a sharper voice:

"No buts, andale - - inside now"

She looked at the other two with her forehead creased and grunted with a whisper-shout:

"You too, after him demonios"

They ran inside washing the laughs off their faces, but that didn't deny both of their heads a smack on the **b**ack as they **jo**gged past her.

"Ouch!"

Icarus looked at them stepping insi**de**, and so did their mother after a brief glare at the Palo-verde tree.

Icarus rushed his steps to enter before she closes the door, but the Mingan knew he couldn't run for he had no control over his speed yet. He quickened his steps to a silly walk, one a person do when burdened with diarrhoea while rushing to the toilet, **and** even with that ridiculous walk, she en**ded** up **c**los**i**ng the door in his face.

Icarus huffed at the door in his face, painting an annoyed expression, but before taking **a** step back, he saw the **f**r**o**nt part of his foot ghosting halfway through the solid door. He dragged it out slowly, then back, to see his toes ghost through again.

"Why - - does all this feel normal!" Icarus sighed, closing his eyes, thus walked through the door like it wasn't there.

"Erini Se Sas," he whispered

The invisible guest opened his eyes on the naked wooden floor, pushing his foot down on a loosen plate. He lifted his head up as his sight started adjusting to the slightly dark interior of the house. It was simple and clean; a kitchen on the right, where the humming mother was preparing the table, a living room on the left, where Flaco and his brothers were still arguing and exchanging discreet blows, and a long hall in between that leads to the back door, before it, one door on each side. Icarus looked back, thus thrust his hand in and out through the door, a simple gesture out of instinct, to make sure he wasn't trapped. He did the same thing to the walls and furniture whilst exploring the small house. The only thing he could physically interact with was the floors.

"Valeria, go call your sisters," said the mother to her youngest. The little girl hurried to the hall, then the room on the right.

"You three go wash your hands," she ordered her three sons with a spoon clatter

The family gathered aro**und** the table for dinner, and even in the presence of their mother, Flaco's brother kept harassing him every time she looked away, until she turned sharply to place the bread basket and caught them.

CHAPTER TWO

"Stop it," she scowled, pointing the wooden spoo**n** in their f**ace**s like a long saber, then in Flaco's, but pulled it back quickly.

"Mi amor, go call your father," she ordered

"Papa!" Flaco started calling loudly before leaving his chair. He walked through the hall and out of the back door, foll**ow**ed by Icarus.

Flaco looked at his father, pressing down his harsh brown moustache, **f**oc**u**sed while reading the newspaper.

"Papa, dinner is ready," Flaco said low

"I'm coming," replied his father si**m**pl**y**, standing up with his eyes still fixed on the newspaper.

Flaco ran back inside, and when he reached the table, he smacked the back of his brother's head before he got **to** his chair. His brother wanted a payback but feared the wrath of his mother.

The old man followed while folding the paper to put it under his armpit. He looked at his wife's behind as she was serving the food, to notice his six ch**ild**ren looking at him whilst suppressing a grin. He shamelessly winked back with a **p**l**a**yfu**l** smile.

"Still striving to read that stupid thing," Agile, his wife gibed in a derisive tone, pointing out his poor English, **bu**t her husband was always quick to reply,

"I learned English to read this - - not to recite poetry about your fat Culo," he quipped back quickly, making the kids free a group nasal chuckle, Flaco even spitted the water back inside his cup.

"Shush!" s**tu**nned, she slapped the side of his arm for being vulgar. But all it took to draw a smile on her angry face was a quick kiss on the cheek.

The family was poor, but rich in heart, and seeing that, curved a spontaneous warm smile on Icarus's face.

The old man sat down, joining his child**re**n, thrilled to share what he read with his wife.

"I finished the one Mr. Orange gave me," he said, grabbing a glass of water.

"The one about the Morgan's office bombing last year," he added with his lips touching the cup, then drank the water with one sip.

"Tell us about it Papa, please," begged Flaco, filled with excitement.

"Yes Papa, please." said his older brother, scornfully mimicking him, and right before telling them, his wife interjected reluctantly:

WHAT CAN A TWIG DO !

"It's no story for chil**d**ren"

She forced a second breadbasket to her husban's hand while giving him a sign to shut up. He acted like he was clearing his throat, to avoid his wife's glares.

Icarus's bracelet glowed faintly, while his lashes fluttered for a moment like they did every time he received a sudden memo**ry** or information.

"Twenty-two dead and more than t**wo** hundred injured!" stated Icarus with a low voice, loo**king** down at the bracelet, thence Flaco, who got off his chair to push the chair of his little sister closer to the table. His mo**the**r sat down and stretched both hands on the table, palms up.

"Mi amor!" she called **F**l**ac**o back to his seat, wiggling her fingers to rush him. He hurried back to his chair, then grabbed his little sister's hand and his brother's with the other. After joining hands, everyone closed their eyes, allowing their mother **to** recite grace.

"Amen," said all of them after she finished

While eating, Flaco looked **at** his sister's plate to notice her piece of chicken was too small. He looked at his parents and siblings with a side-eye then sneaked his piece into her plate. His little sister tried to **r**eject, but he forced it on her plate anyway.

"Shush, eat so you can get bigger," he hissed with a smile, pressing her long hair behind her ear so it doesn't bother her while she eats.

"Say that to yourself, idiota," said his older brother with a **w**hisper, punching his thigh under the table, then gave him his piece of chicken. Icarus curved a faint smile of pleasantry after seeing how they care for one another.

"I love you t**oo**," said a snide Flaco, mocking his brother.

"Eat and shut up," replied his brother, reaching for a piece of bread.

"So, tomorrow is your first payment," chatted the father, waggling a brow at Flaco while stuffing a piece of bread inside thus asked with his mouth full:

"Have you decided how to spend it?"

"He will give it to charity," interjected the mother with a fake smile, serving more soup into his plate.

"Right mama!" she said, blowing a short air-kiss.

Her husband looked at her, rubbing his lips against each other. She already knew that was his expression before a sharp comment.

"I thought you said '*God is rich*'," he interrupted, arguing her proposition.

_ (6-7) (17-10) (7-3) * (15-5) * (8-12) * (21-12) (24-4) (1-5) * (10-5) (13-3) (5-8)

"Why would he need a nineteen cent from the poor kid?" He asked in a snide tone while **t**aking another bite.

The eldest squeezed her lips shut, keeping the spoon inside her mouth to hide her smile, while her religious mother found no counter to what he said. Noticing her daughter's suppressed laughter annoyed her even more. She stood up, rolling her eyes while praying low.

"Oh Senõr forgive us!" She grabbed her plate, then went for her husband's plate.

"Hey! I'm not done yet," he protested, l**ook**ing at her putting both plates in the sink,

"Why?"

He looked at his kids then sank his bread into his eldest daughter's plate.

"Papa!" she whinged, pushing his hand away.

"Thank you, Papa," blithe, he said, pushing the juicy bite inside his mouth.

Later at night, the children prepared their beds to sleep. While Icarus peeked through the window, standing not so far from Flaco's bed. He looked up the **st**e**ep** slope, wondering if Gray were still there, and right before he tried to ghost through the wall to go check, **a** low susurration caught his attention.

"Flaco! Laco!" whispered the little sister, gently pinching Flaco's back.

"Yes!" a drowsy Flaco replied with a faint whisper

"What - - you will - - do with the money?" she asked with a stutter and mixed up words, poking his back again. Flaco turned around, facing her while rubbing the smell of old wool off his stiff nose.

"Save it of course. Then one day, I will buy a big house," he answered, adjusting Val's blanket to cover her shoulders.

"Not of wood but bricks - - like a castle," optimistic, he added, patting her head.

"Can I - - live with you?" asked Val in a low voice

"Of course; you, Mama, Papa and all of us," replied a dreamy Flaco with a warm smile.

His older brothers started chuckling quietly like piglets until they burst with a slightly louder laughter.

"Too early to be dreaming twiggy," one of them badgered Flaco, thus hammered him with his pillow.

"Ouch! Just wait and see," F**l**ac**o** dared, pushing the pillow away to slam him with his.

Their secret fight woke their elder sister, so she shushed them both with a drowsy yet angry sigh,

"Sleep now," she whisper-shouted, making them hurriedl**y** hid their heads under their **b**l**a**nkets.

The night passed, and before the sun peeked behind the high plains, Flaco and his father woke up for work, likewise his mother, who always woke up even earlier to prepare breakfast for them **and** a lunch to go.

After a healthy and mode**st** meal, the father and son left the house, followed by a ghostly Mingan. Before he headed to the road after them, he decided to pass by Gray first. Instead of climbing the slope, all it took from the Mingan was a high leap, only to find his **m**entor still asleep on his serene, cloudy bed.

"Hey - - wake up," Icarus said, shaking Gray's shoulder, but he refused to respond or react. Icarus shook him again, but rougher:

"The kid is moving"

"Go then, we will follow later," somnolent, he answered with a faint yawn

The Mingan surrendered to Gray's slothfulness. He rushed his steps, following Flaco and his father. All three walked on the side of the road for thirty minutes nonstop, telling silly jokes as entertainment.

But Icarus wasn't having much fun, for his wings kept gliding on the sandy ground, and the harsh grain gave him a bothersome sensation of an unp**l**eas**an**t tingle.

"Stupid wings, stay - - up," he whinged low, hunching his back and tightening his shoulder-blades in an attempt to lift them.

"Stupid body," a ponderous Flaco groaned synchronously with Icarus and with the same tone, trying to walk straight with the heavy bag on his back.

His father, who was slightly ahead, looked back at Flaco with a smile.

"Let me have that," said his father, trying to grab the bag off his back but Flaco refused, **c**r**e**asing his forehead.

Flaco knew he was weak compared to boys his age, but he hated to be pitied because of it. However, even while showing a strong character, he always questioned his fragile carcass and the reason why he was born that way. Also, listening to his mother repeating what they preach in the church, that all humans were born with sin, m**ade** his naïve mind think that maybe he did something bad, and for that god **p**unish**e**d him.

"Papa, why was I born like this?" a frustrated Flaco grumbled, tightening his grip on **the** bag whilst lowering his head down, thus added with a faint voice:

"I wish I was **s**trong like you - - or mi hermanos"

"Listen to **me**, Laco," his father interjected, painting a serious look.

"If I learned anything from life, is that everything happens for a r**e**a**s**on," he slammed his chest with his left twice and said with a confident smile:

"You may not grow **to** be a muscular man, but - - I k**no**w damn well you will grow to be a very strong one. You just need to find your way, the one suited for you and your poten**ti**als"

He patted his head then gloated:

"And you will, because you're my son"

I**ca**rus heard his words as if they were meant for him. His tense muscles and shoulders relaxed, so did his inner unease.

"Concentrate," he mused low

Icarus closed his eyes, taking a deep breath while heightening his senses, feeling the flow of his **bl**ood rushing through his veins.

"I can feel it now!" focused, he whispered with a smile as his w**ing**s started to straighten up then flutter as he pleases. Finally, it was the moment when the Mingan found the way to fully control his new limbs, and just flap them close and open.

"All I need now is to train you guys," he smirked proudly, but got interrupted by a truck that parked over his immaterial body. His head was the only part showing out of the cargo on the back, where a dozen men were sitting haphazardly on the cargo's floor, wearing thin stained shirts and loosened stirrup leggings. **F**l**ac**o and his father mounted in, greeting their fellow workers.

"Oll wright," an impassive Icarus said, walking away from the truck. He stretched his arms up, looking at the dirty lorry departing, leaving him behind.

"You guys need to wait until I control these two," he grinned, talking to his wings and referring to his legs with gentle smacks on his right knee whilst taking a trotting position. He waited for the truck to advance far away, giving it a head start, just in case he flashes past it and gets lost - - again.

"That should be enough," said an excited Mingan, looking at the mechanical box turning into a bug-size dot in the narrow road. The moment Icarus bolted **in** full speed; he tumbled hardly on his chest and face, rolling on the harsh road like a human-tumbleweed.

"What the - -" agonized and baffled, Icarus groaned, raising his beaten carcass to a sitting posture. He shook his head while widening his eyes confused to see his legs tied up with a bronze chain, coiling both of his legs from ankle to knee. Bewil**dered**, the Mingan tried freeing his legs but couldn't.

"That damn sorcerer!" Choleric, he whisper-shouted with his teeth pressed, looking at the truck fading away. He used his hands to stand then kept hopping in the same spot with his arms spread to the sides to bala**nce** his body.

"Oll wright, challenge accepted kopanos," he insulted with an angry grin

First, the Mingan spread his eight feet wings to their limit. He fluttered them lei**sur**ely at the beginning then faster, shaking all the surrounding dust off the road.

"Here **I** come!"

Icarus started leaping forward like a giant rabbit while fluttering his large wings vigorously. He flew several feet above the ground to fall not far after, and the same thing happened over and over, but that didn't stop him from continuing with the same process.

"Come on," he grunted tightly, floating higher for seconds, and as he was ready to wear a **s**m**ile**, he sensed a faint pull of gravity driving him back to the ground. He creased his forehead, fed up.

"*Not this time*," Icarus snarled, curving his legs to their limits whilst joining his thighs with his chest, and right before he landed, the Mingan stomped the ground with full st**ren**gth while adding to it a strong flap; the push propelled him high like a reversed swoop, breaking the cage of gravity.

"WOUH!" jubilant, Icarus shouted his lungs out, enjoying the cold gust on his face. He paused in mid-air like a floating astronaut in outer space. The Mingan took his time before locking his enhanced vision on the wagon.

After consuming a long breath of clean air, Icarus speared towards the truck like a hawk, joining his arms with his body to increase his speed.

Finally, the truck parked at a wood factory, releasing the workers out, in the meantime, the flying man landed slowly on his joined feet then knees. As he was observing Flaco giving his bag to his father before he jumped off the truck,

Icarus felt something sl**it**her**ing** on his lower legs. He looked down to see the rope transforming into living serpents.

"Damn it!" an unhing**ed** Mingan groused, shaking the crawlers off his feet. He then grabbed the last one and kept slamming it on the ground while furiously snarling:

"What - - is wrong - - with that man!"

The snake slipped from his grip then tu**r**n**ed** to a fading black **s**moke. Icarus was building the worst expression because of Gray's frenzied ways. The only thing that kept Icarus un**will**ing to leave was the binding oath and the fact that he couldn't even if he **wa**nted to.

Flaco and his father checked into the factory, followed **b**y a f**e**d up Icarus, who passed through the wall instead of the open gate. The Mingan locked his **ey**es on Flaco, scrutinizing him from far. He wondered why was he special in the ey**es** of Gray.

Icarus looked round the gate, hoping Gray steps in to **f**eed him answe**r**s, yet h**e** kn**e**w that won't be anytime soon. He approached Flaco, who was changing his **clo**the**s**, taking the chance to check for any special marks on his skinny body, and the only marks he found were the bone-lines showing under his scraggy skin.

Icarus scratched his chin, disillusioned, yet slightly curious.

"Show me something - - anything kid," he said, but this time, focusing on his aura to see if he had any hidden talent. After a brief examination, a disappointed Icarus sighed:

"Really - - Nothing!"

Raising a white flag, Icarus walked away, accepting that Flaco was simply a skinny and fragile kid, however, he didn't intend to fail the first task giving to him by his mentor, therefore, even while believing nothing special will happen, he monitored Flaco from a distant.

After hours of work, Flaco's father shouted to the rest of the crew:

"Time, time"

He walked to a head-size bell hanged on the side, close to the factory's gate. While looking at the clock on the wall, he shouted louder:

"Time"

He rang the bell so the others would hear him over the noises of the other machineries. He then waved a hand at Flaco.

_ (12-14) (13-14) * (17-1) (3-4) * (10-4) (1-4)

"Go get the bags," he **screa**med high, exaggerating the movement of his mouth while pointing at the balcony upstairs so Flaco could understand him.

Flaco nodded his head, then went running up the metallic stairs, and when he reached the pile of bags thrown there, he started looking **for** both of their bags inside the cloth mountain of sacs, pressing his nostrils shut, for some bags reeked of unpleasant odours of garlic and onions.

"I remember putting it here," perplexed, Flaco **m**us**ed** with an adenoidal voice. He then walked to the balcony's open edge, cautiously overlooking at his fa**th**er.

"Papa, did you move it somewhere else? The bags - - did you move them?" He shouted from above, putting one foot near the edge and one behind.

A careless Icarus looked at him from down while standing not so far from Flaco's father. Suddenly, all the machinery noises reduced to a flatulent silence. Icarus looked righ**t** and **l**eft at the moving machines, making no sound, thus the workers. Their mouths were moving as they spoke to one another, but he couldn't hear **a** word. He used his palm to smack his right ear, but nothing changed. Everything was on a mute mode.

An echo of slow footsteps stomping on a metallic ground broke the silence. Icarus followed the sound up to where Flaco stood to see Gray slithering behind the boy, wearing a white suit and cowboy hat.

"It took you long enough. Hey, why are you muting everything?" Icarus exasperated with a disturbed whisper then shouted his question but received no answer. Gray didn't even bother looking his way.

Icarus narrowed his eyes. Feeling something odd about his partner, and seconds after it was clear for the Mingan. Gray's killing intent rose with every step taken closer to Flaco.

The man in white looked round Icarus, smiling maliciously while waving slowly. He then used the same hand to give Flaco a gentle push, one **that** caused him to lose his balance. After a surprised gasp from Flaco, all the noises of workers and machineries rose up again.

Bug-eyed, Flaco looked down to where his body was heading. He stretched his leg back as his upper-body slowly leaned forward, a **de**sper**a**te attempt to pull his cadaver away from the edge.

"No!" the frightened boy shirked before he plummeted with a slow front-flip.

(4-11) * (16-2) * (32-11) (9-1) * (28-15) * (1-6) (7-8)

CHAPTER TWO

"Blow!"

Flaco landed on his feet first, thus his back before slamming his head onto the conveyor belt of **the** wood-chopping machine.

Witnessing what happened, Icarus and Flaco's father shrieked ghastly at the same time:

"No!"

The shock of that fall caused the convey**or** belt Flaco fell onto to move, driving him to the massive blades; four rotating choppers shaped like giant cleavers, while the poor boy closed his eyelids on them getting bigger and bigger.

While Flaco's father had to go all the way around to reach his son, Icarus dashed through the machines that blocked the way, all thanks to his ghost form.

"You're safe now kid," hasty, said Icarus, grabbing Flaco to see his hands going through. Icarus forgot that.

He sighed audibly, then tried for a second time, but his hand ghosted again. He clutched his eyebrows frantically while his breaths became faster and more vocal, repeatedly switching his **vi**sion between Flaco and the blades. He then tried to push him instead of pulling. Nothing changed. His hands went through Flaco's body.

"F**K! F**K! F**K!" jittery, Icarus cursed, while repeatedly trying to pull and push Flaco away, but couldn't. He lost his co**ol**, screaming and threatening Gray whilst continuing on his failed attempts to save the boy. The Mingan's hands moved so fast they started multiplying, but if you multiply a zero by a hundred, it stays a zero.

When Flaco was a few feet from the blades, Icarus turned his face away while squeezing his eyes shut to avoid seeing Flaco cut to pieces.

The Mingan kept his eyes shut, painting a tight down smile on his face whilst waiting for the unpleasant sound of what he couldn't prev**en**t from happening.

Moments passed and more, yet Icarus heard nothing of what he expected.

"Laco, Papa! Oh thank you god, Thank you!"

Icarus heard the shaking voi**ce** of Flaco's father sobbing joyfully. He opened his eyes slowly, then hesitantly looked back. There was no blood on the blades or the moving belt. Baffled, Icarus glimpsed the father's head behind the blades as they slew **d**own, then stopped. He approached him to get a better look to see him hugging Flaco and kissing him, whilst wiping the tears off his smiley cheeks.

"How!" taken aback, Icarus said low with his mouth agape.

Flaco was unharmed, not even a scratch! Because of his skinny and sm**all** body, he **missed** the deadly bl**ades**.

"No way!" Icarus sighed deeply, putting his hands on his head, not belie**vi**ng what happened. He released another long breath of relief, enjoying the overwhelming scene. Then he remembered who caused that entire tremble he felt.

Icarus shifted his vision up to the balcony with a sharp stroke, to see Gray's back as he was about to leave. The Mingan jumped high with his wings open, landing on the balcony, **but** Gray was already gone.

He looked down, seeing Flaco regaining consciousness while **sur**rounded by the bunch of workers, wearing joyful smiles on their faces.

"**I**'m really glad you're safe kid," Icarus smiled then flew away through the wall.

After a quick flight, Icarus landed be**for**e Gray, who was still lying under the tree the same way he left him, but the **bl**ow Icarus made when he landed woke him up.

Icarus ambled towards his master, folding his wings whilst wearing a cold yet angry face.

"Why - - Why! You almost killed him," a glowering warrior snarled, tightening his fists. He stood on Gray's side and mo**ved** his lips with the same question without saying the word. Then, he snapped and lifted Gray aggressively from his shirt:

"Answer me, you demon"

"To train you of course," a placid Gray replied, slowly grabbing Icarus's hand, and without losing a sweat, he easily twisted Icarus's grip off his clothes. Not only that, he squeezed it tight to show his apprentice who had the upper hand.

"We said it before. We are not here for a picnic," he reminded

Icarus released Gray's shirt, thus slapped Gray's hand off his grip. He massaged it then gave it a wave to shake the pain off.

_ (10-3) * (13-1) * (11-9) (5-13) (21-10) * (15-7) * (3-13) * (16-10) (4-5) * (4-2)

CHAPTER TWO

Gray sighed and snapped his finger, turning day to night in an instant. **S**econds after, the sky continued changing from cyan to Prussian blue repeatedly in a flash.

"What is - - what are you doing?" puzzled, Icarus asked, orbiting his body whilst looking heavenward, then down beyond Flaco's house, observing the town changing, as if it were an old movie speeding forward. **S**o**m**e buildings vanished, others grew bigger **and** t**all**er. An entire city was built in seconds. Then, every**thin**g stopped with a second finger snap from Gray.

"What's going on?" Icarus perplexed in a disbelieving tone, looking at Flaco's torn house turning into a vast villa.

"We moved time - - forward," answered Gray, leaving his place to stand aside I**ca**ru**s** at the edge of the steep slope that transformed to a green space.

"Do you like what you see?" Gray asked, resting a hand on Icarus's shoulder.

The Mingan stupefied in his place, speechless with the sudden transformation he witnessed; the prominent buildings, the stea**my** towers and the **car** noises with their engines and honking. But mostly with the mansion that replaced Flaco's house.

"Are we - -" baffled, Icarus asked, nuzzling Gray's hand off his shoulder before taking a few steps closer to the edge.

"Yes, the *Where* is the same, we just - - changed the *When,*" Gray clarified while following Icarus with slow steps.

As the Mingan had his eyes locked on one of the chimney tower, releasing a gray cloud, he felt a flick on his ear. Gray tapped his ear to drive his attention to a couple sitting on a fancy white table at the mansion's veranda, laughing whilst having tea and enjoying their luxurious life. The man was in his late forties, but

(14-6) * (7-1) * (6-4) * (5-11) (6-5) * (14-10) (11-1) (1-14)

even with his fancy clothes and pleasant look, his skinny and fragile body gave him away.

Without delay, **I**carus flew down closer to them, and the moment he landed, he heard a **str**ange wind behind him. He looked back to see Gray on his tail with a blithe smile.

"Do you recognize him?" Gray asked, walking closer to the couple whilst observing the beauty of the vast garden; the perfect**ly** mowed bushes and the roses of different species and colours.

"F**la**co!" replied Icarus with a suppressed smile, pleasant, seeing the happy face Flaco had while talking and la**ugh**ing with his beautiful companion. Gray joined their table, but before taking a seat, he snapped his finger again, pausing everything but him and Icarus.

"Correct," he confirmed Icarus's assumption

"After that accident - - incident," Gray said while taking the pot of tea from Flaco's hand to serve himself one, and just as he was about to pour the tea into his cup, he looked at the fixed waterfall of r**ed** tea Flaco left when he was serving one for the lady. So he grabbed his teacup and swayed it to collect the floating tea inside. Gray took a sip while pouring another for Icarus. But the Mingan was busy making sure the chair was solid to make sure it was safe to sit on, and when he did, he fixed his eyes on Flaco. Gray placed the pot down, thus continued:

"Flaco here started to look at life with - - an optimistic eye. He cared less about his fragile body and focused on what he had"

"His father's advice," Icarus commented low

"Yes, and - - he was very good with money, and ideas"

Gray told Icarus of what happened and how Flaco pursued his dream, then introduced the lovely lady sharing his table, she was Valeria, his little sister. Icarus enjoyed the story al**ong** with the sweet taste of tea, and that was the first time him and Gray sat down like normal friends.

A while after, a moment of silence took over, allowing the sips of tea to be audible. Icarus placed his cup, creasing his cheeks.

"But why?" He asked curiously

Gray widened his eyes bluntly, waiting for a less vague question.

_ (3-3) * (9-1) (10-7) (16-9) * (4-3) (27-4) (7-9)

CHAPTER TWO

"**I'm** - - Why do you think I needed such a childish lesson?" sour, Icarus argued, joining his hands while resting one elbow on the table.

"Well, you are so full of - - guilt **and** Ifs," replied Gray with a tone that carried a slight of disgust mixed with disappointment,

"Piling this - - negative energy, one in your case, destructive"

Gray rested his palm on the table, then started giving it a slam with every sentence said.

"If only I was stronger, if only I was faster, if only I p**la**nned better," upset, Gray jabbered, knock**ing** harder while increasing the volume of his voice as he spoke the last sentence:

"If only I chose - - another road them"

The last slam dropped the silver spoon from the table, clanging in a moment of silen**ce**, and when it stopped, Gray added with a soft voice:

"If only I stayed behind - - instead of them"

Gray's words irritated Icarus, as if they were hinting to a hidden truth, one that Gray could know only if he had his eyes on him for long.

Suddenly, a calm Gray turned aggressive. He rapidly gripped Icarus's neck and shouted in his face:

"They are dead, and none of it was your fault. You need to stop - - Stop"

Gray unclenched Icarus with a faint push, leaving him stupefied, agape, looking at his temperamental mentor speechlessly, for he found nothing to say. Who was Gray speaking of? Icarus's twitching eyes revealed an expression of loss. His lips moved to ask, '*how did you know?*' but no words were spoken, for he already knew the answer now. Choo**sin**g him was no coincidence, but planned for way before his fall.

Gray grabbed the spoon from the floor and placed it on a glass of water.

"No more Ifs, accept your fate. This is life and life is meant to be shitty," Gray admonished, pointing at Flaco with a slight nod.

"And choose, live in regret, or be like him," he compared Icarus's will with Flaco's,

"Otherwise, you will live a very - - Very dark one"

Gray sighed after his speech, back to enjoying his tea as if nothing happened. He left Icarus to his tho**ugh**ts, locking his eyes on Flaco while evaluating his will compared to the man before him, remembering how small and significant he thought of him, just to find out he bore a stronger spirit.

WHAT CAN A TWIG DO !

The Mingan placed both hands on his face, leaving his mouth free to breathe. He inhaled profoundly then vigorously **s**lammed his hands on his cheeks, and another o**ne**, painting t**w**o burlywood hand-marks on his face. He released a longer breath while Gray stared at him weirdly.

"Indeed, your words are of an inexorable truth, I cannot bear to argue," Icarus admitted with an honest tone

"When life throws a lemon at you__" he added, grabbing a lemon slice fr**om** the table then squeezed it inside his **c**up,

"__you grab it, and make a lemon juice"

Gray looked at him with a sly and **s**urpri**s**ed smile, then hid a chuckle with his cup of tea.

"We forgot you made this proverb," Gray mumbled his words inside his cup before he drank then gave his apprentice a fake grin.

"What!" Icarus asked dully

"Nothing," Gray smirked, while extracting the vermillion book out of thin air.

"Time to head back," said Gray, **pl**a**c**ing the porting book on the table, then s**m**oothl**y** slid it closer to the Mingan.

"Oll wright, Lead the **wa**y," said Icarus with a mute smile, thus placed his hand on the book.

"I wonder what's nex - -"

Gray teleported Icarus before he finished, then took another sip in silence.

"I love doing this, next round on you," he said **joy**fully, looking up then followed Icarus,

"Swish!"

(22-11) * (18-5) (2-5) * (17-1) * (3-1) (3-3) * (8-8) (7-14) (16-7) (10-9)

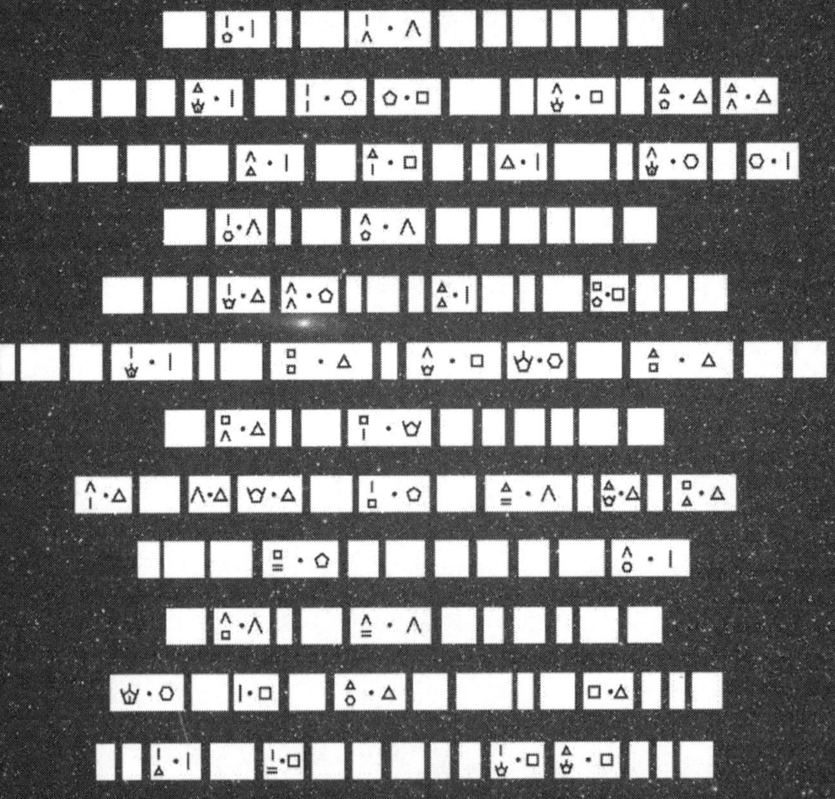

CHAPTER THREE
THE FEARLESS AND THE BRAVE

Kara **was** enjoying her alone time in the library, humming while munching a b**it**e of her juicy apple.

She glimpsed the mermaid rug before her moving! Curious, Kara approached the carpet cagily to see it transform into the vermillion book of Flaco. Soon after, she heard a faint wind behind her. When she looked back, **G**ray appeared out of the bookshelf like a chameleon, fully hued with the same motif of the books behind him. His clothes, skin and mask transformed to their original colours as he walked past Kara to grab the book.

"The cask, hurry," he ordered Kara, pointing at the corner of his desk.

Kara ran as if she were waiting for that order.

Gray thrust his hand inside the book, thus pulled Icarus out like a magician pulling a bunny out of his tall hat.

The Mingan fell on his knees to find Kara standing before him with an empty bucket. With **no** delay, he hugged the bucket with one arm before he shoved his head inside and started puking.

"Gibber!" Kara patted his head to ease his pain, mindless of the sti**nk**. Unlike Gray, who walked away to his desk with two fingers blocking his nostrils.

"How does vomit - - can smell **thi**s bad!?" Gray groused with a nasal voice

The man in black took his fingers out of his nose, thus shook the air away. And while leaning over the desk to blow the fetor further, he glimpsed the kitchen's hidden door, cracked.

He shifted to Kara with his eyes suspicious.

"Speaking of smell," he said in a leisurely and dubious tone

"When we walked in, we sniffed bananas. Come here," he beckoned the little creature with two joined fingers

Kara walked to him, painting an innocent face, an unconvincing one.

"Whoop!" she chattered slowly while pointing at her open mouth.

"Don't lie. **You** hate bananas, you can't even hold one unpeeled," Gray objected, narrowing his eyes **thin**ner. But Kara insisted and denied his accusation until he challenged her:

"Very well. Go get yourself a fresh one - - and eat it - - before us"

CHAPTER THREE

Kara forced a weird grin while rubbing her belly, hinting that she's full. But Gray saw through her. He painted a cunning smile.

"The truth - - or we will make you stuff an entire hand of big, yellow__" Gray said in a slow and teasing manner while Kara tried **to** maintain her innocent grin,

"__mushy, shaped like an elf poop"

Kara surrendered. She stopped him from continuing with a nauseated screech.

"Bwaack!"

After making a revolted grimace, she started chattering fast while using hand signs, pointing at the kitchen, thence to the corridor.

Upset, Gray shushed her, squeezing his hand into a fist.

"We told you - - **not** to feed him," Gray huffed the words from the depth of his tight throat, trying to maintain a low voice, **but** that didn't deny her a proper scolding.

"Never again - - never - - Let Pixie do **it**, understood?"

"Screech!" cogent, Kara argued, pointing her finger to the long corridor again, but Gray silenced her, raising a finger in her face,

"Even if he called you," he said with a fixed emphasis, leaning down, thus gave her forehead a sharp flick.

"Don't - - go - -there - - alone," he added in a serious tone

Kara rubbed her forehead while lowering her head shamefacedly.

Meanwhile, Icarus looked at Kara being rebuked, so he attempted to help her.

"What's going on? Leave her alo - -" wan, he said groggily, before he throws up again.

"Just - - shut up, please. Get up and go **was**h yourself," a disgusted Gray replied, expelling the reek with desperate hand waves. He then patted Kara's head.

"Love, show him to his shower, and how to use it," Gray said kindly

Gray's gentle pats painted a pleasant smile on Kara's face.

She ran to Icarus and grabbed his hand, helping him up thus towards his chamber, and he obediently followed, shuffling, with a hand blocking his mouth.

Gray placed the book back in its place before heading to his chair, listening to Icarus blabbering inside.

"Pitter patter!"

"Woo! Now that's what I call magic," Icarus's gravelly voice echoed, along with Kara's chatters.

"Wait! It can be hot and cold! But how?"

Gray rested his forehead on the edge of his desk, then **si**ghed:

"We need a break, it's your turn"

"Thank **you**, little one," Icarus said

A blushing Kara walked out, giving Icarus a wave before she closed the door. And while she was painting a big smile on her chanted face, she turned around to see Gray glaring at her with his six white.

"Eek, eek!" she chattered, coyly avoiding eye contact whilst running towards **the** hidden door that leads to the kitchen

"Yes, get him some fruits. Don't mind asking us if we want some," an unpleasant Gray said with a satiric manner, drumming his fingers on the desk.

Kara chattered back before entering the kitchen, asking if that meant he wants something to eat as well.

He knocked on the desk with the soft part of his fist.

"Yes we do, thank you for asking," he peered, looking at Kara rushing her steps **in** confusion. He then peeked at the bucket **left** by Icarus, curving a down-smile.

"Tsk! Lee - - Lee, co**me** here," he shouted

A cru**de** broom ran out of the first section, on legs formed from its body of straw; followed by a flying duster-brush of black ostrich feathers. Both stopped in front of Gray's desk like trained troops.

"Vi, not you," Gray said to the floating duster then ordered the broom:

"Lee, take that bucket away, and can you please do something about the smell!"

Lee bent the top of his wooden stick as a yes thus dashed to the bucket, forming two hands of straw. He used one to grab the scuttle whilst placing two fingers on the bottom of his wood, as if he were blocking his figureless nose.

Meanwhile, Vi kept floating around Gray like a flying puppy waiting for a Frisbee to be tossed so she could go and grab it. In Vi's case, the Frisbee was a chore to do so she could feel like an adult.

"Go clean the lanterns," Gray sighed

The duster flew rapidly to the closest lantern, shaking the non-existing dust as if she were dancing while doing so.

CHAPTER THREE

After a refreshing shower, I**c**a**r**us walked out of his room to first glimpse Vi fl**ying** from a moon-lantern to another.

"Your magic is useful when it comes to cleaning," he **sa**id with a sardonic tone, thinking the shower was a work of magic too. He then saw a smiling Kara standing by the couch, pointing at the fruit basket on the table, filled with various kin**ds**.

"Is this for me?" Icarus asked pleasantly, stepping between the couch and the table with a sidewalk,

"Thank you, little one"

Kara nodded her head yes, drawing a wider smile while taking a seat, thus giving him **the** space to sit by her side.

Icarus shrugged, pulling his folded wings back inside with no difficulties, then th**re**w his back on the couch.

"You're used to them n**ow**, very good," Gray praised, taking a bite from the apple on his right, while intentionally showing his sharp fangs.

"By the way, we like your outfit," he added, pointing at the black sweatpants Icarus wore, along with the black hooded sweatshirt.

The Mingan m**is**understood Gray's words. He adjusted his hood and said awkwardly:

"Thank you! I hope you don't mind. The clothes I had - -"

"All of what's inside that room is yours," Gray interjected with two sharp taps on the desk. He then raised his apple as if it were a glass of a fancy wine.

"Cheers," Gray said, taking another bite. While Icarus grabbed a red apple from the fruit basket, thus imitated Gray without saying the word.

Icarus admired the sweetness of his apple with an audible sigh, finishing it wholly with three bites

"I'm starving," He said with his mouth full

Kara lingered, staring at him with her vision fixed on the fruit he grabbed while nodding with a broad mouth. Her smile made it obvious to Icarus. She was simply waiting for praise or a pat on the head.

"Mm! This is exquisite. You picked my favourite fruits," Icarus said, faking an exaggerated expression of delight, only to cheer his new little friend.

Turning to the side, Gray noticed the door of his room was slightly open. Without leaving his place, he swayed his hand, shutting the door. He then locked the doorknob with a slight reel from his finger.

"Click!"

The man in black saw a hint of suspicion on the Mingan's face, so he changed the subject,

"Deceiving the pure girl with a fake smile! Where is your nobility," he smirked, exposing Icarus. He then captured Kara's attention with a quick finger-drumming on the desk.

"Kara dear, go wake that somnolent Pixie," he sent Kara into the fourth section, thus continued, **no**t giving Icarus the chance to inquire of who was this Pixie.

"And you, young Mingan," he said, leaning down **to** open the desk drawer.

"Can you please get us a book titled **Y**aashva - - from that bookshelf over there," he requested, pulling a wand out of the drawer whilst pointing to the same section Kara ran into.

"Oll wright," replied Icarus, standing with a banana in hand.

He peeled it, looking back at Gray while stepping inside the hall. He just remembered his su**rr**oundings were still unknown. The only places he was familiar with were his ch**a**m**b**er and the common room.

After stepping inside the section, he noticed an atmosphere change, as if he travelled between t**wo** continents with one step.

"This one?" uncertain, Icarus inquired, while pointing to the bookshelf on his right.

"Yes, just call for it," Gray replied simply, organizing some papers whilst shredding another pile before using the wand as a lighter to burn it.

"Call for it!" a perplexed Icarus puzzled low while looking at the bookshelf, tall, all the way to the ceiling.

The Mingan sighed then lifted his hand and wiggled his fingers, incorrectly imitating Gray when he used magic.

"Yaashva," Said Icarus with a silly tone, then stood there waiting with his eyebrows lifted. But no**thing** happened. So he intended to call again but got interrupted by a cracking sound.

The wood on the side split, giving him a brief spook. He focused his eyes on the crack, spreading silently, and while he moved warily closer to investigate, a wooden hand surged **out**, thus another from the other side.

"Shit! Oll wright!" cautiously, he whispered, taking a step back while resting a hand on the pommel of his sword.

CHAPTER THREE

He observed the **w**ooden hands elongating whilst rising halfway up the bookshelf. Both grabbed a thick book with a celadon cover.

"*The book - - of* ***Y****aashva*"

Ic**a**r**u**s heard a singsong voice coming out of the bookshelf, while the wooden hands descended to hand him the book; however, a hesitant Icarus left it hanging, for he **was** momentarily stunned.

"*Young master!*"

The voice said again but with an annoyed tone, pushing the book against Icarus's chest and forc**ing** him to grab it, then swayed back.

"Wait - - wait," Icarus said with a loud whisper, stopping the hand from retreating, and one of the hands complied.

"Is there a book here - - talking about **me**?" A curious Mingan asked, looking at Gray with a side-eye.

The wooden hand joined all four fingers, placing them on its thumb to form a head-like shape, one **you** do to draw an earless dog shade on the wall. It carefully looked at Gray, then nodded yes.

Icarus looked at Gray again, who was busy organizing his desk then turned round the hand, excited.

"Can **I** have it?" he whispered, but the hand refused, putting down his cheerful expression.

"You parsimonious twig," annoyed, Icarus cursed with his eyes half-closed. What made the wooden hand give him the middle finger, but Icarus didn't understand it.

"One?" baffled, Icarus asked, looking at the hand di**sa**ppearing back inside

"Hey, what do you mean by one?" he whisper-shouted, slamming a hand on the spot where the wooden head sank to.

A disappointed Icarus walked back to Gray with a puzzled face.

He stood before the desk, roaming in his thoughts. He cared little about what the hand meant by '*One,*' but rather, why does Gray have a book about him? Was it like Flaco's? And if it were, did it mean that his book held information about his future? However, the Mingan kept it all to himself, at least for the time being.

"Thank you," said Gray with his hand stretched towards Icarus, waiting for the Mingan to hand him the book.

_ (15-5) * (24-9) (1-4) * (12-8) * (19-2) * (6-3) * (4-1) (3-4) (9-3)

"Ahem! The book," Gray said with a higher pitch, stretching his arm longer.

"Ah yes!" Icarus gasped low, handing the book to Gray, then headed b**a**c**k** to his place and sat down.

He exchang**ed** stares with Gray while his face screamed '*Questions.*'

"What does this mean?" **a** reluctant Icarus asked, giving Gray the middle finger.

Gray looked at him with a slack jaw.

"What the fu - - **wh**o tol - - That means - -" a confused Gray stuttered, thus reluctantly postponed, standing up sharply:

"We have to leave now. We will tell **you** about this later. Or on second thought, ask the bracelet"

Gray rushed his steps to the lone chair facing Icarus.

"But now, we have a question," he changed the subject, then asked with a curious tone:

"Tell me young **Ica**rus, would you rather be - - brave - - or **f**ea**r**l**e**ss?"

Hearing his question, Icarus leaned back, scratching his chin whilst thinking, not of an answer, but curious of the **me**ans behind this sudden and odd quiz, or was it just to avoid answering his question?

"Of course to be brave," he answered confid**en**tly

"Why?" Gray asked eagerly, leaning forward whilst nodding his head to rush the answer off Icarus's mouth.

"It's simple. If you're fearless, it only means you haven't yet met the thing you fear," deadpan, Icarus answered, taking a bite from the banana he forgot he had in his hand.

He swa**ll**owed, thus continued:

"But being brave means you can overcome your fears no matter what"

He then took another bite.

"Brilliant young Mingan, brilliant indeed," a pleasant Gray praised Icarus for his answer

"You are absolutely right," he added, walking closer to the table, thus placed the book next to the basket.

"However, unfortunately__" Gray said, slowly sliding the book closer to Icarus, while speaking candidly at once,

"__you do not know fear. Therefore, he - - will teach you"

CHAPTER THREE

Gray tapped a claw on the book, causing the scrambled letters engraved on the cover **to** change location.

A curious Icarus was about to touch the book, but **r**etrea**ted** his hand after seeing that.

"What do you mean?" bewildered, he asked for an explanation. But instead of providing one, Gray placed his hand above the book, palm up.

"Give us your hand," he said, wiggling his fingers as if he were craving a touch.

He waited for a moment, but **I**carus was also waiting for an explanation. So he jolted his hand towards Icarus's arm, aggressively snatching his wrist.

"Good," he whispered with a hiss, pulling Icarus's hand inches above the book. He then used his claw to cause a minor cut, mindless of his apprentice's protesting. Gray's full focus was on pushing the blood out.

"Hey!" A disagreeable Icarus groaned, observing drops of his blood fall on the book, making it throb for a few seconds as if it were a living organ then stopped.

Gray grinned pleasantly, looking at the cover absorbing the drops of blood.

"You see, we want a brave partner, not a fearless one," he **sta**ted, looking at Icarus with his nine eyes glowing while Icarus was trying to free his hand from Gray's grip.

"All done," Gray said, releasing his disciple's hand, then looked down at the book as it opened on its own, releasing sh**out**s of agony meddled with faint cries.

"We **sh**ould go - - now," a hasty Gray said

"Hold it, what exactly do you mean by done? And what did you do with my blood?" a sulky Icarus quizzed, using his hand to put pressure on the cut.

The man in black placed his hand on the open book, giving Icarus a virulent smile, then replied with a malevolent tone:

"Oh, you'll know - - soon"

The book sucked Gray inside in an instant. Then his hand sprouted out, pulling Icarus from his shirt,

"Swish!"

2013 – India. Icarus opened his eyes to a strong wind slapping his face. He was plummeting down from the sky.

"Shit, not again!" he grunted. But remembered he's not the same, for he could fly, until he noticed he **was** unable to spread his wings.

Seeing the gap between him and ground closing up, the Mingan used an air-kick to flip his cadaver from a diver position to feet first, hoping his new strength could take such a blow. However, **it** was not what Gray had planned for him.

Icarus's carcass slammed the ground, shatter**ing** into forty-one marbles. They scattered on an empty sidewalk across a local market. Then each one popped into a house-mouse size Icarus.

"What in Zeus's bolt is **thi**s!" flabbergasted one of the mini-figures of Icarus with a squeaky voice

"That's my question. Who the heck are you? All of you!" A**noth**er one replied with an angry tone. And not seconds after, all of them started arguing and throwing insults until Gray stepped in.

"Hello adorable," a scornful Gray smirked, leaning down and closer to the protesting minions. He grinned provocatively at their shouts and squeaky questions:

'*Why are there so many of me? What have you done? Where are we? What is this smell?*'

"Shush, shush! All of **you**, shut up," a loud Gray said, clapping his hands, and all the mi**n**ions stopped tal**k**ing for a moment, then one of them tossed an insolent reply at Gray:

"'You shut up, Jerk"

Gray painted an angry smile on his face while the other minions stepped away from their mouthy friend. Gray snapped his finger, igniting the little Icarus with black flames that ate him from the bottom up in a second.

"What the - -" all the minions gasped, stepping further from that spot.

"That one was obviously a fake. Now, who is the real one," said Gray simply

'*I am, I am, No I am,*'

All forty claimed to be real in a chaotic way. Some even started throwing punches and kicks until one defiant little Icarus stepped in and stopped the ruckus.

"Stop, all of you, don't you see. We won't be able to solve this dilemma if we don't work together. Let's stop this fight, because you are all the real Icarus,"

CHAPTER THREE

The wise minion said, gaining the others' respect with his brief speech. He then added confidently:

"**<u>But</u>**, I'm the real - - real one"

That selfish statement gained him a hard slap on the nape by one of his fellow minions, and the clatter departed again. The arguments and shouts became even sillier.

'*I'm the real real real one,*'

A group launched a race on who could say '*real*' more.

The amused Gray lost his mood. The funny became irritated, turning his laughter in**<u>to</u>** a down smile.

"Quiet," he shouted with a penetrating voice, putting an end to the fight. The scared minions lined up closer to each other, facing their giant master.

"Good. Now, only the real Icarus can fly, so step out," Gray stated.

The minions stared at one another awkwardly. Then, one minion spread his wings and flew up fast, leaving the throng while stomping one for tying to clutch onto his foot.

"Ha! Losers," a flying Icarus cheered with an insolent tone, flapping his way above the crowds onto Gray's shoulder. His behaviour stunned Gray. He burned the first minion for being childish, thinking the real one would never say or do such a thing, and from what he saw from his apprentice, Gray **<u>was</u>** extre**<u>me</u>**ly thankful he did not burn the real one.

"Screw you," the fallen minion gave the real Icarus the finger. Which was an educational coincidence for the Mingan; thanks to the bracelet, he now knows what the wooden hand meant. The Mingan knocked on the side of Gray's mask.

"Now, transform me back," Icarus ordered, looking into Gray's giant eyes. And instead of getting his request, He received a smack that propelled him away.

"**<u>Not</u>** so fast. We shrunk you for a reason," replied Gray, swaying his hand and transforming all the minions back to marbles. He then clutched **<u>it</u>** into a fist, combining them into a crystal sphere. Icarus tried to fly towards it, but Gray snapped his finger, freezing Icarus's wings and forcing him to land.

"We said - - not so fast," Gray repeated with a higher but relaxed pitch, putting his apprentice's wings back with a quick reel from his forefinger.

The mini Icarus tightened his muscles, trying to show them out, but couldn't.

"Your task is simple," said Gray, then blew **a** long puff at the floating sphere, driving it away, through the crowded open mark**et**; tables on the sides from entry to end, covered with traditional **clo**the**s** and souvenirs, and topped by square-tents of fawn, orchid and dandelion. The **s**ph**e**r**e** flew over oodles of heads, then stopped above **a** smoky grill. Gray grinned with a slight of excitement.

"For you to grow back, **all** you need to do - - is to touch the sphere," he explained, thrusting his hands inside his pocket.

"A prior warning, **you** can't ghost through," he added, notifying the fact that his apprentice could be stomped under the jostle feet.

Icarus zoomed through the giant feet before him, then **sm**irked.

"Oll wright," **he** said, tilting his head left and right then stretched his arms up, followed by quick jogging in place as a warm-up. The Mingan clapped his thighs gently and without hesitation, he dashed inside the chaotic track of giant feet.

At first, avoiding being crashed was easy, but the task became harder as he ran deeper into the market.

_ (8-4) * (4-6) * (1-9) * (10-10) (6-6) * (3-5) (2-8) * (10-1) * (4-6) * (5-2)

CHAPTER THREE

Gray followed his moves with a te**le**pathic vision, seeing everyone as transparent figures except for the small Icarus.

After a long run, the sharp Mingan thought **it** would be easier to clutch into one of the moving legs instead of dodging with e**x**haust**ing** flips and side-jumps, and that was exactly what he did, choosing the biggest passerby he could find then glued himself on**to** it with both arms and legs.

"This is much better," a sly **I**carus grinned, enjoying his safe ride.

"Not under our watch," Gray whispered, raising his hand slowly. Synchronously, a hand of thick fog manifested behind a blunt Icarus, and when Gray swung his hand, the black hand smacked Icarus off the man's leg.

The small man bumped **in**to some of the walkers before falling on his back, seeing the b**ot**tom of a flip-flop swooping his way.

"Shit!" Icarus gasped, quickly reeling to the side to escape death by an inch. But to normal size, it **was** a few millimetres.

Without rest, the tiny Mingan went back to hardly dodging the bulk feet, until he glimpsed a long and narrow tube at the bottom of the occupied sidewalk. He waited for an opening, thus took a long leap towards it. The leap was more than enough to get him to his destination, but a child's knee came at him while he was in mid-air; however, Icarus smoothly avoided being slammed by the boy. Instead, he used him to **p**ush his body even faster.

Finally, The Mingan landed before the tube's entry. Wasting no time to barge in, Icarus **r**an through the dark and cold tunnel, clanging his feet against the wet iron, whilst using his hands to keep a straight trail. When the bright end of the tunnel became **v**isibl**e**, Icarus heard a weak tin-cry, then a louder one, to notice the tube shrinking slowly. That was no surprise, for he knew Gray won't let it slide that easily.

A**ft**er calculating the remaining distance, Icarus had a slight doubt that he won't reach the end in time. Also, Gray took not only his wings, but his speed as well. So he had to push himself beyond his limits while groaning loud as a motivational support. To him, it sounded like an echoic warrior-shout, but what Gray heard was like a bee buzzing inside the tube.

The fearless bee-Mingan used the wet smooth surface to skid with his feet ahead, sliding out a moment before the tube shrank to its limits, locking on a small lock of Icarus's hair. He panted, looking at the threads of hair stuck on the tube that turned into a thin rode, thinking that could've been his crushed skull.

Icarus released a long and audible sigh, gathering his strength back. He then bolted to his near target.

He locked his eyes on the high grill instead of the **sp**here, thinking of a way to climb up, then shifted his vision to a long leg swaying his way.

'*Why climb if you can fly*'

That **was** his alternative plan. He waited for the giant man to take a step then jumped on the tip of his foot, using the push he gave him to jump high, straight to the sphere.

Icarus grinned proudly, imagining the l**ook** on Gray's face, but moments after, his grin washed off as his spe**ed** slew down. The Mingan stretched his arm until his bones and muscles freckled, his stretched finger was so close he could sense the sphere's vibe, but that threadfin distance widened, pulling him down to the burning grill. Only a man who lived a life of danger like Icarus can keep his cool in similar situations. The Mingan hunched his body forward, doing a front flip, then used the back of his foot to kick the sphere. The ball blew up and Icarus turned big inches away from the red coals, saved from death, but **not** the painful slam.

"Ouch!" he reeled away then stood up in a hurry, trying to take his ignited shirt off, and before he did, Gray splashed him with cold water.

An annoyed Mingan shook the water off his hair and face, giving Gray a stinky eye.

"Thank you!" said Icarus in an ungrateful tone, pressing his hair back. He then stretched his damaged shirt with a frowned smile, checking the holes caused by the burning coals.

"**I** liked this one," he complained low

Gray smiled then tapped his shoulder, and the shirt got fixed instantly. A cheerful Icarus gently smacked Gray's chest with the back of his hand, painting a wide beam.

"Thank you," he chirped, adjusting his shirt and hood.

Gray smiled faintly, seeing how easy it **was** to drew a smile on Icarus, but even that faint curve on his mouth washed off for what was going to happen next.

"Oh, don't thank us just yet," Gray said, looking at a charcoal Achkan with a grey scarf fused on its eastern brocade from both sides, hanged on one of the merchants' tables. He raised his arms to the sides, thus clapped them against his pockets. His black clothes transfor**med** from the top down to the blue outfit he locked his eyes on. He looked back at Icarus with a faint grin then said:

"This next lesson may cause you to hate us"

Gray walked behind a confused **I**carus then gently reeled his head round the market. He kept his eyes fixed straight as if he were waiting for something to happen. **In** less than a minute, a young boy freed a loud **cr**y in**side** the bulk crowds.

"No! Stay away from me," **frightened**, he shrieked his lungs out, squeezing his eyes shut whilst using his hands to block his ears. He then fell on his knees crying with a quivered voice:

"Please help"

An older kid ran towards him. He shook his shoulder, befuddled and **e**mb**a**rrassed, for everyone was giving them a weird stare.

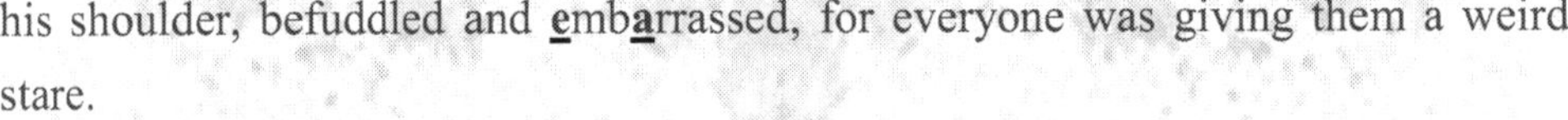

"Shut up, you're embarrassing me you freak," ambivalent, the older one whisper-shouted, shaking the weeper roughly, then forced him to stand straight. The two held hands and rushed out of the market, walking towards Gray and Icarus.

"It is time, for the fearless Mingan to meet his opposite. Icarus, Champion of Crete, meet Yaashva," Gray said loud, staring at the two boys approaching them.

A Malicious Gray turned sharply to Icarus, who coiled his shivering arms around his quivered body, bug-eyed, like one who saw a ghost, but why?

Gray moved closer to Icarus as the youngsters walked past them both. He grabbed Icarus's arms, which made him cowardly shake and squeeze his eyes shut. The Mingan sniffled and breathed as if he were about to cry. But a pitiless Gray painted a **s**adist look on his facade instead of easing his apprentice's sudden terror. He forcefully rotated Icarus towards the two kids, then placed his chin on Icarus's trembling shoulder.

(9-6) * (4-6) * (29-3) (8-2) (16-5) (1-5) * (7-1) (8-3)

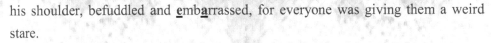

"Now you know why we needed your blood," a wicked **G**ray said with a breathy whisper, whistling cold air on Icarus's **e**ar.

"So you - - can feel__" Gray whispered, roughly pressing Icarus's wet hair back and forth then pulled a lock back, forcing the Mingan's sight up, careless of his unwilling sobs,

"__every**thing** he feels," he continued **with** a sharper hiss, pointing his canine-like finger at the crying boy.

Icarus couldn't differentiate if Gray's hand transformed or if it was his wan imagination.

"You shall know fear," G**ra**y grinned

"P - - Please, make it st - - stop," terrorized, Icarus stuttered, trying to hide his sobbing face under Gray's arm, but Gray nuzzled him while focusing on the steps Yaashva was taking.

"Three, two, one," he counted down, then looked round Icarus, giving him a gentle tap on the shoulder,

"Now"

Icarus fell on his knees, panting h**ea**v**i**ly, as if he were released from a prison of water. He coughed roughly, then breathed deeply. It took him a couple of minutes before gaining his respiration back. He glared at Gray with a side-eye, slowly standing up, then clenched his qui**ve**red fist and snarled:

"You - - demon"

The angry Mingan threw a quick upper-cut, but Gray easily dodged it with a step back.

"What have you done? What was that?" A vacillating Icarus quizzed, giving his hands a quick shake.

Gray raised his hands halfway, palms facing the Mingan, playing innocent.

"That was n**ot** us," he replied cunningly, thus pointed at Yaashva with a slight nod, adding with a provocative grin:

"It was the boy"

Icarus placed both hands on his face, then sighed through the gap between his hands. What Gray did, irritated him, but at the same time, he knew it was necessary for him to get stronger.

"I understand now," he murmured then dropped his hands down, creasing his forehead.

"That **was** a blood link," disgruntled, he stated, giving Gray an annoyed glare, then glowered at Yaashva.

"But that kid - - From what I felt, **it** would be an insult to the word if I were to call him a coward," he insulted resentfully, blaming what he experienced on the boy

"Don't call him that," a hostile Gray interjected

"Don't," he repeated himself as a serious **th**reat thus turned towards Yaashva.

"**You** have no right to call him that, not you. And the boy is ill, not a coward," he clarified, walking ahead after Yaashva while beckoning Icarus to follow.

"A mental illness, a phobia," a despondent Gray explained, slowing down his pace for Icarus to walk by his side the continued, giving Icarus a serious look:

"The fear you suffered for moments, he endures all the time"

"Don't you **think** a coward would take his own life if placed in the same situation? Tell us, M**ing**an, wouldn't you?" he asked, stripping Icarus the right to answer with a mission:

"Your task is to overcome the fear you receive from him, only then, the champion of Crete will k**no**w courage"

Icarus listened obediently, while inside his head, he repeated Gray's question, doubting the possibility of him taking his own life if cursed with the same illness. He gave Gray a serious stare.

"Never have I thought, that my spirit is this fragile, but you saw through me," dismayed, he grumbled, placing his right on his chest then rubbed it slowly, it seemed like he was comforting an invisible pain inside his heart.

"You're an excellent mentor, sharp, talented, knowledgeable. I can't deny that. If only you lose these - - I don't even have a word for it, well, your extreme ways. Anyway, just tell me what to do next and I will"

Gray stopped. He tilted his head to the side, surprised at what he saw as a sudden compliment; however, he decided to not show emotions. He locked his eyes on Yaashva, then heavenward to the tangerine sun behind the lower clouds.

"You will get used to our ways. It will be dark soon," he said low, slowly dissolving into mist from his feet and up.

"Stay inside his range, and survive for a day," furtive, Gray smirked, and right before his head vanishes, he added with a teasing tone:

"Good night"

Some of the mist coiled Icarus's head, **but** he shook it away with a wave.

"Like talking to a brick wall," he com**me**nted low then spread his wings wide,

"At least I got you two back"

Icarus leaped high, following Yaashva from above. His intentions were to keep a safe distance first, **not** knowing he made it worst. The moment he glimpsed the crying boy, Icarus received a sharp stab thrusting his heart. Shocked, he clenched his grip against his chest. The black of his pupil distended, turning his eyes p**it**ch-lack. He saw the ground underneath enlarge, moving away in a fazing way. The horrified Mingan panted heavily yet seemed suffocated, feeling his heart getting squeezed as it throbbed visibly through his shirt.

"Thumps!"

This bizarre state was a first **to** the fearless Mingan. He had no clue on how to escape fear, nor the control lost over his own body. His wings stopped flapping, surrendering his numb body to gravity with a slow spin.

Icarus crashed on his chest like a scorpion. The blow **was** drastic, but the pain helped him gain a foggy conscious. He pulled his face out of the dirt, thus rested his right cheek on the ground to see that he landed a few steps ahead of Yaashva. The two staggered his way, and one thought imprisoned the Mingan's dazed head:

'*If approaching the boy is awfully terrorizing, then how would it feel if I made contact with him?*'

A question he didn't want to know the answer to. Icarus pushed the side of his forehead up, trying to stand.

"Move," he whispered, begging his cadaver to obey, but the increase of that frantic feeling denied him the ability to flee off their way. The boys stepped on him, shoving their feet inside his prostrated body, and that really done it for him. | An agonized Icarus shrieked silently, feeling a throng of stomping feet crushing his carcass. It was a delusion, but the pain was real. He cried as high as his lungs could bear until his throat got injured. He experienced what the poor boy really felt. Not only that. All the terror and horror Yaashva held inside, the

Mingan received all at once. In one second, he experienced falling from the sky, being buried alive, drowning into darkness - - and more. |

Yaashva's foot exited Icarus's shoulder-blade, and with it, the end of Icarus's trip to Mind-Hell.

He coughed strings of red spittle, wetting the dirt beneath his stained cheeks. The Mingan breathed shakily, expelling the light dust with his nostrils, while dropping a tear that painted a trail on his sandy face.

Icarus slid his forehead against the harsh ground to orbit his head towards the **you**ngsters whilst trying to stand but failed. He worried he may lose them but luckily for him, Yaashva and the elder lad entered a house **ju**st across the street.

"G - - good," a wan Mingan whispered low, shutting his eyelids into a moment of tranquillity.

"I will - - in a second," he panted, then rested his head on the ground.

Minutes after, Icarus opened his eyes to one of the house's lights switching on, turning the window's curtains from brown to **be**ige.

"Time to move," **said** Icarus, using his hands and every ounce of strength to push himself up. When he finally managed to stand on his shaky legs, he used his wings as support, like a four-legged creature.

"Ugh!" Icarus li**mp**ed across the street, then observed the loft from the bottom up be**fore** he barged in. It was the only house that had a clean painted facade, unlike the crooked walls the neighbours had, matching the crooked narrow allies that separated each house.

Icarus climbed on the three steps at the house's door.

"Erini Se Sas," Icarus sighed, walking through the door and into an incommodiously cramped hall of two steps large and twenty feet long, then a straight stair to the second floor

"Shit!" Icarus whispered low, for he was in no condition to clamber up. Still, he had no choice. He staggered up then headed right, following the light to hear a faint sobbing.

The intruder glimpsed an open room, so he walked closer and took a peek.

"Agh! Will **you** please stop it already," begged the older boy exasperatedly, standing next to the bed where Yaashva was sitting on the edge, still weeping his nose down.

"I was trying to help," he added

"Creak!" A sharp sound interrupted his lousy attempt at co**n**s**o**lida**t**ion. It was an easy sound to recognize by the boy, because of its unique squeaking tune. He knew it was the front door opening. Quietly, he dropped an ear outside to hear heavy steps climbing the stairs.

Spooked, the boy froze for a second, thus stared at Yaashva with his eyes expanding. He rushed two long and silent steps towards Yaashva then block**ed** the weeper's mouth with a nervous hand.

"Shush! Stop it," he beseeched with a scared whisper, then sl**i**there**d** to take a peek **th**r**ough** the door.

He **sa**w a man holding grocery bags, stepping inside the door before their room.

"Baba is ho**me**, you will get me in trouble," appalled, he whisper-shouted, quietly running towards Yaashva.

The man's footsteps were audible, **al**ong with short beeps, one made by the cell phone buttons.

"**I**'m really sorry," he apologized, forcing Yaashva into the closet then shut the door, using his back to block it whilst locking his eyes on the door.

Meanwhile, **I**carus felt the air trapped inside his throttle, refusing to sink in or to be released out. The Mingan coiled his neck with one hand, then used the other to shove two fingers inside his mouth and deep to his throat. He kept **push**ing until he coughed harshly, falling on his knees. He panted horrifically, crawling to the room's corner like an infant.

Icarus cocooned his shivered body like a newborn, looking at the man standing at the room's door, then closed his eyes, catching only a few words from their jammed **c**onvers**a**tio**n**.

"Please, hurry - - get him out," Icarus sobbed, begging the man to get Yaashva out of the closet and free them both from that terror.

The man stepped in, adjusting a long lock of hair away from his glasses whilst casually thrusting two fingers between the loosened buttons of his shirt.

"Where is your brother?" fixed, he asked the kid, who replied with a quick stutter:

"Baba! The bathroom - - I guess"

He slowly stepped away from the closet, to drive his father's attention away from its door. His father picked up a pillow from the floor, then tossed it on the bed.

(19-14) (6-12) * (11-3) * (13-6) (9-2) * (15-1) * (10-2) (8-11) * (17-2) * (24-2) (1-10)

CHAPTER THREE

“Your mother is parking the car,” he said calmly, then added before stepping out of the room:

“Go prepare the table **for** dinner. And Amir - - wash your hands first”

“Yes Baba,” replied Amir with a nervous tone

When his father walked out, he sighed, relieved, turning back to free his brother from his pris**on**.

“Ah yes, I got you the book **you**__” said his father, walking back in to see his son looking at him ghastly, w**it**h his hands on the closet’s knob. He tilted his head slightly to the side, narrowing his eyes,

“__What are you doing?” **s**c**e**pti**c**al, he asked, walking closer.

“Barf!” he then heard a voice coming from the closet. He rushed his steps **t**o**w**ards the s**o**und as if he knew what lies inside.

“Step back,” he grunted, pushing his son away to open the door.

He found Yaashva hugging the bottom of his legs with both arms, squeezing his knees against his chest; while his mouth and chin stained with a moister mixture of vomit and saliva, and some **was** spilling on his shirt.

“Baba!” a horrified Yaashva cried in a very low voice. His father placed his han**ds** gently beneath his armpits, trying not to scare him.

“I’m here, I’m here Baba,” he whispered low, carefully pulling him out,

“Baba is here”

He hugged him and patted his back to ease down his heart, while his older brother took a slithering step back, ashamed of what he did to his little brother.

“Baba, I was just__” Amir tried to justify his deed, but his father silenced him with one furious glare,

“__Sorry,” he said low, walking behind his father, who held Yaashva out of the room, leaving the Mingan alone, trembled in fear and pain.

“F - - Father,” shivering, Icarus sobbed, squeezing his eyes shut whilst burying his head between his chest and joined knees. The Mingan waited for the awful sensation to fade with Yaashva walking away, but it didn’t. Instead, his hallucination got worst. He saw a giant vulture hand coiling his curved body, squeezing his bones until cracked. But then, a hand patted his head, making the giant hand dissolve and fade. It gently patted his head and face, followed by Gray’s soft voice:

‘*You can do this. We trust you*’

_ (8-6) * (16-6) * (12-1) (12-3) * (10-5) (6-3) (18-1) * (3-5) * (7-8)

The hand he felt pressing into his hair vanished. But its kind **s**ensa**t**i**o**n re**m**ain**e**d, showing the fear out of Icarus's heart, and giving the Mingan a chance to breathe relieved. He relax**ed** his muscles, slightly stretching his legs to a crescent posture.

"Thank you__" Icarus whispered, relaxing his eyelids as his panting slew down,

"__father!" He slept

— —

A faint clinging woke Icarus up. He opened his eyes to a colourful sunlight shed on his face, one caused by a rainbow drawing on the window.

"Morning!" he **m**us**e**d, then lifted his u**pp**er body in a rush, looking at the empty room whilst remembering what happened to him.

Icarus pressed his hair back, then held the last knot with a puzzled look.

"Was it a dream!" blank, he wondered, then stood up, rubbing his welled eyes with a right thumb and forefinger.

The invisible guest left the room, looking right, then left. He walked left, following the clinging, then through the door on his right, to find the entire family inside the kitchen, having an uncomfortable breakfast in silence. The father was obviously s**ti**ll mad with Amir, who sat on his skewed chair, crestfallen, with his plate untouched. Yaashva had his hands on his cup of milk. As **for** their mother, she buried her head in her newspapers, while stealing sips of coffee every ten to twenty seconds

"Clank!"

A noise from the outside grasped Icarus's intention. He walked to the side window and took a peek to see Gray wearing his usual black suit. Icarus was about to call on him, **but** paused with an open mouth, lifting a brow, wondering:

'*What's that large orange bottle he's holding? And why is he splashing its content around the house?*'

Icarus broke his silence,

"Hey!" he shouted, but Gray didn't bother to reply.

"What are you up to?" A suspicious Icarus said low, trying to walk through the wall but ended up bumping into it,

"What!"

Confused, he gently knocked on the wall to find it solid. He then gave it a gentle kick, to be certain.

CHAPTER THREE

A **n**erv**o**us Icarus peeked through the window again to see Gray joining both hands into a fist then stretched both indexes, making a pistol figure.

"Hey!" Icarus shouted louder, uncomfortably punching the window but it didn't move an inch. He had a feeling his mentor was up to no **g**ood.

The Man in black leaned down, getting his forefingers closer to the wet ground. He smirked maliciously, thus shot a **thin** bolt that ignited the liquid he spilled.

Icarus looked at the fire growing swiftly around the dwelling.

"What - - what are **you** doing?" unhinged, he hollered, turning his blunt face into a creased one.

"What are you doing you sick bastard!" he shouted, trying to open the window then break **it**, but failed. Confused and out of options, a hasty Icarus looked back at the family.

"**Think**!" he said, scratching the back of his hand while switching his eyes back and forth, trapped between a growing fire and a family who's ignorant of their near doom.

"Can they - -" he wondered low, fixed on Yaashva's family.

Icarus walked slowly to Yaashva, for he **was** the nearest. He raised his hand to touch him then paused, wetting his dry lip. His hand quivered while retreating. Icarus wasn't ready to relive those dark moments, so he poked the father instead; however, his finger went through the man's head. But that didn't stop him from trying a different approach.

"Hey -- there is a fire -- you need to run," he shouted in his fat ear over and over but no reaction.

Icarus gave up and ran out of the kitchen towards the stairs to see the flames eating their way through the door.

"Tumult!" a loud fuss outside caught the father's ears. Curious, he tried to ask his wife to check but changed his mind after seeing her too focused on her newspapers.

He headed to the window to see his neighbour intending to throw a rock but stopped when he saw him. He ghastly waved with both arms, thus pointed at the blazing fire surrounding his house, alarming Yaashva's father.

"Badra, take the kids to the bedroom," he told his wife while suppressing his fearsome expression. His wife knew something was off. She tried to ask, but he rushed her to leave,

_ (8-4) * (13-1) * (11-4) * (17-8) * (1-2) (6-7) (4-15)

"Now," he said with his teeth shut, rushing his eldest to get up as well.

Confused and blunt, everyone **but** the father left the kitchen, heading to the back, while he headed straight to the door out, making sure it was safe for his family **to** flee.

The hot air slapped his face twenty feet away from the stairs. When he sauntered closer, He saw the fla**me**s eating their way up towards him.

"Malek!"

He heard his wife screaming his name. Wary, he dashed to the room to find her looking through the window, frightened. She stepped back, looking at her husband whilst pointing her trembled finger towards the cracking glass. In the meantime, Amir **was** hugging Yaashva with one hand while blocking his l**it**tle brother's ear with the other, shushing his cries.

Icarus, who followed their father to the bedroom's door, glimpsed a ghost version of Yaashva bursting from the boy's nape; dark skinned with grimy white eyes that cried blood, his slacked jaw spilled a tar-like liquid, while his neck was covered by a slime of eyes slithering on his skin like parasites. The phantom shuffled towards Icarus with his hands up.

"I killed her - - Thor - - save Uniss - - Oran__*Squeak!* The bull lives - - The Gra - - The Gra - - The Gra," the ghost boy echoed random words with different voices like a broken record, while a panting Icarus took a shaken step back.

"**Not** now - - please," Icarus begged with glossy eyes, but the ghost rushed his steps then plunged inside the Mingan's chest, divining inside him like a possessing demon.

A suffocated Icarus dropped to his knees, ripping the upper parts of his shirt while releasing a breathless roar. His ears elongated then transformed to baby-size hands, blocking his mouth then fuse with his face to leave him with no mouth to scream. He whimpered faintly, crawling away from the room, hoping to set himself free by widening the distance between him and Yaashva, and it did, his mouth appeared back.

CHAPTER THREE

Badra and Amir ran out of the room, passing through Icarus, followed by Malek, holding Yaashva. **I**c**a**ru**s** squeezed his eyes shut, embracing for a horrified Yaashva to penetrate his al**rea**dy weaken cadaver, but they passed through without making contact. E**ve**n with the pain he was feeling, the Mingan meddled sighs of re**lie**f with his groans of despondency.

A**l**l four stopped in the middle of the hall, followed by a slothful fifth. They all glanced at the ceiling.

"Get the chair," Malek ordered his eldest, who ran to the kitchen. Then back with a tall chair.

Icarus staggered closer to them then leaned his back on the wall, looking at Malek mounting the chair. He grab**be**d a small rod merging from the ceiling and pulled it down, revealing a squ**are** door to the roof, and out of it slid down a stretched ladder.

"Hurry," Badra rushed Amir to m**o**unt first then followed, holding Yaashva.

Meanwhile, Icarus looked at the opened ceiling, thinking:

'*I had to go up before they close the way out*'

And so he did. He shuffled to the ladder and started ponderously climbing after Badra whilst carefully avoiding any horrific touch from Yaashva.

Halfway through, the kitchen's electricity wires crackled, and right after, all the light bulbs crashed down.

The unexpected noise caused Yaashva to shriek his loudest cry, and so did Icarus asynchronously. The Mingan hugged the ladder, dropping a warm tear on its cold iron, while Malek started climbing up, fazing through him.

Icarus had no choice but using pain to overcome the shock, or else - - he will be trapped inside a deadly inferno. Quick to think, he bit his bottom lip until it bled, then rushed his feet up and plunged out the moment Malek closed the door. The Mingan bit his curved thumb, falling on his back. He looked at his left foot to see half of his sliced, but no blood was gushing out; however, the pain was there. Icarus released an inner scream, squeezing his eyes shut while **p**unc**h**ing his thigh to drive out some of the pain from his lower limb.

"Baba, here," Amir called for his father from the side edge, beckoning him with hasty waves.

"We can make this jump," he suggested, pointing at the neighbour's rooftop, for it was lower and only a few feet away.

_ (29-11) (14-6) (1-1) (2-3) * (12-6) * (3-4) (6-1) * (17-1) * (11-6) (4-14) (4-2)

Malek overlooked down for **a** moment, glancing at the blazing fire underneath, thus rubbed his son's back, approving his plan.

"You and your mother can go first. I will take care of your brother," he instructed, then **t**urned to Badra, who placed Yaashva down, but kept her arm on his face.

Mal**e**k pointed to the neighbour's roof, using simple hand signs to let her know of the plan. She nodded, understanding what had to be done.

Malek walked his youngest a little closer to **the** edge, thus whispered in his ear calmly:

"Baba, we have to do something, and I want you to trust me"

Malek uncovered Yaashva's eyes slowly, allowing him to see **whe**re they were.

"**N**o, no!" A spooked Yaashva shouted, trying to move far from the edge, but Malek b**lo**cked the way.

"Son, we have to do this, just this time, please," a frantic Malek persuaded h**is** frightened child, then nodded to his eldest, giving him a sign to jump.

Amir waited for Yaashva to look his way first then took a leap to **sa**fet**y**, making it look like an effortless task. He then waved to Yaashva with a confident smile, encouraging him to follow:

"See, so easy"

But that didn't change Yaashva's mind.

"No, no please no," haunted, he sc**re**amed, trying to run away, what made his father grab him tight then gave his wife a serious stare,

"Go, **I** know what to do"

Hesitantly, Badra stood still, worried about leaving her son behind.

"Go," Malek repeated with a whisper-shout, asking Badra to trust him with an honest stare.

Badra took some steps back, then dashed and plunged ahead. Her jump was weaker than her son's. She landed on her feet first then stumbled forward, falling on her stomach, but still made it safe and unharmed.

"I have to go too," Icarus quavered anxiously, standing up, then crippled to the edge.

The pain decreased the terror he received from Yaashva. It was a good trade for a Mingan for he could endure the physical pain. After leaving a decent a distance between him and the edge, he ran ponderously, and right be**for**e he took the jump, he glimpsed Yaashva being tossed over by his fa**th**er.

Icarus breathed deeply as time slew down. He knew his body was a **mo**ment apart from **re**ceiving a shock-wave of horror, but he already had his legs stretched and ready to push h**is** body off the ground. There was no way to fall back. Icarus felt the lo**we**r muscles of his legs freezing, reducing the jump's strength, but his body already left the roof. Halfway, he looked down at the blaze, painting screaming faces like ghosts waiting for the Mingan to fall. Even his horrified comp**an**ion was leaving him behind.

Certain that he won't make **it** with that weak leap, the Mingan closed his eyes, surrendering to despair.

"Your Wings!"

A penetrating shout stunned Icarus! He spontaneously spread his wings and fluttered, jumping in mid-air. One flap was enough to drive him onto the other rooftop alongside Yaashva, who was received by his older brother.

Moments after, Malek followed.

"Ugh!" Icarus opened his eyes to see a pair of shoes on his face; topped by black trousers.

"You did well," said Gray, standing before Icarus, but the Mingan was still shaking in **fear**. He grabbed Gray's leg tightly.

"Please," faint, he begged with watering eyes, climbing Gray's leg then embraced his knee,

"Please, take me away"

"Very well," said an obedient Gray with a soft tone, hugging Icarus with the book in his hand. He looked at Yaashva with a down smile, then teleported Icarus and himself back to the library,

"Swish!"

Five days after the fire, Yaashva and his father walked into a building. The squeaky gate spooked the boy, but his father calmed him with a warm pat on the head.

"I will be there with you. I won't leave you for a second. Don't worry," said Malek calmly, brushing Yaashva's thick hair down with his fingers. He then opened a door with a glassy sign that said '*Therapy Counsellor.*'

Embracing his son's head with one arm, Malek approached the receptionist on the side.

"Hello, we have **a**n ap**po**intmen**t**," he said with a faint smile, resting his free han**d** on the counter.

"Name please!" **as**ked the receptionist while typing on the computer.

"Shiva, Yaashva Shiva," he replied, gently pressing Yaashva's hair whilst wait**in**g for the young lady to check the appointments.

"Yes, the doctor was waiting for you," she said with a sudden smile, stepping out of the long counter to open the door behind her.

"Pl**ea**se come in. Yaashva Shiva is here, Doctor," she invited them in, then spoke inside faintly.

Yaashva and Malek stepped inside **th**e doctor's office but found no one.

"Hello Mr. **S**hiva," gr**ee**ted the doctor, walking out of a second door on the side.

It was Icarus, wearing a more mature and professional look, but the doctor was the Mingan in the flesh.

Icarus sat on his chair, then invit**ed** the two to take a seat with a warm smile and a simple hand gesture.

"Dr. Gray Trueman, at your **serv**ice," he introduced himself

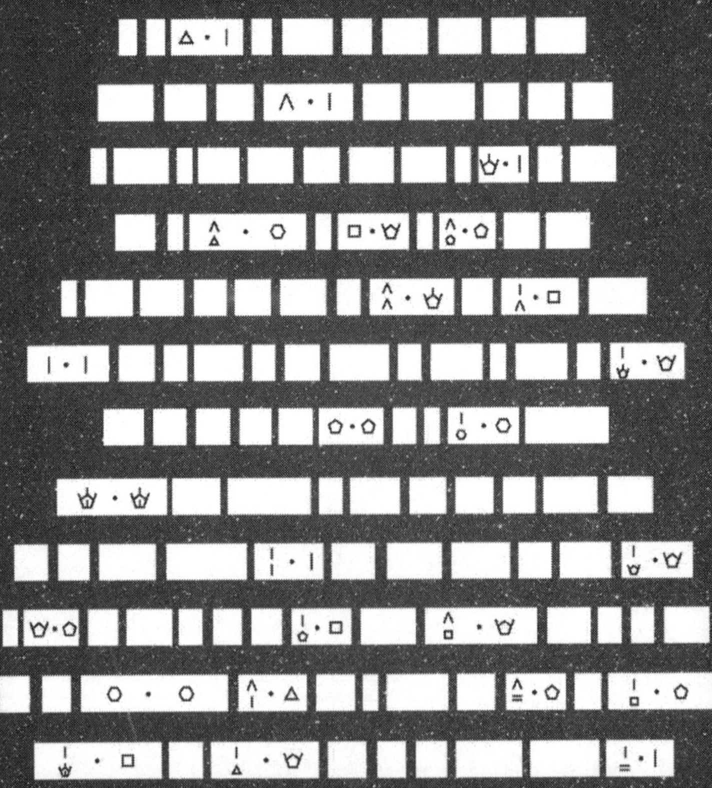

CHAPTER FOUR
HUMANISH

Twelve hours after returning to the library, Icarus stepped out from his roo**m**, wearing a w**is**tful face. He turned left and saw Gray's stretched arm out of his chair, facing the w**al**l of books while reciting poetry. But that wasn't what caught the Mingan's attention. **It** was that Gray had his mask in his hand. A golden chance **to** see what lies behind it.

Icarus sli**the**red quietly while stretching a neck to peek over the tall back of Gray's chair, but his me**n**t**or** busted him on his first step.

"Good morning, how do you **feel?**" Gray said, putting his mask on before he orbited his seat round Icarus.

Icarus curved a side smile, trying to veil his disappointment. Also, admitting his foolishness, thinking a person **who** is as sharp as Gray would be the type to drop his guard that easily.

"Good morning," the Mingan replied low in a dead tone, walking towards the couch.

Gray rested his hand on his desk, noticing Icarus's frustration. His secret plan to change the appr**en**tice's mood failed.

He sighed audibly, thus started drumming a boring tune with his fingers.

"Hey, think of what happened as - - not a failure but an experience," he hinted in a sil**v**er**y** tone

"Now you know something about yourself, which is a necessity if you seek to evolve. You **can** make it as a starting point" he added

After a minute of silence, Kara walked out of the third section, holding two flat boxes over each other.

"Ah! Just in time," a cheerful Gray chirped, changing the tune of his drumming to a faster **one**.

"We brought you the perfect food to brighten your mood," he beamed with a big smile, rushing Kara to hand him the second box, after placing the first on the table before Icarus.

He grabbed the box and placed it on the desk, allowing Kara to open it after jumping on his lap. As for Icarus, he grabbed the box with two hands, baffled yet curious, he tried to shake it, but got stopped with a loud and quick '*No!*' from Gray.

"Put it down, **and** open it - - gently," **s**uggested Gray calmly, slowly pointing at how Kara opened his box.

The Mingan replied with a faint grimace, for Gray spoke with a manner you use with kids or a dull person.

He opened the box and creased his brows, you could tell he **hate**d what he saw; a round baked bread fitting the box, topped with tomato sauce, two small cups in each corner, filled with a marmalade and parchment viscous sauces.

Imitating Gray, Icarus pulled a piece up to see thick strings of cheese stretching out of the galette.

"What is it?" Icarus asked with a disturbed face

"Pizza, one of the best things you can stuff your mouth with," Gray answered, then took a big bite while patting his Kara, who grabbed a slice for her own.

"**This** Pizza - - looks awful," Icarus criticized, dangling the slice gently then looked at Kara, too **emotion**al, shoving her share inside her mouth while painting a pleasant face. An uncertain Mingan looked round Gray to see him taking a second slice, and so did Kara.

"We know four turtles ~ who would waste your **life** just for saying **that**," joked Gray derisively, later added with his mouth full:

"Just eat - - you'll **love** it once you get a taste"

"Oll wright!" said Icarus low, taking bite.

He munched slow at first then faster, raising his upper eyelid when he swallowed, and without saying a word, he took another bite, and another thus said unclearly because of his filled mouth.

"Mm! Thim - - thaste **real**ly good," a delighted Icarus complimented, snatching a second slice, what painted a faint smile on Gray's face.

"Why is your bracelet non-functional here?" a curious Mingan queried, closing his eyes pleasantly while slowly chewing his food.

"it **makes** no sense. I should have known about this when you mentioned it!" he added, then shouted low in a vindictive tone while looking rightward, referring to the wooden hand:

"Or what - - that branchy piece of crap did"

"Branchy! You mean Soul-Aymen? Don't mind him," Gray deadpanned

_ (21-4) * (7-13) * (3-4) * (16-5) (3-8) * (19-13) * (30-2) * (15-1) * (19-9) * (26-4)

"And for the bracelet, we **can't** exchange memories without a link, so the books plays that role, for they **a**re portals to events we saw are worthy to keep safe in case **this** brain gets boomed one day," Gray explained simply, putting a long napkin around Kara's neck **with** one hand while using the other to imitate an explosion near his head.

"That makes sense - - not really, but you know what **I** mean. **I** understand how it goes," Icarus replied franticly then roamed in his thoughts for moments. He looked to the bookshelves facing him, then at the ceiling.

"So - - is it your memories only? Or others as well," he quizzed, putting his unfinished slice **of** pizza back inside the box. Gray smirked in silence for several moments.

"Only ours of course; not anyone can be a worthy source of information," a calm Gray answered in a fixed tone, noticing that he **was** being investigated in a sneaky **way**, but that didn't prevent him from being partly truthful with his apprentice.

"I see now! Does it include the newspapers? They looked **bor**i**n**g but Flaco's father made it seem interesting to read one," Icarus asked, giving Gray his full attention.

"Yes - - especially newspapers, for once upon a future time, they will be the source of all lies," Gray smirked, resting his **el**bows on his desk whilst joining his hands into a relaxed fist. He leaned forward as if he were asking Icarus,

'*Is there anything else you wish to know?*'

The Mingan saw that his intentions were unveiled; however, his curiosity was **st**rong**e**r. He bit his lower lip softly, tilting his head slightly to the side, ready to play detective.

"One last question," he said with a fixed tone, then added:

"Are you really a Gois?" he waggled his brows and curved a faint side smile, **heart**ily waiting for an answer but received a chuckle instead.

"You sounded certain and confident when assuming we were one, why the change of mind?" Gray asked with an obvious grin and Icarus smirked back, adjusting his posture slightly to the side to face Gray.

"I swallowed the possibility that a mage could maybe - - maybe, do the things you can do," Icarus said with a cynical tone then stated confidently:

_ (6-10) * (1-6) * (6-12) * (13-11) * (16-11) * (3-3) * (14-2) * (4-5) * (2-7) * (28-1) * (10-3) * (24-1) (20-9)

CHAPTER FOUR

"But the **a**ge, giving where **y**ou took me, or I should say when, that's at least tw**o** millennia. Isn't too much for **a** mage?"

"Mm! We know mages that lived for long - -"

"**Yes**. But four - - or five hundred years maximum," Icarus interjected Gray's answer, placing one foot on the table while maintaining a sly smile.

"Maybe we just travelled from the future!"

"Everyone knows Goises are near extinction. **I** don't think they will survive that long," he interjected again, thus offered a stronger argument:

"Or how about your strength, when you forced my hand to bond with Yaashva, **not** a hundred Goises combined **could** be that powerful," he hinted, while beckoning Kara to his box after finishing Gray's.

Looking at Kara throwing the napkin away before she ran towards Icarus, Gray freed a long breathy laugh.

"In our defence, we never claimed to be one," replied a cunning Gray, while calling for Vi, who was cleaning the bookshelves on the side. He ordered **he**r to clean the mess Kara left on his desk, thus added:

"Mages survived by the way. Adding to that, they actu**al**ly evolved and **p**ro**s**pered in modern times. They have their own lands now. With their own laws, facilities and even schools for their youngsters," Gray clarified, joining his fingers into a steeple.

"Sadly, we can't say the same for Mingans. Your kind became as rare as ice age **disease**," he grinned, stunning Icarus with a shocking fact. Mingans, the powerful specie that was built to survive, will perish! While Goises, who lived a life of a prey survived! Icarus found it hard to believe.

Gray knocked on the desk, interrupting Icarus's thoughts.

"Do we sense - - fear," he grinned provocatively, a hint that the Mingan started experiencing new feelings.

Icarus gazed at Gray, thus admitted straightforwardly:

"I believe it is!"

He straightened his posture back, glancing down on the table.

"Therefore, our last trip was a success. You just don't see it," Gray stated, leaving his **ch**air then added in a passionate tone while heading to the chair facing Icarus:

_ (4-1) * (2-7) * (18-1) (1-6) (32-3) (2-1) * (1-3) * (22-2) * (7-7) * (10-7) * (10-2) * (15-14) (17-10)

"Our means were to introduce you to fear, not conquer it - - well not yet. Remember young Mingan, in this life, you need to bend down so you can jump high"

The man in black sat down with his upper half leaning forward.

"Introduce me! If **I'm** being honest, after going through what I felt, I wish I did**n't** have feelings to begin with," said a spiritless Icarus, gently scratching the back of his hand. Even a memory of what he suffered trauma**ti**zed his heart.

"All they do - - is weaken one's spirit," a despondent Mingan murmured faintly

"**Do** you really think so?" Gray asked, but Icarus maintained his silence.

"Hey, look at us, do you really - - believe so?" A serious Gray repeated, crossing his arms while casting a displeased vibe.

"Do you think your emotions - - makes you weak!" he asked with a tone that held a slight **of** a disenchanted mockery in it.

Without lifting his head, **I**carus looked at Gray with dead eyes.

"You disagree?" He asked, showing a line between his brows as he suppressed his ire. To Icarus, Gray had no right to disagree.

'*You're the last to speak of emotion after what you* ***care****lessly did to me*'

That was what the Mingan wanted to say **but** kept unspoken.

"You saw what happened to me over there," he added calmly

Gray gave him a sour stare as if he read his mind, then sighed, slightly shaking his head no.

"Every time we fix something - - another breaks," he lowe**red** his head then mumbled low. He then looked at Icarus with a side smile.

"Stand up. Common, stand up," said Gray rudely with two sharp claps.

"Go get the book titled Oscar six five, five one, two," he ordered with a fixed tone, stretching a hand partly towards the corridor then added tardily while exaggerating the movement of his mouth:

"You'll find it in that big corridor over there; fourth shelf on your left"

The way he spoke irritated the Mingan, it sounded as if Icarus were dumb enough to lose his way in a straight line like some three swords bushido ~

Annoyed, Icarus stood up, intentionally bumping the table's edge with his knee.

When he stepped inside the arc, he started soundlessly repeating the numbers with his lips, sauntering with his sight fixed on his left,

_ (15-5) * (10-1) (6-1) * (18-11) * (19-9) * (5-4) * (7-12) (23-9) * (14-4)

CHAPTER FOUR

'*One, two, three, and four*'

He counted the separated shelves with air finger-taps then stopped at the fourth one. But, he felt undert**ra**i**n**e**d** if he had a mixed up between the bookshelf's number and **the** numbers in the book title. Icarus squeezed his lips shut; the last thing he wanted was to show Gray that he forgot such a significant thing.

Gray, on the other hand, read it on his face. He nodded slowly, **sp**ar**in**g Icarus the embarrassment of asking. The Mingan rolled his eyes back to the bookshelf, acting like he knew.

He lifted his head up whilst taking a step back.

"Oscar six five, five - - one two!" he said out loud, thus remembered his beef with the wooden hand, it was the perfect bowl to empty his frustration.

"C**om**e out, you piece of shit," he snarled in a low voice

The side of the shelf cracked, and out of it sprouted Soul-Aymen. Icarus grinned then said with an insolent tone:

"H**el**lo, you thrall"

The extended hand ignored his insult, thus pointed rudely at a thick **wh**it**e** book in Icarus's reach instead of grabbing it for him like last time. Icarus shook his head no and said with a provocative smirk:

"You - - give it to me, you useless THRALL"

A Peeved Soul-Aymen vibrated while curving into an angry fist, while the Mingan maintained a bitter grin intact. The duke grabbed the book aggressively.

'*The book of Oscar six five, five one, two*'

The bookshelf chorused in an annoyed tone, ha**n**d**ing** the book to Icarus while shivering resentfully; however, the Mingan wasn't done teasing. He stretched his right arm to the side, palm open.

"Put in my hand," he demanded provocatively

Quivering in rage, Soul-Aymen obeyed, and when he tried to place it on Icarus's hand, the Mingan lowered it quickly whilst raising his left.

"Not there, here," a playful Icarus said, to hear an angry shout from Gray, who saw what he was doing:

"Are you a freaking child?"

Stunned, Icarus looked round Gray, giving the hand a chance to smack his face with the book then rapidly shrank back inside.

(6-14) (23-8) * (4-3) * (3-5) (12-1) * (16-13) (15-1)

“Ouch! **What**! You wooden FFFU - -” the Mingan fell down on his knees, pressing one hand against his face and the other on the book.

“That piece - - of shit,” he groaned then stood up hastily, punching the shelf several times while rubbing his reddish nose.

“Leave it **to** that,” said Gray from far while heading to his desk.

Icarus tightened his grip on the book and kicked the bottom of the shelf bef**or**e walking back. He slammed the book on the desk.

“You’re welcome,” a heated Mingan said, turning back to head to his spot whilst checking if his nose was broken, but before departing, Gray stopped him.

“Wait! Ahem!” coughed Gray with a croaky voice. He forced another cough then showed his teeth as if he were hardly pushing down something locked in his throat.

“Can you hold on **to** the book?” Gray requested with an unclear voice while gently sliding it closer to Icarus.

“**What**! Ah Yes,” a blunt Icarus deadpanned, grabbing the book and it in**s**t**a**ntl**y** sucked his body inside.

“I**d**i**o**t**!**” said a sly Gray, then followed,

“Swish!”

2000 - The suburbs of New Jersey. Under the warmth of a radiant star, a canary flew over four large squares of fancy houses, all topped with black pyramidal roofs of painted bricks. In the middle of each square an open green garden, serving fresh air to the residents, or simply a place to run from the polluted puffs and mechanical noises.

Inside one of the gardens, a submerged blow disturbed the sound of tranquillity. Right after, one of trees trembled, scaring away the canary who just landed on one of its branches. It shook again with the sound of another blow, then an echoic yelling and squeaking meddled with minor blows that caused some dry leafs to fall. The sounds became louder, and moments after, a shrunken version of Icarus emerged out the tree hollow! Again!

Aghast, the Mingan plunged forward; rapidly spreading his wings then flapped his way up, and after him, leaped a hungry weasel mounted by a cheerful mini-Gray. Like a shark jumping above the water for a tasty meal, the ferret tried to clutch Icarus’s body with one bite but got a furious punch in the nose instead. Seconds after, The Mingan grew back to his normal size before landing, and so did Gray, after jumping off his furry ride.

CHAPTER FOUR

"No - - more - - **sh**rinking," a sullen Icarus groaned with an emphasized tone, pulling his wings back while approaching Gray, who like usual, couldn't miss a chance **to** bark a laughter as long as it irritates his apprentice.

"Look at the bright side, you haven't puked your guts out this time," chuckled Gray while climbing the tree to pull the book out of the tree-hall**ow**.

"Maybe because I opened my eyes to that damn thing chewing my leg; you know what, just forget it," Icarus surrendered. He stepped away while adjusting his clothes and shaking the dirt off.

"**Whe**re are we anyway, it looks - - too clean a**n**d quiet," he asked irreverently, grasping the backyard of a house.

"Not this one - - that one," Gray corrected his attention to another house on the other side of the garden.

Avoiding the wet dirt, Gray stepped to **a cons**truct**e**d trail of flat stones, heading toward the house he pointed at, followed by Icarus, who curiously observed his surroundings, glimpsing m**or**e houses on both sides. Then, his eyes squinted a slight, as if a thought landed on his head. Dubious, he looked at Gray while slowing his pace to increase the distance in between, then discreetly raised his wrist closer to his mouth and whispered:

"Gois and Mingans"

Icarus closed one eye while keeping the other on Gray, receiving as much information as he could get before getting caught.

"Huh!" he freed a spontaneous gasp, capturing Gray's attention.

"There are only twelve of us left yet millions of mages still exist!? WHY? And why does one of the Mingans look like a damn clown?" a st**a**rt**l**ed Icarus sputtered the flooded datum loudly. He glanced at the ground without blinking, then turned left to one of the houses, jaw slacking,

"And the fat blond who lives there is a Gois? But I thought all Goises are of a dark-skin! Oh! He's cheating on his wife!"

Gray, who tried hardly to maintain a calm **smile** and ignore the annoying comments turned back sharply.

"Come here," a fed up mentor said in a sharp tone, rushing his feet to his apprentice. He grabbed Icarus's wrist, then took the bracelet off his hand forcefully.

"This - - is not a tool - - for you to spy on people, and can't you see? Using it much is changing your behaviour and even the way you speak," the master

(9-1) (9-9) * (3-2) * (1-3) (5-14) * (13-8) * (29-9) * (15-3) * (13-9) (24-14)

scolded his apprentice while highlighting a serious fact Icarus missed seeing bef**or**e.

Gray placed the bracelet on his chest pocket, thus walk**ed** ahead, adding in an an**no**yed tone:

"You'll need this soon, but until then - - **we**'ll be keeping it"

"Spying! They're your memories, dipshit. You're the one spying. Oh shit!" Icarus murmured low then **not**iced that he was acting off **ch**aracter. He kicked a small stone under his foot then rushed his steps to catch up with Gray.

The two sauntered out of the group of trees **and** into the house's backyard, where **a** tall man with hazelnut skin sat calmly, reading his newspapers while adjusting the neck of his shirt then his boring granola sweater.

Gray walked towards the man with a faint grin, taking his hands out of his deep pocket while snapping his neck by tilting his head to the sides.

"This one is really, really interesting," he said in a tone that carried a hint of excitement.

Gray stopped before the two long steps that separate the wooden porch from the pear lawn.

"Kid, meet Oscar, your next **train**ing session," he said, smiling slyly.

Gray's words teased out Icarus's curiosity, so he sharpened his eyes to scrutinize Oscar. His first thought was that the man before him looks like a **killer**, for even behind those inl**ine** clothes, his veiled muscles were obviously forged for combat, likewise, his body went belligerent eyes. However, after a brief examination, the Mingan sensed nothing off about him, just a mere hu**ma**n reading the news.

"What's so special about this - - man," he deadpanned, giving Gray a boring look.

Oscar's wife stepped out, pausing Gray's reply. She approached her husband with a hot cup of coffee.

"Hun, your coffee," she said, c**are**fully handing him the cup, followed by a quick kiss on the cheek

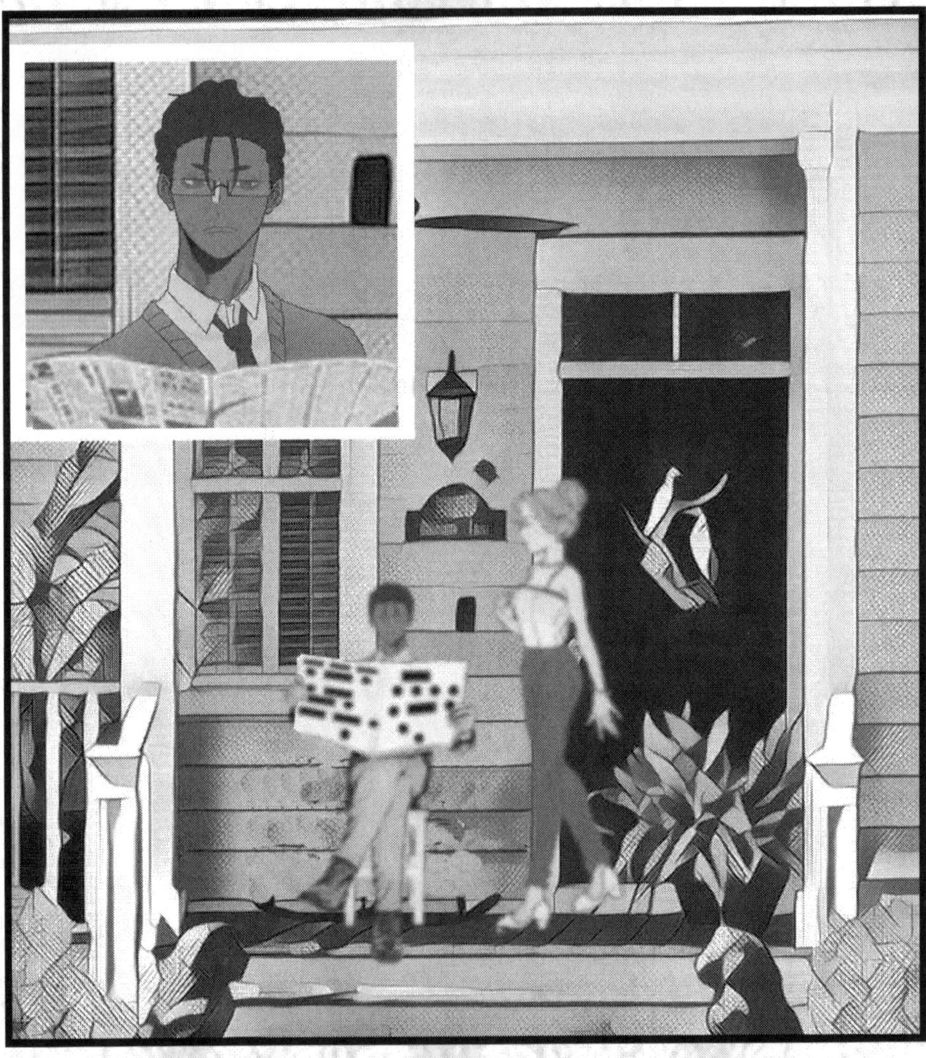

“Thank you sweetie,” he replied **with** a blissful s**M**ile, grabbing the cup with one h**a**nd while folding the newspapers with the other.

A swift Gray to**ss**ed the bracelet t**o** Icarus.

“Wear it - - and just w**at**ch, do not - - move,” Gray grinned, walking to the wife with l**O**ng steps then without w**A**rning, he vigorously punched the young lady while Icarus gaz**ed**! The blow was vi**ci**ous enough to reel her head twice

_ (2-2) (3-4) (3-7) (6-7) (4-5) (6-3) * (1-6) * (1-9) (3-1) (5-3) (5-7)

before it stopped facing Icarus, dropping her on her k**ne**es first, thus prostrated; freeing a last breath out of her broken jaw.

Benumbed, Icarus's eyes enlarged slowly as his petrified face turned pale, disbelieving **what** he witnessed while fixed at her soulless stares, he said low:

"What did you - - What did you do?"

He then raged with a shout while unsheathing his right wing:

"Why did **you**?"

Icarus arrowed the wing's lar**ge** thorn towards Gray but - - a relaxed Gray snapped a fing**er**, freezing Icarus in his place; one foot on the porch and the o**the**r jabbing the grass underneath, the Mingan snarled, trying hard to stab Gray, f**or** the tip of his wing was inches from the man in black's chest.

"Don't look here, look at him," Gray said with a deep voice, pointing Icarus's vision towards Oscar with a slight head-tilt.

Icarus couldn't move his head, so he switched his sight left towards Oscar to be amazed further more.

He gazed, switching his snarls to a silent stare of confusion, as his clutch loosened. The reason was Oscar's unexpected reaction.

The husband who witnessed his young wife taking her last breaths stood straight, carelessly loo**ki**ng at her lifeless cadaver. He released a puzzled sigh while throwing the newspapers on the chair. He **cal**m**l**y leaned down closer to her whilst checking if there were any passersby in the garden. There were none.

He placed two fingers on her neck, checking her carotid artery, but noticed that it was a stupid thing to check for a pulse after hearing her neck snap, there was no chance she survived, but what was really strange was Oscar being quizzical about what to do with the body and not what caused his wife's neck to snap on its own! Was this usual in this man's life?

Icarus reflected quietly, eager for a reasonable explanation, but there were none; '*is he in shock?*' but his dead eyes stated he wasn't. '*Or does he hate her?*' but his reserved expression showed that he didn't.

"What now!" Oscar sighed casually, standing straight while thinking of a convincing cover-up. After a while, He grabbed his wife's legs to drag her body halfway down the steps, mindless of her head bumping onto the hard step. He adjusted her sku**ll** above the step's edge to make it look like she fell and broke her neck.

(10-13) * (4-2) * (7-3) * (20-8) * (9-16) * (19-2) (33-3) (9-3) * (8-5) (1-10)

"**A**h, much better," he said low, gently tapping a palm on her cheek then shoved his hand inside his pocket, pulling a p**l**ast**i**c vial of eye drops.

In the meantime, a smiley **G**ray walked behind Icarus, adjusting his **st**u**p**efied head slightly to the left, to grant him a better view of what was about to happen.

"Just watch," he whispered c**al**m**ly**, resting his hands on his apprentice's shoulder.

Os**ca**r looked heavenward, fixing his head back whilst using a hand to pull his lower eyelid down, and the other to squeeze several drops into his eyes.

"Ouch!" he yelped low, squeezing his eyes shut. The content was a le**mon** compound to force tears out of his dry eyes.

"This will do," he mumbled, pulling his cell-phone out to make a nine-one-one call.

After the bib an operator answered. Oscar faked a cry and a sniffled tone while talking,

"My wife - - please Hurry - - I think she broke her neck," he stuttered in a brittle voice, panting rapidly while answering the operator's question:

"Ah - - 315 Benson Place - - ok, I don't know what to do, please hurry"

After a demonstrated pretence, Oscar ended the call, stopping his fake cries in an instant. He looked around, then dropped more lemon drops inside his eyes before sitting next to his wife's dead body.

"Now **we** wait," he said, thus blew a bored whistle.

"That's enough," said Gray, reeling his index against clockwise. Time reversed rapidly, then stopped when Oscar's wife stepped out of the house.

"Hun - - your coffee," she said, gi**ving** him the cup, followed by a quick kiss on the cheek.

"Thank **you** sweetie," he replied with a blissful smile, grabbing the cup with one hand while folding the newspapers with the other.

Gray used a quick flick on Icarus's nape to unfreeze him. He then lowered the Mingans's shirt to reveal the contract's rune on his chest, glowing red in reaction to his actions.

"Next time, obey, or there will be unpleasant consequences," Gray said in a serious tone.

"What you saw just now, was a made-up scene, it never happened, but, if it did, that would be Oscar's real reaction," he cl**ar**ifi**e**d with a brief explanation, approach**ing** Oscar with steady steps then added, mimicking Icarus's boring tone:

"To show you, what's so special about this - - man"

The Mingan stared at the glare on his chest fade back to a **g**lauc**o**us tattoo, then placed the pieces toge**th**e**r**. Him wishing to be emo**tio**n**l**ess and now this, a man that shows not a shred of empathy after seeing his wife drop dead before him. The reason behind this j**ou**rney was revealed.

"You mean - - he has no emotions!" an unsure Icarus inquired, strai**gh**tening his stand whilst pulling his wing back:

"Is he a non-Human?"

Gray puffed his cheeks then started drumming his teeth while thinking, as if he struggled between yes and no.

"**Same** as you now; he is, but not completely. After all, he's missing the thing that makes most humans - - humane," Gray answered indecisively, leaning closer to Oscar, who was casually talking to his wife about a potential storm somewhere in the country.

Gray placed his nine-eyed face next to Oscar's then poked his chest, penetrating his flesh.

"Which makes this hollow individual a very, very rare one," he grinned, taking his finger out. Meanwhile, a disturbed Icarus grabbed his bracelet off the g**rou**nd and wore it.

"What do you mean?" he asked, stretching his arms like a cat, thus rotating his shoulders to loosen his stiff muscles while his lashes fluttered.

"Why tell you if we can show you? Then, you will see why it is bad__" he paused, pointing to Oscar with both of his hands open, drumming with his mouth as if he were a showman presenting his great finally, then grinned with a singsong tone,

"__to be - - a Psychopath"

Icarus stood still, looking at his mentor with crinkled cheeks, a down-smile, and a slight headshake that says '*Stop*'

Gray misunderstood Icarus's upsetting grimace with him not understanding the word, so he gave him a lopsided grin then tapped his wrist, indicating the Mingan's need for the bracelet.

"Oh, I know. I already received the information while stretching. Just - - please stop acting like a clown," the apprentice didn't waste the chance to acerbically hu**mi**lia**t**e his mentor. He then turned round Oscar with a frowned face, gently scratching his neck.

"And believe me, a**f**t**er** seeing that - - consi**de**r me convinced. We can go back already," he groused

"Ahem!" Gray faked a shameful cough then adjusted his stand, placing his h**a**n**d**s behind his back, but it was too late for him to act high and formal.

"Unfortunately, there are still two things **we** have to show you. Follow me," he said in a serious tone, walking past Icarus to a black door with a golden frame, standing in Oscar's backyard. Icarus raised a brow, musing silently:

'*Where did that come from*'

The man in black opened the door, then slid to the side, waiting for Icarus to walk through first. When the Mingan ap**pr**oach**e**d the door, he noticed that the blackness was actually a screen of matte smoke.

Gray cleared **hi**s throat to rush his apprentice in, and so he did. Icarus shook the smoke coiling the door knob then barged in to find himself entering a vast and crowded salon; filled with small squared tables, occupied by couples of the oppos**it**e gender, acting as if they were on a date. **For** a reason Icarus didn't know, there was a sand hour in the shape of two hearts in every table, resides on the right side of every woman, and an orchid on their left.

Icarus got used to the view; the sound of chatters meddled with soft jazz. Suddenly, all men stood up and changed tables with the one on their left, swapping their dates. It was very confounding to Icarus, thinking that these men are exchanging their **w**om**e**n.

"Speed dating," said Gray, raising Icarus's hand, the one with the bracelet, while closing the door behind him.

The Mingan looked at his bracelet, thence Gray. He received the explanation of that idiom while looking at the black door transforming to a vintage door with a glass window in the middle.

"Night!" he commented in a low voice, peeking outside through the glass as the sky went dark, making the moon more radiant.

In a flash of a lightning strike, Icarus glimpsed a shade of a winged man on one of the buildings, one that disappeared so fast he thought he was just imagining things.

"Let's go!" Gray pulled his shoulder to follow whilst advancing through the tables, thus pointed at the one on the furthest corner.

"This is why we're here," he said with a high-pitch to **be** heard over the palaver noises, from flirtations to sloppy coy lines.

Walking closer **to** the corner, Icarus grasped Oscar sitting there with an **anonymous** woman; he had his glasses off, and an attractive haircut, even the vibe he had was completely different.

"You unfaithful - - piece of cow shit," Icarus grinned with a lopsided smile, then added in a scornful tone while looking slyly at Gray:

"And you say - - he's emotionless!"

He swung a sharp smack on Gray's arm, but Gray shook his head no, denying his apprentice's accusation with a dull smile.

"**N**ever be quick to judge. He's not **being** unfaithful, well - - he is partly but not what you're thinking," he replied, tilting his head both sides, uncertain on how to explain. He stood two f**ee**t apart from Oscar and said ambiguously:

"He's doing this - - looking for something he doesn't have"

"Two things - - obviously," Icarus was quick to reply with a snide joke, hinting that Oscar's date had bigger breasts **than** his wife.

"This is serious," Gray interjected in a serious tone meddled by an uncontrolled chuckle, trying to straighten his apprentice's behaviour.

"The first thing we want to make clear__" Gray stated, walking to the other side of the table. He leaned over it, locking his eyes on Oscar's relaxed face,

“__People like him - - desire, loathe and yearn to be natural - - normal in the eyes of their kind, to love, hate, cry and all of that, and believe us, they can do anything to get what they want,” Gray clarified, pointing Icarus to the watch Oscar wore.

The **Mi**ngan leaned closer to take a better look. He concentrated his vision on its screen to see that it didn’t tell the time, but the heart ratio, and before he asked of the reason, he read the brand on the watch’s frame, ‘*Daedalus.*’ engraved in Greek.

Gray continued with his explanation. But Icarus’s mind was roaming somewhere else,

“This watch unable him to measure his heart rate, therefore he comes here. Hoping that one day he may meet a woman that can raise his heart beats to a certain digit,” Gray smirked, straightening his stand. While Icarus, who joined the conv**ers**a**t**ion late, felt pity for Oscar, one that society rushes to judge his kind as a killing machine.

A distracted Mingan st**ood** silently for a moment, thus remember to inquire Gray about the watch’s brand,

“The watch - -” he said but got interrupted by a a reluctant Gray:

“**We**’re done here, let’s move to stage two”

He walked towards the exit door. Icarus looked inquisitively at the watch then gave Gray a suspicious gl**are**, following with a ponderous pace.

The two walked out of the golden door and back to Oscar’s backyard, nothing changed but the dark sky.

Without saying a word, Gray headed to the side passage, heading to the front yard, followed by Icarus, who kept his eyes on the portal while vanishing.

“He’s already here,” said Gray, to rush his apprentice.

The two met Oscar in the driveway, parking his car inside the garage; it was large enough to fit four other vehicles like his, but since his car was the only one there, Oscar parked in the middle.

After wearing his fake spectacles and pre**ss**ing his hair back, he stepped out to head straight to the door that lead into the house. He glanced at the far corner before opening the door, thus shouted with an orot**und** voice:

“Hun - - I’m home,”

“Here - - in the kitchen, dinner is almost ready,” she replied with a shout that he barely heard, for the kitchen was on the other side of the house.

_ (18-1) * (20-5) * (5-2) (29-7) (31-9) (13-1) (15-4)

"Be right **the**re sweetie, I just have something - - with the car," Osca**r** replied

C**o**ncurrently, Gray and Icarus stepped int**o** the garage, pausing on the vast unoccupied **s**pace.

Oscar locked the door **t**h**e**n ambled to the corne**r** **w**h**il**st reeling his keychain around his finger. Whi**l**e, the snoopers stood there awkwardly silent, observing everything he does.

"This is the thing we want **you** to see most," said Gray in a serious tone, hyping Icarus's enthusiasm.

Oscar leaned down on one knee. He looked back to the door be**f**ore thrusting **a** key size rod from his keychain inside a sm**all** hole in the floor. When he did, a small plate clicked open, revealing a long handle.

Seeing that thrilled Icarus, he swallowed his spittle, waiting for Oscar to unveil the secrets he hid behind his friendly smiles. The Mingan stretched his neck without leaving his spot, peeking as Oscar opened the secret hideout underneath.

"Hello friend," said Oscar, pulling a half human size boxing-puppet out; one with a heavy round base to keep it balanced.

Icarus crossed his arms then looked at Gray dully, he said nothing but his expression spoke louder, '*is this a joke?*' Gray replied with a faint sly smile thus pointed Icarus's attention back to Oscar, who carried the torn doll closer to the car.

He wearily looked back at the door again then used his thumb to push the doll's stiff forehead.

"Click!"

Oscar released a long audible sigh, and a few seconds after the click, it sounded **like** a record st**a**r**ted** playing inside the puppet's head.

"Hello Oscar," said the record with Oscar's **v**o**i**c**e**, but fuller and deeper.

"Hello," replied Oscar, taking a step back from the doll.

"My **mo**ther died," said the record with a sad tone, meddled with cries of different people.

Oscar breathed in and out, s**tre**tching his neck up then slightly to the side.

"I don't care," he deadpanned

"What the - -" a baffled Icarus tried to ask but Gray shushed him, so he could focus on the rest.

CHAPTER FOUR

"Oscar - - I have great news. I won the lottery," said the record blissfully, fo**llowe**d by **ch**eers and faint sounds of fireworks.

Oscar stretched his mouth broadly to a terrible fake smile that showed most of his teeth.

"I don't care," he replied, maintaining that awful grin, then loosened his face muscles back and sighed.

"I love you, do you love me?" said the record with his wife's dulcet voice

Oscar looked round the door, then back to the puppet, rubbing the nape of his neck while squeezing his eyes shut. He then slid his tensed **ha**nd up over his head and clutched his hair tightly.

"I - - don't f**king know - - **w**h**at** love is," angry, he huffed with a whisper-shout then punched the puppet's head, causing its neck to twist back, looking straight at Icarus with its creepy plastic eyes.

A panting Oscar stood sil**en**tly with his eyes closed, while a Mingan screwed up his face into a frown, glaring at Oscar after an unpleasant thought crossed his mind.

"Was that anger?" He queried in a serious t**on**e

"Worst," Gray replied, walking closer to Oscar. He rubbed a palm on the puppet's head, thus Oscar's, while moving behind him. He then rested his chin on the man's right shoulder, peering at Icarus.

"This, my dear Icarus - - is Frustration," Gray clarified with a solemn tone

The man in black tapped Oscar's back, then stepped back as if he triggered something. Not long after, a grimy dark smoke vaporized out of Oscar's carcass.

"Living a life - - unable to love, to be sad - - or to be angry even," Gray said, walking back toward Icarus while raising his hand, palm up, gathering the black mist Oscar freed into a black sphere, floating inches above the rest of his hand. He presented it to Icarus then added with a low voice:

"What would you do if we let you have it?"

The gloomy vibes liberated from the sphere penetrated Icarus, affecting his state. He clutched both fists vigorously. His veins throbbed while his shoulder blades swell, as if his wings were fighting to dash out.

The Mingan took a step away, then admitted with a faint voice:

"I would kill myself!"

A few seconds were enough for Icarus to make such a serious statement.

Gray clutched his ha**nd**, making the sphere pop back into mist, thus gave Icarus a l**o**psided grin, as if he were expecting those words out of his dry mouth.

"That was exactly what he did," Gray **sta**ted, thrusting his hands inside his pockets then added whimsically:

"But fai**le**d"

"H**un** - - Leon is on the phone," Oscar's wife interrupted with a loud shout from inside the house, driving the eyes of all three to the door at once.

"Coming," a hurried Oscar replied with a shout, carrying the puppet back to its hideout in a rush. He shoved it down and closed the door without locking it, a peccadillo that only Icarus noticed.

"Time for us to leave," said Gray, pulling the book out of his coat. **But** Icarus stared at him as if he were still asking for more, for not all his ques**tion**s were answered. However, his mentor made up his mind. He opened the book with a faint smile and the Mingan knew what was going to happen next. He att**em**pted to take a step back, but the book sucked him inside before he got the chance to retreat.

"We should've changed that damn brand or hid it. Some things are better hidden - - for now at least," said a sly Gray, then followed like usual,

"Swish!"

Oscar left the garage, rushing his steps down the hallway to find his wife in the living room, talking to his friend through the phone.

"Oz is here - - here you go," she said, handing Oscar the phone, then walked back to the dining table.

With his hand on the speaker, Oscar walked away to the furthest chair in the living room whilst checking on his wife, thus answered with a fixed, low voice:

"I told you not to call me here anymore"

The man over the phone released a deep and throaty laugh.

"And mi**ss** hearing your wife's sweet voice. I just - - can't resist," cunning, Leon replied in a provocative tone then jested:

"It's not like you care, my **de**a**r** friend, or do you?"

"What do you want?" A deadpan Oscar asked, keeping his eyes on his wife, while hearing his friend drumming his fingers on a wooden surface. Leon sighed audibly then said with a croaky voice:

'The Canons - - the big guy says it's time for them to go"

CHAPTER FOUR

Oscar drew a slightly surprised expression, yet impassive. He swallowed his dry throat, thus said with a lower voice and a questioning tone:

"What about the twin?"

"Mr. True**man** said '*they're not to be h**ar**m**e**d,*' so don't screw this up," a serious Leon replied, then immediately hanged up.

"Bib Bib!"

"**Hu**n, did you get the red wine? Ozie!" Oscar's wife asked, approaching him while wiping her **we**t hands dry with a white napkin.

"Ah yes! In the car," replied Oscar, hastily standing to get it for her, but she stopped him, for she was already next to the hallway that takes to the gar**ag**e.

"I'll get it," she said with a faint honest sm**ile**, curving her lips to a quick air-kiss.

Oscar blew a fake air-kiss back then sat down, playing with his keychain. Then noticed the key to the hidden-door was missing.

- -

Back in the Library, the white book fell off the ceiling, open. Icarus climbed out of it to see Gray already sitting in his chair. The book closed and flew back to its place.

"You arrived first this time!" said Icarus gruffly, with his fist close to his mouth, then barfed soundlessly.

"And you - - didn't stain our floors this time," Gray grinned, scratching his chin.

"I had some unanswered questions. Why did you force me back?" Icarus quizzed, approaching Gray's desk whilst continuing a shower of questions:

"Why was my father's name on **that** watch? And why didn't the bracelet show any information then?"

"Your story with your father and that - - bull is famous in the modern times, known as a Greek myth. But all they know is a pile of bullshit," Gray answered acerbically

"Me, a myth!"

"No thanks to us - - It was all you. You hid your story **fr**om history and chose to live like a ghost, yet you keep accusing us of being discreet. Huh! Like master - - like disciple," Gray clarified snidely, clearing all Icarus's doubts.

"Have a drink, we will leave soon," he invited Icarus to the couch, dropp**ing** his leg down, thus stood straight.

He walked towards the fourth section while Icarus grabbed the bottle of the drink offered to him, still processing what he had **be**en told.

"There is somewhere we want you to visit," Gray added, walking into the section and appeared instantly out of the first one. Icarus spat his drink after seeing him do so, confused on how he moved across the room in a flash.

The man in black walked towards his blunt apprentice with a silver book in hand.

"Ready or not," Gray smirked, offering the book to Icaru**s**.

CHAPTER FIVE
I DON'T MIND THE PAIN

2018 – Athe**ns**, Greece; on a **g**old**en** dry macula of a cracked floor, circulated b**y** damaged pillars of a stone and marble mixture, surrounding a winged-warrior statue of gray; wings spread tall while holding the sword low w**it**h both hands, a heroic posture.

The sculpture qu**iv**ered a slight, then aga**in** but harder, causing small cracks in both arms and legs. The fissures fulminated **al**l over its stony carcass, thus up to **it**s wings, until the figure exploded, propelling the shattered scree in all dire**cti**o**n**s.

Inside the fading harsh cloud of powder, stood a dusty Icarus

The Mingan coughed the d**i**r**t** out of his mouth as puffs of smoke, shaking the scraps off his shoulders and wings while trying to fore**se**e beyond the fog.

"Can't we for once - - travel normally," Icarus protested with a suppressed angry tone, stomping his foot on the ground to drop some stuck gravel down his p**an**ts, and while doing so, he noticed that the floor he stood upon seemed somehow familiar, he rushed a wide flap **to** clear his surroundings at once.

The Mingan gazed at the surrounding columns as the sight became more apparent; standing tall like damaged guardians to a destroyed chamber; however, Icarus saw everything around in its best state, re**pai**ri**n**g what was broken **with** images from his own memories.

A little boy of w**hi**te smoke ran past him, as if he were a ghost from the past. Icarus tried to grab him, but the boy van**is**hed.

"School!" he whispered with a sigh, ambling out of the ruined ground, and continued walking to the near edge of a cliff.

The peripatetic stood high, smiling at the view of the vast blue sea capturing the sunlight and turning it to sparkling grains of white, covering the featureless water. He curved an even wider beam while his eyes welled.

"Piraeus! Home!" a blissful Icarus grinned, cl**os**ing his eyes while respiring deeply and enjoying the salty breeze.

With a face filled with nostalgia, he stretched his arms both ways as if he wanted to embrace the surrounding atmosphere, smells and sounds - -

"Loud honking!"

Icarus's relaxed eyes twitched. He fought the urge to open them and confirm what he heard, but he had to know. The traveller raised his right eyelid slower than an electronic garage-gate, but a second loud honking rushed both of his eyes open.

A boat passing by shattered his joyful spirit. His smile fell, and so did his arms **dr**amatically.

Icarus squeezed his eyes and lips shut, stifling a shout of frustration, and when he threw his neck back to shoot it out, he heard steady steps coming from behind; steps that he could identify anywhere, the recognizable sound of Gray's shoes.

He opened his eyes after a relinquished sigh, then facepalmed, looking at the boat on his left through the gap between his fingers. He followed its trail to see the port of Piraeus crowded with more advanced ships of mostly white and sapphire, and behind it, a modernistic series of buildings, interspersed with paved roads of concrete; a pleasant view for a tourist, but not for the Mingan.

"Why now? Why not my time?" A disappointed Icarus asked in a subdued tone.

I DON'T MIND THE PAIN

Gray approached his melancholy apprentice, holding a brown paper bag with one hand while snacking on a crunchy bar of pastry with the other.

"You're not ready for that yet," deadpan, Gray answered, licking the sweetness off his forefinger and thumb.

He stood on Icarus's side, who **g**azed at the port while trying to imagine it the way he remembered it instead.

Gray interrupted his thoughts by shaking the paper bag before his face as an invitation.

"Have some, **friend**," said Gray, shaking the bag again to show its content.

Icarus p**eek**ed inside before grabbing a slice. He knew the pleasant smell of hot honey before he had a glance. Even with its smooth modern shape, he recognized what it was.

"Pasteli!" he **said** with a feeble smile, then thrust a lazy hand inside the bag to take one out.

"Mother used to make it for me," **I**carus remembered, whilst both he and Gray took a bite.

"Well, at least this one survived," he added, subduing his unpleasantry.

He took another bite **and** so did Gray, standing there in silence, observing the admiral sea while enjoying one of Icarus's childhood snacks.

The Mingan grabbed the bag off Gray's hand before speaking his mind cal**mly**:

"A whisper and a distant shout may sound the same, but - - it doesn't mean they're of the same volume"

"Mm! We will make sure to remember these wise words," Gray extolled humbly, reflecting on Icarus's words before adding a controversial reply:

"However, you also need to remember that if the voice was of the same source, time won't change its real essence"

After stating his argument, Gray walked to the other side of the cliff, where the view was free of all of what's human.

"I see! Home is Home," Icarus said in low voice, understanding the meaning behind Gray's words. But now, he was curious about the means behind this journey.

Following Gray while observing the medallion slope above, he sighed and wondered with a curious tone:

"So, why are we here? Is there someone I need to meet - - or observe?"

CHAPTER FIVE

Gray stood before a flat rock, taking his time to reply. He shook off the harsh dust a**wa**y with his naked palm before taking a seat, facing the sea. He then beckoned Icarus to approach him while pulling a hand size bottle from the interior pocket of his jacket.

"**W**e are here - - for you to do as you please, go wherever you want. Think of this as a break, or a vacation," he stated with a honeyed tone, handing him the bottle while taking his shoes off with his feet like a toddler.

Icarus lif**te**d a brow distrustfully, grabbing the bottle with a hesitant hand, then **qu**esti**o**ned with a slight of mockery:

"And you - - will stay here?"

"Yes," Gray answered simply, placing his **sh**oes on the side while resting h**is** bare feet on the dank dirt.

"Ha! Ha ha!" Icarus forced out a sardonic chuckle, shaking his head no while suppressing his discreet chuckles from turning into laughter. He narrowed his eyes askance while smelling the content of the bottle.

"A break huh! Mm! Do I look like a kid to you? Because believe me, you look more like one to me," said Icarus, referring to how Gray was toying and jerking the dirt with his feet.

"The **way** I see it; you're waiting for me to leave, then abandon me here. So, just tell me, is **this** a starvation test? Or is there a door I should find to escape? Huh. Or any of your vagary ideas," he huffed with an accusatory tone, standing on Gray's face and blocking his view.

Gray grumped. He opened his mouth and moved it as if the words were trapped inside then got freed seconds after,

"Are we this evil to you!?" he inquired aggrievedly, giving Icarus a sharp kick on his tibia to step off his view

"No, that would be an insult to the word evil," a hassled Icarus exasperated acerbically, pushing Gray's foot off his leg like an irritated teen.

Gray sighed, then forced a grin and said with a soft yet provocative tone:

"We believe you're confusing us with your father!"

He then curved his mouth down, realizing he shot the wrong words. For a reason only he and Gray knew, Icarus was excessively sensitive when **it** came to h**is** father.

Fixed, the Mingan glared at Gr**ay**, raising his forefinger in the man's face; however, no words were spoken, and he didn't need to, his feelings were **sh**o**w**n by his tight expression and twitching limbs that **cau**sed his wings to spread. Gray nodded his head regrettably, then apologized sincerely:

"We apologize. That was an od**ious** thing to say,"

Icarus put his finger down, giving Gray his back, while slowly absorbing his wings back inside.

"Accepted," he replied low

"Now, go **be**fore we change our mind," said Gray, stretching his legs whilst yawning. He threw his head back and a pillow of fluffy smoke appeared behind his nape, like a floating cushion.

Icarus crackled his fingers bef**o**re tilting his head right and left. He then **r**an **to**wards the edge with a speeding pace, and before he reached the end of the cliff, he leaped forward like a human spear then swooped towards the sea; arms stre**t**ched ahead, the Mingan dived deep, leaving an underwater trail of jumbled foam before swimming inches below the surface like a hyped dolphin. He broke the surface above into a smooth crescent, then spread his wings, raising them high like two large fins cutting the ocean.

Icarus flapped his wings vigorously, blowing the surface of the water as he burst out, spreading his wings to fly high with a shout of excitement.

"Wouh!"

The winged man headed to the port first, focusing his vision on a horde mounting a cruise boat. He roamed the coast first, then made a sharp turn towards the city, zigzagging through the buildings at high speed then heavenwards. The Mingan stopped halfway to the clouds, floating high like an angel while enjoying the view; a city painted as a round galette of buildings. He then noticed a large rectangle of white and red, and driven by curiosity as always, he swayed towards it in a flash then down a slight to see it was a vast strange coliseum. Thanks to the bracelet, he realized it was a football stadium. Not soccer ~

Icarus landed on the empty field of sleek grass, looking at the uninhabited seats of pale red.

CHAPTER FIVE

As one who used to love attending gladiators' matches when he was a child, it was a chance to live a dream; a dream he lost **when** he knew of his true nature, | the same truth that **fo**rced a seven-years old boy to travel to the eastern Sahara, to be men**t**ored in the hands of a known Mingan at that time.

Being away from **ho**me caused the little Mingan to feel a great deal of abandonment and loneliness, until one **day**, while carrying a love letter from his mentor, he walked across **a** horde hosting similar sports, but mainly wrestling. The boy lost track of time while watching giant-like men fighting to death. It caused him a long scolding and a harsh punishment, but after that, his master allowed him the attendance of all the wrestling matches, saying '*it's a part of yo***ur** *training,*' but Icarus knew he was only **try**ing to cheer him up, for he was far s**u**perio**r** to all the gladiator**s** there. |

Icarus silenced the faint cheers inside his head by unsheathing his sword and giving it an acrobatic wave before fixing its sharp edge towards the bleachers. He closed his eyes calmly while walking in a small-ranged circle, hearing much louder cheers calling for his name. Icarus started performing highly skilled sword moves to his imaginary crowds, and while doing a high back flip, he heard a honeyed woman voice calling for him from behind:

(4-1) (2-12) (11-6) * (3-4) (10-13) * (5-4) (11-15) (12-1) * (7-5) * (6-6)

'Icarus dear!'

Alarmed, he rapidly looked back **t**o assess, but there was no one, and from his expression, it seemed as if he **k**new to whom that voice belonged.

Icarus looked heavenwards **whilst** shea**thin**g his sword, then flew out of the stadium with one jump.

Wasting no time, he headed straight to **a** place called Kallithea.

The **Min**gan pulled his wings inside before landing gently on a crowded sidewalk. After a brief walk, he made a turn to a quiet ally that sloped down; the cramped sidewalks fit only one person, while the street could barely fit two cars, and being made of bricks instead of concrete showed it was only for footers and not wheels. Icarus had to lean a shoulder forward to walk on the incommodious sidewalk but gave up a few steps ahead and jumped to the road, the sidewalks were m**or**e pleasant to look at than to walk on, for they had different textures of different colours on each doorstep, **it** was artistically chaotic.

The Greek walked slowly with slithering steps, enjoying the faint smell of night musk, then paused before a two-storey house of caramel. **You** may be wondering why he paused before that house, one he saw for the first time, or **is** it obvious? Even with all the modern changes, the Mingan would never forget this spot.

"Home," Icarus said low with a faint smile, looking at the house from the bottom up. He glimpsed a couple of birds nesting below one of the windows' edges, and **when** the Mingan focused his vision to get a better look, he noticed their nest was manmade, and so were several empty ones.

Standing there alone was enough to give him a pleasant vibe.

While observing his surroundings, his eye caught an old man sitting on the side, next to a small shop, similar to the fruit shop next to his door back in the days.

"Click!"

The door of the house opened, and out of it walked a young blushed lady; wearing a long pearl-wihte peplos and leather sandals with thin flat stripes coiling her ankle, and golden earrings, matching her blond, silky hair.

CHAPTER FIVE

Amazed, Icarus gazed with his mouth agape, curving his brows up, then whispered low:

"Mo**t**he**r**!"

When the Mingan blinked, he saw the young lady in her actual state; she was wearing a black pants and **sh**o**e**s, topped by a cotton white shirt with stripped neck and sleeves; a simple modern look.

A confused Icarus squeezed his eyes shut then opened them after a slight head jiggle. He shook the bracelet next, uncertain if the young lady was just a split-image of his mother or if he were really just hallucinating as he first thought.

The **you**ng lady locked the door, then kicked its bottom gently; another habit his mother used to do whenever she leaves the house. **It** was then when Icarus knew this was no mere coincidence.

The mysterious girl walked on her way, passing by the old man's store. She gave the old owner a familiar smile.

"Kalimera," she greeted with a slight wave

"Kalimera Uniss," the old man greeted her back with his **ea**s**t**-Asian accent, peeking over the newspaper he was reading.

"The usual?" he added in a questioning tone, affirming her daily order of fresh vegetables and fruits.

"Yes please. I'll be back in - - the afternoon," she replied simply, while checking her watch and walking forward.

"Your voice - - the way you speak!" said Icarus **with** a sad smile, rubbing his eyes.

The Mingan cancelled **a**ll his plans and followed her around to be certain, scrolling through all possibilities:

'*Does she really look like my mother, or is the bracelet tampering with my mind and vision? Or is it one of Gray's plans?*'

The last assumption was his most accurate. He **co**u**ld**n't be blamed for su**sp**ecting Gray's trickery.

After a brief walk of pursuit, Icarus rushed his steps to walk by her side, unable to take his eyes off her face, scrutinizing every detail with suspicion. However, after a while, he couldn't prevent a delighted smile from his face.

"Real or not, it feels so good to see you," a nostalgic Icarus said in an ardent tone, curving his faint smile into a grin, for at that moment, enjoying the presence of his deceased mother was more important than thinking of what games G**ray** was playing.

Walking side by side, Icarus relished the one-sided conversation, while checking if Uniss could see him with a slight wave on her face every few steps taken, until, the two stopped at a crosswalk, waiting for the green lights to permit them a passage.

While waiting, a shady man over wearing his hood stood behind Uniss, jolting his he**ad** left and right suspiciously before sliding a sharp eye into the girl's open purse. He glimpsed her phone; the easy booty was confirmed and locked upon, and it was time to make his move.

The skilled swindler thrust a hand inside the bag, then started pulling the phone out with two long yet steady fingers.

Icarus knew he was up to no good from the start, but Uniss was completely blunt. It seemed as if she didn't even notice a person was standing behind her.

"Hey, you bastard!" an irritated Icarus shouted with a lazy tone, waving his right and le**f**t at the man's arm just t**o** **s**ee them ghost through. He then looked at Uniss, giving her a '*seriously!*' stare.

The Mingan placed his palms on her cheeks, biting his lip and tightening his hands as if he were trying to drive her head towards her purse with an invisible force, he knew it wouldn't work, but did so out of anguish. When Icarus's hand infiltrated Uniss's face, the thief's hand twitched synchronously, moving the pur**s**e down a slight on Uniss's skin. She sneezed dully, spooking Icarus and the thief's hands back. Icarus took a step back, then huffed, surprised that she didn't notice that obvious motion on her arm:

"Really!"

The sneaky wease**l** tried to reach for the phone again, seeing that Uniss showed no reaction or an alarmed expression, **but** the light turning green saved her phone from **b**eing snatched.

She crossed the street with her phone halfway out of the purse, and with the trembling of her rushed steps, **it** fell back, specifically inside an inner small pocket. Seeing that, the thief surrendered to fai**lure**, not to mention the mob of people walking their way.

Walking by her side while observing the thief departing to the opposite way as he navigated for a new prey, Icarus **turn**ed round Uniss with a mixed look of disappointment and pity.

"**You**ng lady, you need to be more careful," he said with a slight headshake.

Not too long **a**f**ter**, the two walked past an electronics shop with a long interface of flat screens, displaying different channels. The Mingan **realise**d something he missed:

'*How was it that there was no fiend-related news or anything of such?*'

He turned to the bracelet for a clarification, but before getting the chance to ask, Uniss interrupted his attention, waving at two girls inside a dinner across the street while exchanging beamy smiles through the wall of glass.

"Hey!"

Uniss looked both ways before slow-running across the street. She tapped a finger against the glass of wall between her and her friends while heading to the entrance. Contrastingly, Icarus walked through it while avoiding any physical contact with the two girls, or in his case, a ghostly one.

The Mingan stood few steps away from Uniss's friends, while his interest was mostly occupied by the dinner's big screen, likewise, the different kinds of food; then back to the girls' table when Uniss joined, giving each one two quick kisses on the cheek.

"I've got something to tell you," cheerful, one of her friends said with a big smile. She leaned closer while grabbing Uniss's hand, then said low with a discreet and sly tone:

I DON'T MIND THE PAIN

"Chri**s** and I kissed last night"

Uniss responded with an agape mouth, blissfull**y** surprised.

"**Tha**t's - - great, congrats," she replied, but the other fri**en**d chuckled mockingly, separating their hands.

"So what, it's not that big of a deal," she interfered, making fun of her friend's enthusiastic **b**ehaviou**r**, then tried to win Uniss to her opinion:

"Right Unie?"

But the one dru**nk** in love grabbed Uniss's hand again, responding to her friend's m**o**c**k**ery while e**x**agge**ra**ting the pronunciation of her name out of suppressed anger:

"Don't mind MARIA - - she's just jealous." She gave Maria a slight shoulder jab.

"Maria isn't jealous, **it's** SOPHIA who's overreacting because it was her first time," Maria sassed, pinching Sophia's arm.

The two started arguing while Uniss watched with a suppressed laughter.

"Mary, let her enjoy it," Uniss said with a faint chuckle, pushing Maria's hand off Sophia.

"I think I'll step back for now," discomfited, Icarus said with a heavy grin while walking away. He wanted **to** stay with Uniss, but as a gentleman, he found it inappropriate to overhear them while speaking of their private life. It was also a chance to explore and learn new things about the modern world.

The curious Mingan roamed the kitchen first, enjoying the smell of food. Then, out to the customers, rudely snooping on some individuals whilst they used their phones; and his last stop was the big screen on the side of the dinner, watching commercials and ads.

Two hours passed in a flash. Icarus saw the girls leaving their booth, so he followed them outside with back steps while monitoring the TV.

After saying their goodbyes, the three parted ways at the cafeteria's gate.

Uniss headed to her usual supermarket for some goods, while Icarus considered it as a continuation to his Modern Times' lessons.

At the end of another short foot-trip, the two stepped inside the supermarket. Icarus learned new things about shopping, how to choose ingredients, also about Canned food, which he really didn't like, likewise, some things he found embarrassing or rather unpleasant to know, the ones that fall in the '*ladies things*' category, therefore, he waited for Uniss outside of that section.

CHAPTER FIVE

Finally, they arrived at her ally, but before heading home, she stopped at the old man's shop. They found him the same way they left him, sitting lazily on the side of his shop, reading the news.

"Hey **The**ios," she greeted

"Hey Un**is**s," he replied kindly, pressing on the words whilst hardly standing up. He walked inside the shop and staggered out with two filled bags, already prepared.

"Fresh - - as usual," he smiled, handing her the bags.

"Thank you," she smiled back, grabbing the heavy weight off his quivered hand.

"**Do**n't mention it," he replied, walking back to his seat while Uniss walked towards her house.

"You're not paying?" Icarus **ask**ed bluntly, look**ing** at the old man casually going back to his seat. He then slow-ran after her, adding low:

"Oll wright, I believe you're not!"

Instead of barging in first, the spe**ct**re stood behind Uniss while she unlocked the do**or**, waiting for her to step inside first, and when she did, he followed with a discreet excitement

"Erini Se Sas! Home sweet home," said Icarus with an obvious smile, walking in.

Uniss took off her shoes at the door to place them in a small shoe closet on the side. She then stepped on a fabric parakeet carpet that wrapped the entire floor like a fuzzy and smooth field of lawn; the walls were wrapped with a stripped paper of golden and denim.

Uniss walked through the short corridor to a big round table of birch wooden legs topped by a marble surface of gray and white, holding random house gadgets, like keys, scattered coins, pens and an empty vase at its midst. The table itself played as a separator between the open living room and kitchen, adding to that, the living room was two steps down from the rest of the house.

While she was putting the bags on the table, Icarus sauntered to the living room, pausing on the side of a long arctic sofa facing the TV. He looked at the remote, but Uniss interrupted his vision as she walked through him. She sneezed before grabbing the TV controller, and Icarus hyped when she turned it on, for he didn't have enough of it.

Uniss switched through the channels to stop at a Japanese anime.

_ (4-2) – (11-1) (16-7) (17-1) * (5-2) * (13-5) (13-7)

I DON'T MIND THE PAIN

Agape, **I**carus approached the TV to an unhealthy distance. It was his first time watching a cartoon.

'*How can these unrealistic images move this way!*' was his unspoken thought.

His memory bracelet fed him **s**ome informa**tion**, but **that** didn't ruin the fun. He enjoyed the **s**how while the main character fought large wild beasts. It was then when his Mingan instinct took o**ve**r, he mused seriously:

"These moves can be very useful for fighting large fiends"

Uniss watched a couple of scenes with Icarus then walked back to the bags, taking only the ones with the groceries to the kitchen, while passionately singing with the anime's theme song.

She placed the goods on the counter but right before taking everything out, the house phone rang. Uniss rushed towards the ringing to a s**qu**ar**e** poll where the phone was **ha**nged and picked it up with a half-wet hand.

"Hello? Oh Hey Mama," she answered, ambling back to the kitchen while talking.

"Yes - - Yes I did. I k**no**w - - you don't need to remind of that too," vexed, she spoke with a heavy tone, rolling her eyes whilst placing the phone between her right cheek and shoulder.

She opened the bags noisily, intending to make her mother hear the plastic screech.

"I know Mama. I have to wash the things now, so talk to you later," she postponed in a reluctant tone, ending the call.

"Bib bib!"

Uniss placed the phone on the side of the counter, then went back to taking the goods out. She placed some in a basket under the sink to be washed, and the rest she put into the fridge.

"Where is it?" she said low, tapping her pockets then head to the table to check for the missing item.

After a brief check-up, Uniss walked towards the living room, pausing before her purse first. She took a glimpse inside then continued to the living room, flipping the cushions of the sofa. She was missing her Smartphone, ignorant that it was inside her purse.

Unlike girls her age, Uniss cared little for technology. She only bought that Smartphone recently because her friends kept nagging her to do so. That was why it became a habit of hers to misplace it.

CHAPTER FIVE

While **s**earching, Uniss released several loud huffs and exhales. However, Icarus didn't mind her and continued watching the show until she stood between him and the TV. She rested her loosened fists on the sides of her waist, taking her time to remember **w**h**er**e she left her phone.

"Seriously!" said an annoyed Icarus. The same person who was flabbergasted when first seeing the face of his mother! Or maybe the reality of her not being his mother finally **sa**nk in.

Uniss rushed awa**y** from the TV as if she heard Icarus's words, heading **to**wards the staircase. She climbed in a hurried pace, skipping three stairs with every step taken; halfway up, her foot slipped and crumbled down in a second.

"Slam!"

A wary Icarus turned round to assess the blow, hurrying to the stairs only to find Uniss on the floor with one hand behind her head and the other behind her back! He didn't know what to do, **for** she wasn't moving, but moments after, Uniss groaned while faintly pushing her body to the side to pull her arm out, and while doing so, Icarus heard a faint snap.

"What happened to you!" perplexed and worried, he said, looking up the stairs as Uniss already stood up on her feet with a casual expression.

Icarus waited for a cry or anything of such, but nothing. His concerned face turned to an impressed one.

"Well! I guess I misjudged you. You really are a sturdy one!"

That didn't last for long. Uniss forced a worried face on the Ming**ans** face again when she suddenly fretted, rushing to the bathroom.

"Please - - let it be nothing," vexed, she begged repeatedly, feeling her arms whilst stepping into the bathroom.

Icarus followed, but something odd about her bathroom's decoration trapped his attention first. She had two large mirrors covering most of the front and back walls; the use for it was to enable her to see her carcass from all sides. He shifted his attention back to Uniss, examining her hands and arms over and over.

"Please please, oh god," a dismayed Uniss murmured repeatedly while switching to check her neck and nape.

The Mingan kept watching bluntly, unaware to what she was stressed about. If she weren't hurt, why was she checking her body while paranoid, like one looking for an injury?

"Kid, what's wrong?" baffled, he asked, frowning his brows while Uniss leaned down to check her feet. She then started unzipping her pants to ta**ke** them off, forcing Icarus to look away and leave the bathroom.

Icarus waited outside. After five minutes of stress, Uniss stepped out with a relieved face.

"Phew!"

She headed to the **fr**idg**e** and grabbed a cold spray from its door **d**raw**er**. While sh**ak**ing the bottle, Uniss looked at the phone she forgot on the kitchen counter, hesitantly sliding her hand closer, she sighed and pulled her hand away.

She took two steps to the side, facing **a** kitchen cabinet with five open drawers except for the one in the bottom, it had a sliding door. She took a first aid kit out of it and moved to the **li**ving room's sofa.

Uniss showed no indications of pain, puzzling Icarus as she used the spray on those bruises that were barely there. This process reminded him of the snap he heard; the Mingan felt then that something was not right.

Exhausted, **Un**iss threw the spray recklessly on the floor, then herself on the sofa. She grabbed the remote, delicately touching the off button. She tapped it twice without pressing it just to end up placing the remote on the floor, leaving the TV on.

Icarus saw through her, it was a piteous attempt to not **feel** lonely inside this quiet house.

The ghostly guest approached her, still dull and suspicious of what drove her to that appalling state if the fall was clearly harmless - - or wasn't it.

Icarus sized Uniss up and down again, focusing on her facial expression as she rolled on her back, measuring the movement of every limb and bone. Uniss, however, was feeling drowsy. She rolled again to lie on her back, resting an arm on her eyes to block the faint light.

"Yawn!"

After a one-hour nap, Uniss opened her eyes partly while trying to push herself up with her right arm but couldn't. Confused, she fought her heavy eyelids open, and they sobered at the sight of her arm turning mauve and swollen.

A motionless Uniss pressed her lips shut tightly while her eyes glossed, suppressing a cry. She was more sad than surprised.

"I knew it," she whispered in a croaky voice

_ (4-1) * (20-12) * (12-6) (2-14) * (10-9) * (7-5) (8-1) * (16-2) (7-14)

CHAPTER FIVE

Icaru**s** said the same thing, for he had not left her sight and therefore witnessed her arm turning to its current state.

The Mingan observed how he was wrong about Uniss, **se**eing that her tears were actually stronger than her will, she wasn't sturdy or bold as he thought, but a sensitive miss.

"Why - - god? Why?" She sobbed and whin**ed** faintly

Crestfal**l**en, Icarus felt sorry for Uniss. You may think the reason behind his robust heart turning soft was that she resembled his mother, maybe, but an innocent woman shedding tears never failed to move the Mingan's heart, it was simply in his nature, and that - - may have something to do with his mother.

"How did you not notice? **I** mean - - a broken arm! Isn't that supposed to be painful for your kind?" Sounding down and perplexed, Icarus wondered with mixed-up feelings, thus dropped a knee to approa**ch** her.

He knew his presence wouldn't help, b**ut** the feeling of guilt he knew he would experience if he did not try took over his rational thoughts.

Uniss sniffed her mucus back inside her nose whilst wiping her cheeks dry with her sleeves. It took her a while to reali**ze** that crying wouldn't heal her arm, so she forced her body up to a sitting position.

Her current state didn't break her habit of rubbing the bottom of her feet a**ga**inst each other before placing them on the floor. Icarus missed that, for he was focused on her brooding face.

Uniss headed for her purse first to find out that her phone was there the whole time. She sighed audibly and headed directly to the door out. She was partly thankful for the triangle mirror hanged three feet away from the door, alarming her to fix her dishevelled hair before leaving the house.

After sorting her hair orderly and wearing a sandal, Uniss hanged a jacket over her curved arm, using it to hide her swollen limb and avoid attracting any sort of attention, but a jacket on a hot day was a lousy decoy.

Stepping outside, she looked left at the shop owner, then took the opposite route, rushing her feet to the main street.

"Bib Bib!"

An opportunist taxi driver stopped before her without her asking.

"Miss, need a ride?" he asked, peeking through the window.

Uniss hopped inside without saying a word, all he received from her was the name of a clinic. On the way, the two made several fiddly eye contacts through the front mirror; one thinking about hiding her bruises **to** avoid any inconvenient conversation, while the other translated the nervous stares as a possibility that she had no money to pay for the ride, but that cleared out when they reached their destination. **The** driver was relieved when he received his payment with extra and Uniss from the disturbing stares.

She walked through the a**ut**o door into a long white hallway; the cleanliness of the floors and walls, the silent yet bright lights, likewise, the beautiful receptionist that looked more like a model in her feminine emerald suit, all indicates that this private clinic was for those who were blessed with heavy pockets. It was not that Uniss looked poor, but rather that place made everyone look like one.

Uniss approa**ch**ed the receptionist, noticing her arrogant stares and forced neat smile before they spoke.

"Can you please call for Dr. Orange? I'm his patient," she requested with a **tight**-lipped smile, tapping her finger on the polished-wood counter.

The receptionist sighed, fixedly maintaining a decent smile. She doubted Uniss for a moment but complied anyway, for it was the clinic's policy.

"What's your name, miss?" She asked in a silvery tone, lifting her brows whilst stretching her fingers over the keyboard, ready to type.

"Uniss Sonda," Uniss answered, switching her vision between the screen and the receptionist.

She typed on the computer without breaking eye contact, then looked at the s**cr**een. She dropped the fake smile faintly while hiding her surprised expression when she found Uniss on the VIP list.

"Miss Sonda, take a seat please," she said, pointing to the wall behind, where a chrome bench of three leather seats compiled together took place. She then picked the phone, pressing a single button,

"I will let Dr. Orange know"

Uniss walked leisurely to the seats, and the moment she sat down she heard someone calling for her.

"Miss Sonda," Dr. Orange paced towards her. She approached him with quick steps, leaving her jacket behind.

"What happened? Are you Okay?" concerned, he asked.

Uniss looked back at the receptionist, then showed him her arm discreetly.

CHAPTER FIVE

"I **think** - - it's broken" wistful, **s**he snivelled, rubbing her nose with the back of her hand. Her words carried a h**in**t of shame as if it were a sin to get hurt.

"It is," said both **I**carus and the doctor at the same time; however, one was annoyed, while the other was genuinely worried for his patient.

The doctor turned left and right as if he were searching for a certain ob**j**ect, th**us** locked an eye on a stretcher several steps away

"Stay still, don't move. I'll get the bed so please don't move," he instructed **with** a strict tone, then hurried to the stretcher and back while waving at one nurse to come, and she did briskly.

Doctor O**ra**n**ge** placed Uniss on the stretcher carefully, fearing that she may have other fractures that she didn't know about.

"Slowly," he said aggressively to the nurse who adjusted Uniss's hand with a slight force. The nurse looked down, sorry.

"It's okay, I'm okay," Uniss pr**even**ted him from scolding the nurse.

Icarus wondered why Doctor Orange had delivered his command harshly, was Uniss that important to him?

Doctor Orange sighed then ordered the nurse to take his patient to the X-Ray room number thirty on the fourth floor, one kept for important patients only. He also insisted that she helps her with her clothes and not allow her to move. The way he spoke, the expressions he showed, in any way you see it, Orange seemed more like a butler than a doctor when talking to Uniss.

Icarus followed Doctor Orange, heading to the Diagnostics room; a darkish long room, the wall on the right had three whiteboards with bright neon lights on top of each one, and on the left **side**, four computers, topped by a large window that occupied most of the wall, one you could see the radiography room through.

A few minutes after their arrival, Uniss, along with two nurses, entered the Radiography room; She was wearing a long and loose white piece of cloth. The two nurses helped her onto the X-Ray bed then left without saying a word.

Doctor Orange pressed a button on the reach of his hand, allowing him to talk through the speaker.

"Are you feeling okay, Miss Sonda?" said Orange, then squeezed his eyes and lips shut as if he said something he wasn't supposed to say.

"Yes, all good," Uniss replied simply

Orange pressed a thumb on his **f**orehead while breathing in and out d**eepl**y.

"Would you please try **not** to move," he said in a formal tone, sitting on the last computer on his right.

"Okay," replied Uniss, narrowing her eyes in reaction to the radiant light as her bed slid inside the cylindrical space of the ma**ch**ine.

Ten minutes after, Or**ang**e grabbed his cell phone then stepped out of the Diagnostics room, leaving Icarus with two interns. One looked as if she were longing for Orange to leave, and the moment he closed the door behind him, she spoke low with her colleague then grinned:

"So this is the girl - - who **can**'t feel pain. What a bless, huh!"

Her words stunned the Mingan, but everything became clear now as the bracelet clarified it furthermore when receiving a sign. Introducing him to a disorder called CIPA. Uniss wasn't **tou**gh as he thought, rather a poor girl with a rare illness, same as Yaashva and Oscar.

"More like a curse if you ask me," replied the other one while checking the monitors before she jested slyly:

"You know, no pain means no action down there too"

Both chuckled at that inappropriate joke, not knowing the speaker was still on. Uniss heard eve**ry** word, her tears dropped in silence, while two of her nails broke when she clutched to the bed out of frustration and shame.

"Tfou!"

A glowering Icarus spitted on the intern next to him, but his spittle went through her and through the floor even.

"Tsk!"

The truth that he couldn't slap them in his current form made him rage even more, but **this** time, he didn't even attempt an angry wave as he used to, instead, he left the room, burying his fury.

He glared outside through one of the round windows in the hallway, overlooking the ruins of Piraeus, where Gray was.

"I get it now," he whispered low

Another thirty minutes passed since Icarus had left the Radiographic room. The Mingan glimpsed Orange walking back, so he barged through the wall first, hoping the doctor may capture the mouthed interns on the act, however, they were quietly focused on Uniss's results. Icarus couldn't hide his slight disappointment, not knowing that would change moments after when Orange enters.

CHAPTER FIVE

"You two - - out, get your things, you're fired," Orange expelled them both with **a** bitter ton**e** then took his seat without announcing the reasons.

Shocked, they t**h**o**ug**ht of protesting, but Orange's glares denied them that right, so they walked out silently. Meanwhile, Icarus painted a malevo**l**en**t**, satis**fie**d smile. He didn't care for the reasons, as long as they got what they **d**e**s**erve, in his opinion.

Doctor Orange called for the nurses to help Uniss out, for the examination was over. T**han**kfully, he found nothing other than her broken arm. All she needed was **a** splint and rest. Adding to that, Orange made sure she had all the medications she needed before leaving the clinic, so she doesn't bother going to a pharmacy.

"Miss Sonda, I spoke to your grandfather, and - - he's really worr - -"

Uniss's grateful face shifted instantly after the mentioning of her grandfather. She raised a finger in her doctor's face, preventing him from saying any other word. She frowned, then growled in a commanding tone:

"I told you - - to **never** talk about him"

Doctor Orange complied obediently, nodding his head once as an apology. After making sure she wasn't upset with him, he insisted on driving her home, and Uniss accepted.

After a slow ride, Uniss stepped out of the car then towards her house after a grateful t**ha**n**k** you and a good day wish. Doctor Orange waited for her to get inside before departing, and while leaving, he drove by the fruit shop. Orange exchanged fixed stares with the old owner, then nodded to one another.

After stepping inside, Uniss headed directly to the kitchen to eat something as instructed by her doctor.

"Rings!"

Her Smartphone rang. She placed it on the counter next to the apple she intended to eat, and when she looked at the number, she sighed audibly.

"Hey Sophie," she answered in an adenoidal voice, trying to sound casual,

"I really can't talk right now"

"Ah okay! Sorry, we'll talk later then," replied Sophie before hanging up.

Uniss looked at her phone, surprised and disappointed at how fast her friend ended the call,

"You didn't even ask why - - you didn't ask if I'm okay," Uniss mused low, tightening her grip on the phone until the screen cracked. She threw it recklessly on the kitchen counter before walking to the living room, leaving the apple untou**ch**ed

Uniss couldn't feel **anything** physically, but emotionally - - that was a different st**or**y. She felt a sharp pain in her heart, devastated. Adding to that, no one was there to help. She was all alone, just herself and the soft cushion she placed on the sofa as decoration, the only thing familiar with her tears.

"I really wish I could help," **a** brooding Icarus said, lowering his face closer to her sobbing one.

"It really pains me to see you like this. I know loneliness, but know - -that this will make you strong, invincible even. Trust me on that," filled with cingulomania, he said softly, then kindly **kiss**ed her untouchable forehead.

"Sneeze!"

Icarus sat by her side, humming a s**of**t tune until she fell asleep.

The night was already upon him. He bid Uniss farewell before he flew back to the ruins of Piraeus.

The winged man landed quietly behind Gray, who was sitting the same way he left him. Enjoying the sound of tranquillity meddled with the crashing **su**rf of the waves pounding the cliff.

"That was a low move?" said Icarus calmly, sitting on the ground next to Gray, then added with a smirk:

"A break, huh!"

"We told you to do as you please, didn't we? Everything you did was of your own choice - - not ours," Gray replied with a faint smile, stretching his arms up.

"True. So - - emotional sensation, and now - - physical sensation," Icarus said low, gazing at the bright stars and moon. He then tapped Gray's knee gently with a smile,

"Lesson received, and thank you for allowing me to see her face again"

Gray painted a sort of surprised expression for a second, for he didn't expect that mature reaction from Icarus, but then smiled, satisfied.

"You know, this place is special for us as well. This exact spot," he chatted, then tapped Icarus's hand while standing up.

He walked to the edge of the cliff, then took a deep breath that puffed his chest. Gray tapped his foot twice as if he were marking the place.

"Yes, this here - - is where we met your mother for the first time," Gray divulged a surprising confession at his apprentice. Icarus's eyelids rose spontaneously. Gray knew **I**carus's mother!? The M**in**gan couldn't comment nor ask, not because he had none, rather there were too many, how, when and many other quizzical thoughts fell upon the **I**carus's head. Also, he couldn't tell if that was the truth or one of Gray's lies.

Gray knew his apprentice may suspect the credibility of his words. Still, he told him of that day anyway.

"**Sh**e was just a child," Gray smiled

"A child finding a strange man like us, wearing **this** scary mask__" he used a sharp claw to tap his mask then continued, looking heavenwards,

"__ and do you know what was her reaction - - her first words?"

Icarus stood up slowly, nodding his head yes while imagining a little girl standing on Gray's **side**.

"She said, '*are you okay? You look sad*!' can you imagine that," Gray said **wi**th a chuckle then continued:

"No screaming or a hint of fear, only a pure, concerned question. Somehow, those words bewitched a secretive man like us to speak his truth. Now you know why you're such a rantipole"

Gray beckoned Icarus to approach him, and as Icarus walked towards him, he preceded with telling his story:

"We told her we were indeed sad because we lost someone"

The man in black turned around toward Icarus, who stood by his side. He gently grabbed his apprentice's hands and placed them on his shoulders, and his, on Icarus's shoulders. Meanwhile, a ghostly version of Gray faced the little girl, like a flashback created from Gray's memory.

The real Gray spoke calmly, while the ghosts from his past mimicked what he told:

"And then she said, '*I can't help bring back the lost ones, but maybe I can help with the* ***pain*** *you* ***feel*** *inside your heart.*' She asked us to lean and stand on our knees then grabbed us just as we're grabbing you now, and started dancing with us while humming"

Gray soothingly jiggled Icarus left and righ**t** while humm**i**ng a soft and calm tune. The Mingan's emerald eyes glinted aqua in reaction to the moonlight and the tears locked inside. Those words were a doubt breaker for him. Also, the tune Gray hummed. Icarus knew Gray was telling the truth, remembering how his mother used to cheer him up with a dance, and with that same humming

_ (11-1) * (28-6) * (8-10) * (28-4) * (1-7) (12-4) * (1-4) * (14-1) (7-1) * (3-7)

whenever he's injured, beaten by the neighbours' kids or missing his father, a warm dance **with** his mother never failed to draw a smile on his face.

Tears ran down Icarus's smi**lin**g chee**k**s, tears he held for so long, for so many things piled inside. It was the first time that Gray saw his honest tears, making him **the** only one beside Icarus's mother.

Gray rested Icarus's forehead on his s**h**o**u**lder while patting the back of his he**a**d.

"She was one of the reasons we chose you. We knew that a pure heart like hers **can** only bear another like it," Gray confessed, then continued humming, and he kept doing so until Icarus fell asleep while standing up; the **two** then teleported back to the library,

"Swish!"

Twelve days after. While Uniss was getting ready to get out, the doorbell rang. She looked at the door, then her hand wa**tch**, curving a confused face as if she were waiting for someone, but they were too early.

"Coming," she yelled low while rushing her steps to open the door.

A gentleman holding a briefcase raised his hand as a greeting while painting a dull smile.

"Miss Uniss Sonda?" he asked politely

"Yes!" she replied with a hesitant tone

"Great. My name is Matthew Jones," he introduced himself, throwing his hand to shake hers, but noticed her broken right. Uniss shook his hand with the healthy one, adding a smile to spare him the embarrassment.

"I'm your grandfather's lawyer"

Her smile washed off, turning to a frosty glare instead. Matthew frowned, confused by her sudden change of manner but maintained a professional fake smile, adding to it a look as if he were waiting for an invitation inside.

Uniss sized him up first, seeing that he was indeed sent by her grandfather. All from his American accent, likewise, the golden 'S' pinned on his cravat. She painted an obviously fake smile back, thus invited him in:

"Come in, from here"

She walked him to the living room then allowed him a seat on the sofa with a hand gesture.

Uniss sat down on a three-legged stool on the side, sensing that something was off this time. Her grandfather used to send her money, sometimes gifts or people to check on her, but a lawyer, that was a first. However, deep inside, she had an idea of the reason behind this visit. Her main thought was that it had someth**ing** to do with her turning eighteen soon.

Mathew **for**ced a cough out, clearing his throat whilst adjusting his already adjusted **t**ie. Uniss noticed he was struggling on how to spill the reason that brought him there. His face exposed him. Now, she knows she was mistaken. She nodded her head faintly, rushing the words out of his mouth; also hinting that she was ready.

"I hate to be the bearer of bad news, but your grandfather - - passed away five days ago. **I** **am** very sorry for your loss," Mathew delivered the news Uniss suspected then remained silent, giving her the ti**me** to process. He joined his legs together, placing his briefcase on his lap.

Uniss closed her eyes for a moment. She **too**k a deep breath then looked at him fixed.

"Don't worry **much**," she replied, swallowing her own saliva.

"The only relationship we had is that I know he exists - - existed. Never met the guy, never wanted to," an impassive Uniss replied apathetically.

Matthew was slightly stunned by her quiet reaction, but continued with his t**ask** professionally.

"Very w**ell**," he said slowly. He opened his briefcase, and out of it he pulled a contract, then a vintage envelope and a small black box.

"Lor - - Mr. Icarus Sonda left you his house in Prague. All the paperwork is already taken care of; you just need to sign here. He also left you this letter and - - the box. Before you ask, no, I have no idea about their content"

Mathew placed the envelope and box on the small table between them, then the contract, placing his finger on where Uniss should sign,

"Please sign here"

Uniss grabbed the pen off his hand and signed with no hint of hesitation or excitement. She then grabbed the envelope, curiously, but because she had only one functional hand, Uniss tried to use her mouth to open it, and before she did, Mathew tossed a hasty hand to prevent that, rudely snatching the envelope off her hand while maintaining a polite smile, as if it were a divine epistle and not a goodbye letter from a grandfather to his grandchild.

"Here, let me," said Matthew, opening the letter for her then hand it over to her hanged hand

Uniss overlooked his weird behaviour and started reading the letter silently:

'My dear Uniss,

Allow this foolish grandfather of yours to apologize for not being present in your life. However, soon you will know of my reasons, including the one you hated me for. All you need to know is inside the box.

Love, Papa

Ps : trust the Gray, but not Gray'

Baffled, s**h**e folded the le**t**ter then grabbed the black box, l**oo**king **for** a padlo**c**k or a space to open it, b**u**t there was none, and while examining all six surfaces, she gli**m**psed a slightly bright engraved wing appearing on its base.

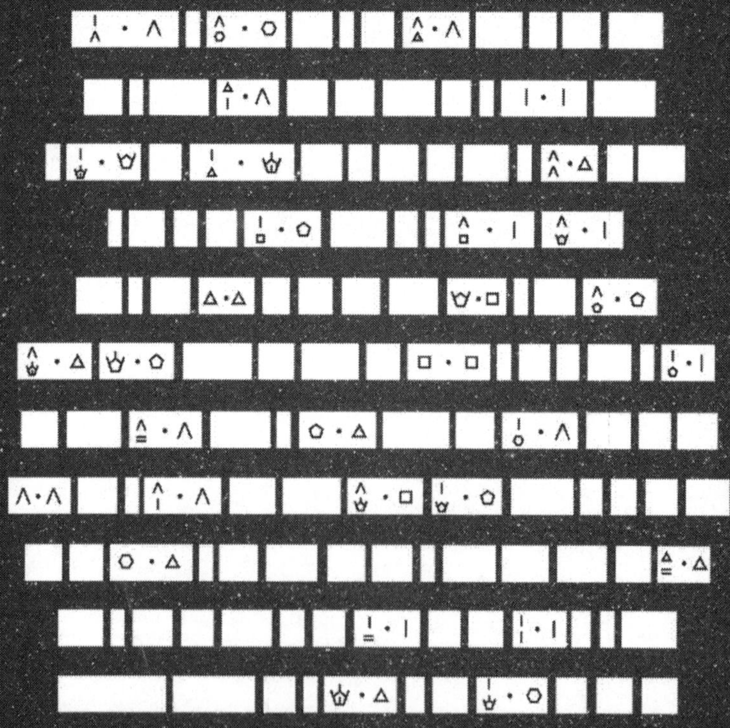

CHAPTER SIX
THE CURSE OF ATLAS

A month aft**er** Icarus's last trip, the common room was noisel**es**s. All you could hear was a scribble of a quill, meddled with Gray's sighs and hums.

The Man in black was lazily sitting behi**nd** his desk, **a**r**m**s crossed and eyes closed, while the quill in front of him wrote on its own, diving its tip into the inkpot after every few **wo**rds written.

"No - - no scratch that, it sounds - - boring," said Gray, tapping his claw on the desk, and the quill did as ordered.

Kara dashed out of the second section, chasing after Vi. The flying duster kept teasing Kara with fast tickles and spanks on her head and behind. That childish chase drove them closer to Gray's desk. He tried to ignore them and focus on whatever he was writing on that ancient scroll of his, but that didn't last.

V**i** flew behind Gray to use him as cover, while he waved a hand at her like a disturbing fly just to notice the huntress leaping to the desk carelessly. Kara hit the ink with her tail, spilling **some** on Gray's papers and books.

"Ah! Shit!" he yelped loudly, quickly adjusting the inkpot before it emptied its content on the entire desk.

Kara spooked! She looked at Gray, vexed and upset, and then down at the scroll he was writing on.

With a face full of remorse, Gray carefully pulled the scroll away from the ink, hoping that he could save the none-speckled half, and when he did, he smiled faintly, but Kara grabbed it off his hand and used her tail to wipe the scroll clean, meaning well, instead, she ended up staining it completely in black.

A devastated Gray freed a long gasp, twitching his hands towards Kara as if he were intending to strangle her. Not that she cared. She just patted his stiff shoulder then proceeded with the pursuit.

Icarus, who had just finished his shower, heard Gray's first screech. Curious, he walked out of his room with his hair wet and a towel on top, to see Kara climbing the bookshelf on his side then pouncing at Vi. Kara's leap was a certain success, her **tim**ing was perfect, and there was no doubt that she was going to catch her prey. But, a very upset Gray used his smoke to coil her in mid-air, a span away from **the** cunning duster.

"Hey, leave the poor thing alone," said a repelling I**c**ar**u**s, sauntering towards Kara. He shook the smoke off a**nd** grabbed her like an infant, patting her h**e**a**d** while she was throwing her hand up towards Vi.

The Mingan didn't like how the duster was laughing and teasing his little friend, so he snatched Vi with a quick move and gave him to Kara.

"Here you go little one. Have it your way," said a p**la**yful Mingan. He placed her on the floor, so she could enjoy her sweet time, torturing Vi by removing some **of** her feathers and slamming her on the floor mercilessly. After taking a decent number of blows, Vi tried to crawl to Ica**r**u**s**, begging for help, but he smirked and walked away towards Gray.

With both hands clutched into fists, resting on the desk, Gray fixed his eyes down at his ruined scroll while thinking if he could at least save some clean pieces of it. The Mingan interrupted his thoughts with a finger tap on the scroll.

"I sense so much hostility even through that veiling mask of yours, and all that for a piece of paper," said Icarus with a cold **man**ner, placing the books away from the spilled Ink.

Gray smacked Icarus's hand away, acting unnecessarily rude to someone who simply tried to help.

"**This** '*piece of paper*' is made of Saint Nicholas's bones. A very limited amount we use specifically to script our poems," an irascible Gray yapped. At the same time, he used his grimy fog to transfer all the clean things from the desk to the table. Icarus noticed he was going to smash the pizza box, so he rushed his feet and pulled it away. He placed the box on the couch while commenting with a teasing tone:

"Poems! And I thought poetry is for one with a passion, or is it just an amphigory?"

In the middle of his discreet chuckles, Icarus noticed he missed more important information in Gray's words. He shrank his eyes, raising a brow whilst looking at Gray with his head tilted to the side.

"Wait! You used a person's bones to make papers," Icarus bleated with a down smile.

"Not any person__ Lee, come clean this mess __Saint Nicholas's bones," Gray replied casually whilst calling for the broom concurrently. He then gave a brief **d**esc**ri**ption while **be**ckon**ing** the running broom to the desk.

"Fat, a long white beard, wears red all the time"

Icarus's eyes enlarged while listening to this Nicholas's description. He then dropped a jaw and perplexed with a whisper-shout:

"Santa Clause?"

Gray turned round to Icarus with his two middle fingers raised, then bantered with a wicked gr**in** followed by a weird sound effect with his mouth:

"More like '*dead by these claws.*' Shink Shink!"

After imitating knife slashes with his claws, he exchanged silent stares with a disgusted **I**carus for a moment, thus washed off the evil grin.

"Bad joke! Noted"

"So - - you killed a good man who used **to** give poor kids toys! You're sick," a disenchanted Icarus revolted. He then pushed Lee away from the desk, pre**ven**ting him from cleaning:

"Don't help **this** psycho. Let him clean his own mess"

Lee obeyed immediately, not because he considered Icarus as his master; rather, he was too lazy to clean the mess, especially one he didn't make. Unluckily for him, his real master wouldn't allow it. He beckoned him back with a glare while manifesting two very long arms of smoke. One smacked Lee while the other one elongated even more to grab a book from the bookshelf on his left. He rapidly sl**am**med the book on Icarus's chest.

"Read this - - then tell us if you still think of him as a '*good man*,'" Gray said with a scornful tone while smacking Lee again for disobeying.

"Screech!"

After putting Lee in a painful snag with his master, Icarus opened the book offered to him on an advanced page, aiming to get a flash glance before he starts reading it.

When mumbling a few lines, Icarus's face turned from curious to shaky.

"Wait! How in Zeus's bolt - - did this man become an icon for children? And check this! '*He wears red to cache the blood of his slaughtered victims!*' Seriously!?" a stunned Mingan rasped, closing the book with a slam.

"The kids getting gifts was probably our fault__" claimed Gray while standing tall before Lee like a warden as he spoke,

_ (23-1) * (12-2) * (3-4) * (3-2) (16-1) * (9-4) (14-9) * (17-3)

"__That criminal left a lot of orphans behind, so after biding him **a** painful **by**e-bye, we had our servant send gifts to the victims' families. We believe you know what the servant looked like"

"Fat, red cheeks, white beard and hair," said Icarus in low voice while Gray nodded yes.

On one hand, **Ic**arus felt disappointed and ashamed with his behaviour towards Gray. And on the other, peeved and upset about how humans twist the truth.

Gray, who was scolding Lee, gave Icarus a taste as well, castigating him along with the slothful broom:

"Next time - - don't be a blunt fool who believes everything he sees on TV. Now, put the book back. We will start cultivation when we're done with this wretched twig"

Aggrieved, the poor Lee hopped on the **de**sk, looking mournfully down. He used his straws to suck the ink off the desk until its last drop, leaving no stains behind. Gray gave him an i**m**pr**ess**ed look, thus tapped on the splashed scrolls.

"Now, can you do the same with these?" he asked with a hopeful grin, showing his oddly intimidating fangs. To Lee, it seemed more like, 'D*o it or we will turn you into a toothpick*'

Lee used his thin wooden forefinger to scratch his planking palm in circles, showing a lack of confidence, for he couldn't give a promise he couldn't keep. Hence, he stretched his **hand** wide open then slowly wiggled it to the sides as a '*maybe.*'

The scrolls were quite valuable to take '*a maybe*' for an answer, so Gray misread Lee's hand sign intentionally.

"Yes, it is," he grinned simply, thus headed to Icarus, who already took a cultivating posture, sitting on a lime round carpet located amid the com**mon** room, one the Mingan made it his cultivation spot during the past ten days.

Legs crossed, right hand on his chest and the left one on his head, while his eyes were closed relaxingly. His breaths were peacefully soft like a calm breeze, but there was no visible motion from his mouth or nose, as if his entire carcass was breathing.

Gray smacked the back of his head as he walked past him, breaking Icarus's focus. He stood tall, facing the Mingan with his arms crossed.

"Not yet, not befo**re** you tell us of what is disturbing your concentration, or else - - we will again hit a dead end," he directed im**pa**tiently, tapping one foot whilst glancing at the silent and reluctant ap**pre**ntice.

"**For** one with your talent, it should've only taken two days, max. Ten days is too much, so tell us what is holding you back, **everything**," Gray insisted with a serious tone while throwing faint kicks at Icarus's knees.

Icarus slapped his master's foot away and stood up, avoiding eye contact. He argued Gray's claim in a sulking tone as he walked to **the** couch:

"You have **b**een asking the same - - damn - - question over and ove**r**. **I** know it, you know it - - so will you just let it go?"

Icarus thought of sitting d**own** but stood **s**traight half**w**ay just to avo**i**d facing Gray.

"What the he**ll** is '*it*'? This is not a f**king therapy session__" Gray grunted acerbically, thus looked at Ka**r**a's eyes w**i**den in reaction to him cursing,

"__Freaking, we mean freaking therapy. **S**orry, lov**e**," Gray corrected his bad manners then sighed audibly.

"Look, we can't infiltrate your mind every time we sense a wall blocking you from progress. It would be better if you were to take that step instead, recognizing your weakness is power," he persuaded with a fixed tone while approaching Icarus. He slowly placed a hand on his apprentice's shoulder and added a soft squeeze.

"You tell us the problem, we help you solve it__" he said with discontinuous nodding, thus paused, looking for the right word to say,

"__Teamwork"

Icarus facepalmed, suffering a lack for words to counter Gray's brief speech, there was no other way but to surrender to his will. He snapped all ten fingers and walked back to the lime carpet, while Gray released Lee temporarily of his duties to give Icarus the needed privacy to speak his mind; but why just Lee? Why not Kara and Vi who were playing in the corner?

Gray sat on the couch while Icarus sat on the carpet with one leg crossed and the other one bent, knee up.

"Just you - - and us," said Gray

One of Icarus's eyes lustred in reaction to the moon lantern floating above him; his brows knitted while his eyes were fixed on Gray. With belligerent stares, the Mingan looked like one getting ready **to** fight, and not one about to speak his heart.

"**D**o you know - - of the Arising?" he asked, resting the face of his elbow on his knee whilst placing the back of his hand against his mo**u**th to hide his tightly squeezed lips that exposed his anger.

"At the age of five, the Mingan emerges, and wh**en** he does, he attracts the nearest magical beast," Gray answered casually.

Icarus saw wings of blue flames before him when he blinked.

"A Glaucous eagle - - I mean in my case, it was a Glaucous eagle," Icarus stated, then chuckled sadly, clutching his hand while turning his vision down to Gray's feet,

"**Just**! What a stroke of luck, huh! One of the rarest and fiercest beasts - - ha**p**pened to be flying by my house on the day I arose"

The Mingan lifted his brows and smirked as he crinkled the corners of his eyes, a weak attempt to hide his frustration. The words were struggling to get out, but it was needless for him to continue. Gray already placed the pieces together, or maybe he already knew.

"Your mother," a pensive Gray concluded **with** a low voice, hinting that the Glaucous eagle was what killed his mother that day, and Icarus nodded yes slowly. He then forced a grin, looking at Gray with welled eyes.

"And the sick part that really ruined me was after he killed her, he kept rubbing his beak on me kindly like a pet, staining my face and clothes with her blood, her warm blood"

Icarus crinkled his cheek while narrowing his eyes, painting a confused expression, for till that day, he was still clueless as to why the beast did what he did.

Gray noticed the hint of bewilderness on his apprentice's face.

"Do you - - wish to know why he did so?" he asked carefully.

"It," replied Icarus

The Mingan shook his head no and said with a clear tone, measuring his words:

"It - - is a monster, and - -It - - does what monsters do, kill. Plus, I know enough, everywhere I go - - death and pain follows"

Gray freed a long and loud sigh. He crossed all his fingers together, thus threw his back on the couch while glancing at the ceiling.

(12-1) * (1-9) * (6-10) (3-1) * (4-12) (13-1) * (18-7)

"Tik - - tok, tik tok," he started imitating a timer with his mouth. Icarus looked at him, confused, as he i**n**crease**d** the ticking ratio.

"Boom!"

He finished it with **a** loud blow while looking at Icarus with his eyes glowing. The vibes he freed were completely different, shifted from remorse to anger and hostility.

"We have a question," **sa**id Gray in a serious tone, as if he were suspecting something.

"Do you still hear it - - That whore's voice?" he asked with a hiss

I**ca**ru**s** stood up heatedly, thinking that Gray badmouthed his mother.

However, Gray stood up calmly, clearing the misunderstanding as he repeated his question more specifically.

"Answer, do you still hear that monkey whore - - Apollo?"

Without warning, he arrowed fast towards **the** confuse**d** Ming**a**n as if his **r**elaxed feet floated an inch above the floor! He used his left to grab Icarus's nape aggressively, pulling his retreating head closer; then quic**k**ly used his thumb t**o** press the Mi**n**gan's for**e**head.

"Hey!" Icaru**s** protested, trying to push Gray's hand a**w**ay but fa**il**ed. His mentor's strength was immeasurab**l**y superior to his, or any **of** the other four kinds that have a human form. Icarus couldn't put an understanding to Gray's nature.

'*He can't be a vampire, his skin is not cold. Also, vampires can't eat normal food, but Gray does. He can't be a werewolf, because werewolves are anti-magic, immune like Mingans but can't use it too, yet Gray uses magic. And he can't be a Mingan, because Mingans can sense one another. Unless, the mask wasn't hiding his aura and presence alone, but his shape as well'*

"What are you?" a **j**umbled Icarus inquired with a snarl while clutching Gray's fixed arm with b**o**th hands. He even threw several punches, but **i**t was like hitti**n**g a mo**t**ion**le**ss wall.

Gray gave Icarus a petrifying glare that weakened his arms down.

"Quiet," fixed, he hissed with a penetrating voice, pressing Icarus's forehead even harder,

"Whoosh!"

CHAPTER SIX

Bright runes flew out of his **for**ehead to form a collar of luminous letters around his head! The puzzled Mingan fixed his trembling head, agape, following the runes with his eyes as they orbited around in a wavy circle.

"The spell **we** placed is still there, but some**thing** isn't right. Where?" wary, Gra**y** murmured, scrolling through th**e** **c**rown of runes right and left then stopped, pai**nt**ing a winning grin,

"There you are, you cheap harlot"

Gray elongated two nails into thin claws and used them to **s**n**a**tch a small quivering ring among the runes. He swayed his hand then clutched it, forcing the collar back inside Icarus's head while walking towards his desk with his eyes fixed on the ring.

"What is wrong with you?" Perplexed, Icarus complained as he rubbed his forehead gently, but a focused Gray ig**no**red him.

"Kara!" he called loudly, looking at the fourth section.

"Kara!" he called again, but louder.

Kara trotted out of the second section, clutching to Vi as she headed to Gray.

"Have a taste," he said, propelling the gleaming ring her way.

Without delay, Kara jumped and swallowed it. She stood still with her eyes large, freeing Vi who crawled away slowly.

Kara's hide buffed up and shined a bright blue light as if she were electrified.

Icarus lifted a torn Vi whilst staring at Kara, trying to comprehend what was going on.

A few seconds later, Kara turned back to her normal state then started chattering with Gray, giving him her analyses about the ring she swallowed.

"Very well - - you, stay here. We know what to do," Gray ordered, rushing his steps to the first section

Kara ran back to Icarus, throwing her hands in the air, indicating for him to give her Vi back, but Vi quivered, embracing Icarus to not do **so**. Icarus sighed.

"I think she has had enough, little one," he said with an abstaining smile, then tossed Vi to fly away

"Tell me, little one," Icarus said, whilst lifting Kara. He patted her head while she was playing with the neck of his shirt.

"Are you really a Kirada? As if your master isn't enough of mystery. Now you! Seriously, what are you both?" he added low, sensing her hide whilst looking at her big gleamed eyes.

_ (21-1) * (8-12) (5-1) * (28-12) * (1-7) * (13-7) (4-9) * (4-3) (6-1)

"Put her down - - now," said Gray aggressively, sauntering with a skobeloff book in h**an**d. He waited for Icarus to put Kara down, thus sighed dis**c**ree**tly**.

"**Per**haps, you're wondering - - why we're acting this way! We just found out she's inside," Gray said with a fixed tone, beckoning Kara to stand behind him **as** if Icarus were a threat. He then conti**nu**ed in a monotonous tone:

"You don't know what can happen, or who may get hurt"

Gray gave Kara a head scratch, reminding Icarus that she could be his first victim if he went berserk.

The Mingan took a step back, he was instantly convinced. The thought of him hurting Kara shook him. Not only that, he **fe**lt shame for selfishly thinking about his state, and secretly investigating the ones that took him in. He remembered the fact that he was the dangerous entity inside that library.

Icarus continued taking slow steps back away from Kara and Gray until he bumped into the couch behind him. He looked back thence down to glimpse stains of blood covering his shirt for a s**pl**it second. He looked up at Gray, holding Kara in his arms, then an image of him holding her dead while covered in blood flashed before his eyes. The Mingan knew he wasn't in his right mind; however, he also knew that these flashes weren't simply hallucinations but possibilities.

"Apologies - - I overlooked the fact that it wasn't me in harm's way," crestfallen, he muttered, sitting down and resting his arms on his knees.

"You have every right to fear for your life - - and friends"

Something in Icarus's words triggered Gray. He dropped Kara, who grunted at him and rapidly ran away.

"Wait! What did you say? '*Fear for your life!*' Us - - afraid?" a jaw slightly dropped, Gray said with a low and breathy voice.

He took a deep breath while crossing eight fingers together to form a muzzle, one he used to block his mouth while tilting his head back.

"Umm!" He released a loud inner growl.

Gray dropped his hands down then glowered at Icarus furiously, whilst reeking of killing intent. Icarus gasted as he sensed a sudden rage filling the entire room.

A heated Gray ambled towards him with heavy steps. He raged with a penetrating voice while taking a breath after every word spoken:

CHAPTER SIX

“Us, scared of a pitiful Olympian!?”

He raised his **ha**nd palm-up to the level of his waist while a dense fume spilled from between his fingers **like** liquid.

“We - - can have her head__“ Gray threatened as he crea**ted** a head figure of smoke above his hand,

“__in the blink of an eye,” Gray stated surly

Meanwhile, the Mingan **was** being suffocated **by** the intense vibe Gray released. Even the lanterns faded as if their source of **li**ght was being sucked by his ruthless presence, leaving the room almost dark with a sourceless cold breeze, turning the Mingan’s pants into puffs of vapour.

Gray didn’t bother going around the table. Instead, he walked through, transforming it **and** everything above into a fading mist. Then he shrieked, emphasizing every word:

“No one scares ######”

Icarus heard a disturbing screech instead of the last word Gray said.

He leaned closer to Icarus, who couldn’t stop his body from shivering, thus hissed in Icarus’s ear with a lower voice and a more tranquil tone:

“Consider yourself lucky - - for being chosen by us”

The man in black gently threaded his cold hand through Icarus’s hair, turning a **fe**w tufts white. It wasn’t magic, but rather the Mingan’s body reacting to Gray’s pungent energy.

The Mingan locked his eyes on Gray’s sadistic grin. That wasn’t the Gray he knew. Not the Gray who tried to look evil but always did things for his best interest, the Gray that he had started to grow a bond with.

“Who are you?” Bug-eyed, Icarus stuttered without moving a muscle, thus shuddered, squeezing his eyes shut:

“What are you?”

Gray poked Icarus’s neck with his claw, causing drops of blood to run down his chest and stain his shirt.

“Exactly what that scroll you signed says,” calmly, he reminded Icarus of the contract,

“We are your master, and you - - our apprentice”

“ROAR!”

A loud beastly shriek pierced its way to the common room, shaking Gray’s hand off Icarus. He turned round the corridor with a cold stare, then stood up straight, switching his vision back to the Mingan, looking down on him with a boastful stare.

“Don’t you ever - - look down on us,” said a fixed Gray, then promised with a silvery tone:

“So - - if you do as we say, you too - - will have the power to crush - - these fake deities you call gods”

Gray took a small step back while lowering his hostile vibe to a minimum, gi**ving** Icarus a chance to breathe normally. The moon lanterns **b**eg**an** to brighten back. He then offered Icarus a hand to shake,

“Even the one standing before you”

Icarus tightened his muscles to stop the quivering, and when he did, he took his time to stand up. The Mingan sighed and puffed his chest, giving Gray a determi**ned** stare.

“Understood,” he answered simply

Icarus shook Gray’s hand, but his vex of his master’s hector behaviour **was** apparent. Gray sighed audibly, curving a side smile of regret.

“We apologize for that tantrum. We tend to overreact when Kara is in harm’s way,” He apologized, using a dishonest excuse.

He freed Icarus’s hand, thus walked back to his desk. He leaned on its edge and saw the mess he left behind? The table turned into a thin mattress of ashes. Half of his books and papers too, while the other half scattered on the floor.

“And now, down to business. We know how she was able to infiltrate your mind,” a casual Gray claimed, ree**li**ng his forefinger, and the table he obliterated was back to its original state.

Icarus sat back on the couch to rest his weak legs.

“Which is?” bitter, he asked low, fixing his eyes on the floor between his feet

“You, condemning yourself,” answered Gray, using his hands as a cushion between his body and the desk’s hard edge whilst slowly drumming his claws against the hardwood. He looked at Icarus’s blunt face for a few seconds, then forced a grin and added with a disappointed tone:

“We - - thought Flaco was enough, apparently not; however__” he straightened his stand and brushed his palms together before grabbing the book **from** the desk,

CHAPTER SIX

"__we now know the right person for this," he said confidently, opening the book. He sauntered towards a blunt Icarus whilst flipping through the pages.

"You wasted enough time - - as **always**, so we will skip this - - and this, this one too. Okay here is good," Gray spoke low then looked up at Icarus with a wide smile, turning the book's face towards the Mingan who immediately squeezed his eyes shut, waiting to **be** teleported - - but not**hin**g happene**d**! Gray looked down at the book, confused. He slammed it shut and open twice and got sucked unintentionally, alongside Icarus,

"Swish!"

When the two left; metallic steps walked steadily out of the second section, heading to Gray's room.

2019 – Tunisia, the sounds of the densely packed merchants and buyers filled a local bazaar like a chaotic Arabian song. The weather was slightly sultry, but thanks to the ceiling of colourful sheets shading the street, the souk had a slightly cold breeze, one that carried the salty smells of the Mediterranean. The customers' route was made of large polished plates of cement, confined on both sides with ceramic floors of different designs, and on the porch of every shop, took place a small table, attracting the buyers with their unique and tempting goods.

Gray walked out of a vintage bookstore located at the end of the street; fashioned in a traditional clothing of the land, he looked **le**ft and right as the crowds passed through his ghostly body. He then glimpsed a big man selling embroidered men-dresses. Gray grinned, looking at him, thence the skobeloff book in his hand. He hurried his steps to that man, then stopped behind him, placing the book on the floor, specifically between the man's feet, muttering with his grin still intact:

"This is for **put**ting us below those mountain monkeys"

Gray opened the book, freeing Icarus out of it. He was tossed high then down to fall on his back while his sight was locked on what was underneath the big man's dress. From Icarus's reaction, it seemed that he wasn't wearing anything under it like he was supposed to.

"Barf! Shit - -" a jumbled-up Icarus grunted, jumping away from the man while blocking his mouth and nose with his hand. Gray laughed his tears out but stopped in an instant before he got caught by Icarus.

_ (3-6) * (6-5) (6-8) (6-9) * (3-6) * (26-4)

"We thought you were over this - - teleportation nausea!" He said bluntly, acting as if he didn't see what reall**y** happened. He then asked in a derisive tone, changing **the** subject:

"What **d**o you think?"

Gray showed off his new look with some man-model stands.

Icarus intended to answer with a dull '*fine*', but the glaucous tattoo on Gray's chest caught his attention. However, it wasn't complete. The slightly opened shirt revealed only a long canine-ear and one hollow round eye beneath it. Gray adjusted his open shirt to hide the tattoo after noticing Icarus scrutinizing it. Icarus had the face of a cat that was caught stealing. He **tr**ied to act casual.

"I just saw what's underneath that man's Thawb. Can you remove that from my memory, please?" he asked, leaning forward with both hands on his knees.

"Are you sure?" asked Gray with a doubtful tone

"Yes - - yes you have my blessings," a hasty Icarus answered, swallowing his **own** saliva

Gray clattered his teeth twice, waiting for Icarus to change his mind but he didn't, so he used his index to poke the Mingan's forehead.

"Very well," Gray deadpanned, then quickly pierced the Mingan's head with a claw, forcing him to cough a sparkling bubble in the size of his head, thus popped **moment**s after,

"All done"

The memory extraction dazed Icarus. He squeezed his eyes shut and shook his head sharply to sober up.

"What have you done?" Ambivalent, he said with an accusatory tone, smacking Gray's hand away.

Gray gave him a poker face for moments, thinking if he should slap the mucus out of his nose, but decided to leave him be and walk away.

"Nothing - - we have to go," he answered, shoving his hands in his puffed trousers' pockets.

Tilting his head right an**d** left, a confused Ic**a**rus looked at the big man on his left while rubbing his forehead, feeling something was missing. He then rushed his feet to catch up with Gray.

"Where to now?" he asked, looking back at the bazaar as they left it behind.

(4-2) (15-1) * (3-2) * (20-1) * (6-1) * (10-10) (2-8)

CHAPTER SIX

"S**tra**ight to the main character; as we said before, this will be quick," replied Gray, making a turn into **a** narrow alley with white high walls on the sides, marked by doors and windows of cyan. Some of the opposite houses had joint rooms on their second floor, serving as arcs, a beautiful construction made by an old tradition in Tunisia.

Gray smiled, looking at the hanged-rooms above his head as he wal**ke**d by.

"What you have now - - is what we call the Atlas curse," Gray **sta**ted, raising his right closer **to** the wall then jutted his claws.

He scratched the wall deep whilst walking; causing a black smoke to gush out of the fissures he left behind. The fume filled the surrounding space before ascending above Gray like a dark cloud.

With a finger snap from Gray, the body of smoke transformed into a human-sized shadow figure of a muscular man, a**nd** on his shoulders, a perfectly shaped orb, two times his size. Icarus recognized it easily. It was a figure of Atlas holding the globe.

"I see, so - - I am Atlas in this scenario," pensive, he concluded, looking at Atlas falling on a knee, then both, and finally, he got squashed by the globe.

Gray snapped his finger with a slight spark, and all that dense smoke was sucked back inside the fissures, and they joined back to its original smooth surface right after.

Back to the noisy streets and crowded sidewalks, Gray and Icarus stood facing a five-storey building across the street. The cracked walls and wiped-out paint indicate that the block was archaic; white satellites emerged out of most of the balconies, some rusted to a cider colour. On the bottom of the building, and specifically the right side of its metallic gate, there was a lousy black graffiti that says '*Girls suck, I love food.*'

Looking at the building from the bottom up, Gray yawned with the back of his left hand against his mouth.

"He's up there," he said drowsily, locking his eyes to the fifth storey.

Icarus narrowed his eyes to focus his vision, thus looked at Gray with a questioning face, waiting for a continuation.

"The incarnation of Atlas, and the key to lock the door that whore is using to get to you," fixed, Gray answered. He then walked across the road, careless of the mobilized vehicles passing by.

"Vrooms!"

Icarus observed how Gray walked with a fixed pace, yet he missed all the cars and motorcycles by inches. When he reach**ed** the other side, Icarus looked both ways, thi**n**king that he should be able to ghost through; how**ever**, he couldn't exclude the thought of Gray making them solid, for he knew it was in his cunning nature to do so just for a laugh, and the discreet grin he had while waiting for Icarus to cross over proved it.

The Mingan smirked **back** then took a high leap, crossing above all the cars, until he looked to his left and saw a large truck on his face. The Mingan used both arms to cover his head, bracing for impact, **but** his body ghosted through it instead.

Unharmed but embarrassed, **I**carus landed before Gray, who smirked provocatively, then walked inside the building. Icarus sighed audibly. He had nothing to say or complain about, so he followed in silence.

The two climbed up the old and crooked stairs to its end to face a wooden door, scratched and doodled with a pen from the bottom up, and on its top, a sign that said '*Chaker Younane'* written in Arabic.

Icarus approached the door, focusing on the words. He then used his two thumbs to cover some dots on the letters.

"Chaker Younane! Younane was one of the first Greek tribes. I see, so this is where Atlas's spirit ended up." Icarus speculated while trying to scratch the dots off. Gray curved a **down** smile, then gently smacked his apprentice's head.

"Step aside," disappointedly, he said, pushing Icarus away from the door.

"First, that was obviously a metaphor. We didn't mean he's Atlas incarnation as literally. Second, his last name is a mere coincidence. But it's really impressive that you can read Arabic without using the bracelet," Gray sagged his lower lip, giving Icarus a pat on the shoulder after smacking him seconds ago.

"We master all Semitic languages," a non-arrogant Icarus replied simply, then painted a slight frown of displease, commenting on the sign:

"But these dots and marks - - are confusing"

"Okay, show off, time to close the deal with your tramp stamp," Gray said, walking through the door with his head high, followed by Icarus, who still used his hand to check before ghosting through anything.

The apartment inside was surprisingly clean, given the state of the obsolete building. However, the walls had some significant cracks; most were hidden behind cheap paintings of fruits. As for the furniture, it was almost empty with the exception of a sofa on the right, likewise, a wooden armoire holding some books **and** files, and a simple **work**-desk facing the door.

The man who was sitting on the desk stood up aggressively and slamm**ed** both hands on the **hard** surface. He glared at Icarus, then snarled loudly.

Gray took a fighting posture, coiling his hands with black smoke.

"What!" an alarmed Icarus sputtered, taking a defensive stand like his mast**er** while unsheathing his wings.

"Is he a threat?" Belligerent, Icarus asked with a loud whisper, taking wary side steps to round the possible menace; a few steps after, he noticed that the man wasn't looking at him but rather at the exit door.

Icarus creased his forehead, puzzled, thus heard an explosive discreet chuckle. He looked at Gray, who acted as if he were checking the paintings on the wall, trying to cover his silent laughter, but his wiggling shoulders exposed him.

A scowling Icarus straightened his stand then walked closer to the stranger while keeping an annoyed glare on Gray, who kept a sly grin and sat on the squeaking sofa.

"That was funny. If you saw your face, you would've laughed too," he jested derisively, placing one leg above the other, thus shrugged.

"Relax, he can't see us," Gray added, putting his partner's mind at ease. However, Icarus remained uncertain. He cautiously waved his hand at the man's face, just to be sure.

"So this is Atl - - Chaker," Icarus stammered, walking around his desk then closer to Gray while keeping a side-eye on Chaker.

Chaker took his time leaning over the desk, looking down with his chin resting on his chest. He then glanced up to the ceiling while using both hands to press his hair back, releasing a long grieving sigh.

"What's with him?" asked Icarus

"Just give him time," Gray answered simply

Chaker sat dow**n** slowly, showing fatigue; not a physical one, but the one **tha**t **s**houts '*I can't* ***rest*** *because I'm holding the world over my shoulder.*'

"Why?" He said with an exhale, resting his chin on his fist whilst reflecting on what was haunting his thought.

"Should I do a Rokia?" Aggrieved, he huffed, rubbing his eyes with his left. **The**y were as red as an Albino-ferret's eyes.

Gray left his place and saun**ter**ed towards Chaker. He stood behind him, leaning over the back of his torn chair.

"In co**mp**a**ar**ison to your - - bad luck, as you would call it. We would call this man's life__" He massaged Chaker's tense shoulders,

"__a bad joke," a fixed Gray asserted, drumming his fingers up from Chakers's shoulders to his neck, then to his forehead, but Chaker showed no reaction.

"Why - - you may ask," Gray grinned, covering the unfortunate man's eyes with his hands.

"Every step this ambitious kid makes towards success fails bizarrely," Gray said with a hissing voice as if he were telling a scary tale.

Chaker's cell phone rang, interrupting Gray's words, but the masked man snapped his finger in a hurry, freezing time before Chaker shoves his hand inside his pocket.

"Not yet, we still need you," Gray said low, tapping Chaker's shoulder.

Icarus seemed bothered. Not with Gray freezing time or manipulating others, he got used to that. What really niggled him was what Gray said. He gave his mentor a slight headshake, curving his mouth to the side.

"Are you serious? Comparing him - - to me. I would say he's living the dream. A wealthy, privileged - - easy life," an uneasy Icarus argued, twisting Gray's words as he referred to how easy modern people have it.

"He - - knows nothing of real suffering," Icarus said in a disparaging tone

"A common mistake__" Gray interjected with a high-pitch then lowered his voice as he continued slowly,

"__many individuals fall into. To compare one's resources and way of living, and not one's feelings, the burdens one can bear in his current time"

Gray walked closer to the left window, blocking the little striped light that illuminated the apartment.

(3-1) (10-2) (8-6) * (2-14) (2-3) * (7-1) * (3-4)

"Humans - - in particular are an evolving kind. They do not see that they're living a better life than their ancestors, so the things you see as wealth or an easygoing life - - is meaningless to them. It's their zero point. You too have yours. Think of the humans before you, the ones that had no weapons to hunt, carriages to travel and so on. Do you think they have the right to deny your suffering for it?"

"**I** understand, but still, he looks like someone who's doing just fine for his time," an unconvinced Icarus interrupted

"Maybe," replied Gray, resting his palm on the window's glass.

"But **please** let us ask you this: would you rather be a thirsty man, lost in the **d**esert, while standing before a bottle of water that you can easily grab, or - - standing before an oasis that somehow you can **never** reach?" Gray quizzed, turning round Icarus with his two fists raised upfront, as if they were choice number one and choice number two. Icarus looked at both fists, answerless. He remained silent until Gray chose on his behalf. He opened his right hand.

"Choice number one, of course," he answered his own question, taking two steps closer to the motionless Chaker.

"The man you see before you__" said Gray, tapping a gentle palm twice on Chaker's head,

"__used to be a bright student; however, on his graduation test, he failed three times," Gray deadpanned, scratching his cheek,

"The first time, his answers were stolen and given to a rich kid. The second time, his answers were lost, and so they gave him random grades instead of admitting their mistake"

Fixed, Gray crossed his arms then continued **with** a slow tone:

"Third, his mother died - - a day before the test. He **was** devastated, therefore he abandoned the test - - and school"

Icarus was moved by the mentioning of Chaker's mother passing away.

Gray walked to the desk's front and used it as a seat. He sighed, then continued, for there was more to tell:

"Not so long after, our boy here found a job in a constructing company, just to get fired on his first day. The owner knew his uncle whom he owed a lot of money"

Gray **s**howed a slight of amusement on his face as he recited Chaker's **se**tba**c**ks, not being evil or out of hate, but rather the irony in the man's bad luck.

Gray drummed his fingers against his thigh, seeing a request for him to continue on Icarus's face, so he did with a continuous grin:

"Thanks to his fluent English, he was accepted as an interpreter for a foreign company. However, they were attacked by terrorists before launching their project. The incident forced them to relocate to another country, and guess what? With a policy of not accepting any Arab employees"

Gray widened his grin, using his thumb to point at Chaker on his back.

"And now, he switched to re**al** estate. A tough field yet gratitude to his slick mouth and contacts, he found a buyer for a nice expensive villa in just a week, and guess what? A day before, the buyer died," Gray grinned, as if he were speaking of a broken toy and not a living **being**.

"Oll wright stop - - Oll wright, I get it," an amazed Icarus surrendered revoltingly. He walked to the couch, thus admitted to stop Gray from continuing:

"I'm c**on**vince**d**, this man is a bad omen - - an incarnation of bad luck, not Atlas"

While talking, he gave the couch a sharp kick to see if it were solid, but his foot ghosted through. A selfish Gray move, making things solid only when it suits him.

"Ahem! There is no such thing as bad luck," Gray stated in a serious tone.

"There is only energy, of different quirks, sizes and vibes__"

Gray walked backwards around the desk while explaining,

"__Some are born with it, and some acquired it along the **way**"

Icarus walked slowly away from the couch and closer to Gray. On the first steps he took, he glimpsed the lime carpet on which he used to cultivate spread on Chakers's floor. He tilted his head to the side and sharpened his eyes, confused, seeing its fibres swaying up then toward him, as if it were calling on him.

Gray looked at him then the carpet, slowly placing a hand on Chaker's head.

"All creatures have two types of energy, positive - - and negative," he smirked and closed all his eyes, entering a concentration mindset,

CHAPTER SIX

"We think you know what type this one has, so prepare yourself for here it comes"

Icarus's in**st**inct triggered him of an upcoming danger. He plunged towards the carpet, with his eyes on Chaker, seeing his face and body melt slowly, then exploded in**to** gushing water. Dam-like, the rumbling water overwhelmed the corners in seconds; thus formed a liquid fist that punched the Mingan away right **be**fore landing on the carpet.

In less than a minute, **the** apartment was submerged. The Mingan realized this was no ordinary water. It was heavier than lead, also suffocating, not to mention the way it moved, as if the water had its own consciousness, one determined to squeeze the life out of him.

Icarus swam hardly and made his way to the carpet, listening to Gray's wobbling words, the words you hear underwater,

'*Just like we showed you*!'

That was the only clue given to Icarus, yet it was enough. Icarus sat on the carpet hardly, trying to take a cultivating posture whilst fighting the pressure. It took him a while, but he succeeded.

"Good boy!" Gray's wavy words were unclear, but enough to **be** understood,

"Now push your aura out"

Focused, Icarus tightened his muscles, and seconds after, the water started retreating off the Mingan's body. The gap enlarged slowly, as if there were an invisible magnetic power wrapping Icarus, one that kept pushing the water away until it created a sphere of air around him. Icarus smiled proudly, keeping his eyes shut.

"Not yet," said Gray, ruining his victorious moment.

He walked towards his apprentice freely, as if the surrounding water didn't exist. Icarus opened one eye halfway to see Gray's image approaching him, wiggling like a dancing cobra.

Gray shoved his head inside the breathable space Icarus created.

'*Not yet!*'

That was the only thought stuck in Icarus's mind, knowing his mentor's sadistic nature meant bad things were about to happen, and Gray's sly grin **af**fi**r****med** it.

"Do you still think this man's m**ise**rable life is so little to be compared to yours?" a smiley G**r**ay asked with a mocking tone, using his hand to sprinkle some of **the** water on Icarus's face. He then retreated slowly while talking with a deep voice:

"The real test starts now. Focus on your pleasant **me**mories. We wonder - - do you have some about us?"

His last words mingled with the sound of water, his snide laughter too.

Icarus noticed an abnormal motion on the surface of the surrounding water. A dozen liquid te**nt**acles emerged around the Mingan, bursting from the surface towards him like slothful large serpents, wrapped in long films holding images from Chaker's memory; one had young Chaker standing be**for**e his mother's lifeless cadaver, another was with him getting yelled at by his father, and many other bad me**mo**ries.

The celadon snakes mugged their fangs, then charged at Icarus. However, they all turned to ashes inches away from the Mingan. It was as if Icarus had an invisible barrier to protect him. Yet, that didn't mean he was safe, for whenever a head evaporated, another one sprouted from the side and rapidly dashed towards him. Little by little, some vipers reached Icarus's skin, whipping him from all directions, causing cuts and scars of light instead of blood, as if the snakes were damaging his spirit and not his flesh.

Suppressing his pain, Icarus snarled discretely, tightening his lips shut whilst trying to maintain his focus through the burning stings. The situation was getting worst with every second passing, and the number of attacks Icarus received kept increasing. Meanwhile, Gray continued on repeating himself:

"Stop avoiding her"

Icarus focused on several flashbacks to maintain his shield. He saw his trainer giving him his first sword for his first hunt, which was a fire goblin, then another flashback, where he was helping his father with one of his inventions. He even saw Kara playing with his hair while eating pizza. For one who lived his entire life fighting and hunting, it wasn't that easy to fish for a happy memory; one might say that he had none, but who was Gray referring to?

'*Stop avoiding her!*'

Every time Gray repeated these words, blue large wings intervened with his flashbacks.

CHAPTER SIX

Gray was fed up with his **a**ppre**nt**ice ignoring his advice, so he decided to speak with his disciple telepathically:

"She didn't live with you for one day. You need to look past that day. Remember your times together,"

Gray's words worked as a beckon inside Icarus's **h**ead. A bright l**ight** filled the Mingan's sight, **and** when that great glow faded tardily into a gleam, Icarus was ported to a more realistic memory.

| A kid on his knees was looking **a**t his mother's dead body while a large phoenix of glaucous and green stood in between. The beast flapped his wings smoothly, winding blue and white flames out of his luminous feathers, turning the Mingan's old house into an inferno.

Both versions of Icarus used their hands to block their eyes then started humming their mother's tune, but the eagle's shrieks were louder.

Some of the flames reached the younger version of Icarus, and with every touch, he lost a piece of his body.

"Fight back!" Gray shouted inside Icarus's head

Icarus lowered his hands and looked at his younger version getting burned. He spontaneously threw a hand upfront, shooting a body of black smoke, similar to Gray's ma**gi**c. The smoke coiled the room, vanquishing the Glaucous eagle along with his fire, and his mother's cadaver too, leaving the room clean and bright, where Icarus stood alone inside his child version.

While staring at his small hands, the door opened, and through it walked Icarus's mother with a warm smile on her face. Without saying a word, she rushed to him and embraced him. |

The barrier around Icarus became slightly visible. It looked **like** a thin glass of yellow spectra, shining brighter and wider, forcing the slimy serpents to retreat, and so did the grim expression on Icarus's face, swapped instead by a faint warm smile.

Gray looked at him with sorrow and remorse, followed by a guilty smile, but why?

All the serpents vaporized, and the space of air grew bigger and greater, pushing the water all the way to the corners of the apartment. Icarus's shield was as large as the loft they were in.

Gray approached Icarus with steady steps, applauding his apprentice's success proudly.

"Well done, this - - is more than we expected," Gray praised, looking up then sideways, observi**ng** the bubble of energy Icarus had created. He then snapped a finger and all the cornered water gathered back to the desk's chair, transforming **ba**ck into Chaker.

Icarus dispatched his shield, thus stood up, loo**king** at his torn body, full of cuts and sharp slashes. He rubbed his thumb against one of them, wondering if it were dangerous, just to see it heal instantly, and so did all the others all over his carcass.

Gray ambled towards **Ch**aker then tapped a claw on the desk, unfreezing time.

Chaker pulled his ringing cell phone out from his ch**est**-pocket.

"Ahleen - - yes this is Chaker Younane," he replied, nodding his head with every sentence spoken,

"Of course - - yes of course - - I will be there in one hour In-Sha-Allah - - yes - - yes, all the papers are legit - - ok good, we meet in one hour - - Salem"

Chaker ended the call while grabbing his clattering keychain. He locked all the drawers then left in a hurry.

Gray looked at him closing the apartment door behind him then turned to Icarus, standing bluntly with a '*what now?*' face

"After him idiot," said Gray

"We will be waiting downstairs," he grinned archly then swooped through the floor.

An annoyed Icarus sighed audibly, tapping a foot on the floor underneath. He moved to the spot where Gray ghosted through. It was solid too as was the roof. He circled the walls while bumping a soft fist with every step, checking if Gray left him a passage. He kept following the wall until he reached the door. Icarus threw a hand and saw it ghosting through the door. He facepalmed quietly then huffed out of his nose like an angry dragon.

Icarus ran through the door and down the stairs in a flash. He paused at the building's exit, searching for Gray and Chaker. He glimpsed Gray on his left, waving with his wiggling fingers like a teen girl.

Icarus sauntered towards his mentor, and on his way, he noticed Chaker standing at the e**mpty** bus stop across the street

The Mingan joined his master. Arms crossed and a tensed face. They stood there in silence for long, urging several thoughts inside Icarus's head. Some he wanted to share with Gray but couldn't. The mentor noticed his **di**sturb**e**d expression.

"What?" he said with a lazy tone

Icarus hesitated f**or** a few seconds then spoke his mind:

"**I** admit, what I had with her is much more powerful than that day. However, that day happened, **and** I was the reason, I accept it, but don't expect me to be fine with it__"

He rubbed his watery eyes then sighed,

"__I **will** keep the good - - and the bad"

"No, no__" Gray interjected with a controversial headshake,

"__don't accept it," he sighed audibly, disappointed with Icarus's conclusion.

He used a simple hand gesture to reduce the horns and engine noises then placed his hands behind his back. A small thread of black smoke spilled from his finger to the ground. The shapeless serpent of vapour sli**there**d away while Gray continued speaking in a clear and flat tone.

"Kid, did you choose to be born a Mingan? Did you know the Glaucous eagle was nearby?"

Icarus **tr**ied to argue but Gra**y** stopped him by rais**ing** his voice for a few words:

"Did you force your mother to stay home that day?"

Gray looked round Icarus with his eyes wide open, loathing for a simple honest answer,

"Did you ask her - - to stand between you - - and the beast?"

Icarus wanted to answer with an honest '*No*,' but lowered his head instead.

"It's okay. It will take time, but we will help you through it. We will always be there. You don't need to be alone anymore," Gray promised while keeping an eye on Chaker.

At the same time, the small nebula made its way up to a food table, dropping an olive from a small bowl. The olive rolled over, missing the feet of all the passersby before falling from the sidewalk's edge and close to the sewerage hole. A mouse peeked from the hole, hesitantly **get**ting its head out just to retreat several times. Smelling the olive; the rodent was hungry enough to leave his safe hideout for a sour meal. He dashed towards it, not knowing a cat was waiting for a chance to onslaught.

_ (6-4) * (5-1) * (9-2) * (30-6) * (14-8) * (4-3) * (1-12) * (18-2) (18-6) (18-10)

"Caterwaul!"

The skinny feline chased the mouse through the street then the crowded road, causing a boy on his bicycle to flip be**for**e falling on his back

"Crash!"

Rubbing h**is** injured knee, the blunt boy stood up to see a speeding car honking while heading his way. He was **st**upefied to dodge, so the driver made a sharp turn to **a**void running the boy over.

"Brakes!"

Icarus w**it**nes**se**d everything in slow motion. At the end, the car went straight to Chaker, who somehow didn't show any expression of shock or fear. Instead, he closed his eyes then spread his arms calmly, as if he were receiving a hug.

"No!" Icarus shrieked, and everything turned white instantly.

A confused and puzzled Icarus orbited, looking around in all directions; all he could see was a limitless white ground and ceiling, and his mentor who was back inside his black suit.

"What happened? Where is he? Where is this place?" Icarus **qu**izz**e**d Gray who replied with a relaxed smile then snapped his fingers and a black door appeared behind Icarus.

"Ladies first," Gray invited Icarus scornfully with a butler-like bow.

Fazed, Icarus opened the door and walked through without delay. He set his feet on a vast and long hospital room; it had several beds on both sides, separated by green curtains that seemed slightly arctic under the bright neon.

"That one," Gray pointed him to the last bed on the **le**f**t**

Icarus walked to that bed to find Chaker laying down in critical condition. Both arms and right leg hanged high inside a splint, broken. Likewise, his neck was coiled with a splint, not to mention the several cuts and bruises on his face.

"He survived!" An astonished Icarus said with a relieved chuckle. Who can blame him? Any *normal* human would've died from that.

The Mingan walked closer to Chaker's side, but his smile faded quickly, showing a concerned frown.

"Will he be okay?"

"He will," replied Gray briefly

"No, I don't mean - - just this," said Icarus, pointing at Chaker's injuries then clarified:

"I mean this **life** of his - - and this dark energy haunting him, will it end?"

(3-9) * (35-4) * (9-2) (23-12) * (5-2) * (7-2) * (16-11) (6-7)

CHAPTER SIX

Gray took **a** moment to think, scratching his c**reas**ed chin then answered with an unsure tone:

"If he learn how to c**on**trol and harness it - - **m**a**y**be"

"Learn, I see," Icarus mused while walking back next to Gray who rested his arm on his student's shoulder.

"Not to worry, **for** after **everything** that **happen**ed, and in this exact moment and while we're talking__" Gray said, narrowing his eye**s** on Chaker who glanced up to the **s**ky through the open window,

"__th**is** brave lad is already thinking of a way to get back on his feet. He knows not how to give up," he praised Chaker with a truthful mouth.

Icarus tightened his fist so hard that his bones crackled while giving Chaker a defiant and determined stare. He didn't speak, but his glares did. Chaker was considered by the Mingan to be a rival whom he had to win against.

After hearing a female cough from the bed next to Chaker, Gray squeezed Icarus's shoulder and teleported him without warning,

"Swish!"

"So, will you be the Atlas who carries the globe - - or the one crushed beneath it?" He grinned then hissed low:

"Behave yourselves, kids." He vanished.

"So you're the one they're calling a Black Cat?" the girl on the side bed asked from behind the curtains.

Chaker turned his head slowly, looking at a faint moving shade.

"That's what I heard - - more like a white cat if you asked me," Chaker replied sarca**st**ically on how he was wrapped in white splints and bandages from head to toe.

"Haha! That bad huh! **Te**ll me what you got?" she inquired with a soft laugh.

"Okay, both arms broken, right leg, all ribs, neck and a possible concussion," he **answer**ed, trying to look at her shade as she moved to a sitting posture then he asked:

"What about you?"

"First, waw! Well - - I had two broken ribs, one shoulder, and a twisted wrist. So I guess you win," she responded with a humorous tone.

"Wait! Were you in a car accident too?" Curious, asked Chaker, trying to move his head more to the side without hurting himself.

"Nah, not that kind of accident," she chuckled then replied while still laughing:

"**This** was actually a training accident, or so he said"

Chaker remained silent **for** a moment, thus asked hesitantly with a frowned face, thinking that she might be a victim of an abusive partner; however, he couldn't ask her that directly, so he had to mingle his suspicion with something else

"You mean - - like martial arts? Or did someone attack you?"

"Yes, martial arts - - kind of. My mentor can be extreme sometimes," she answered with an evasive way, putting his mind at ease, for abusing women was one of the things he hated most, still, he found it wired that a training can cause all that.

"So, this is what they call tough love?" He responded with a fake laugh

"I don't think that thing knows what love is," she sighed then added with a light-hearted tone:

"My name is Uniss"

"My name is Chaker," he replied with a soft voice

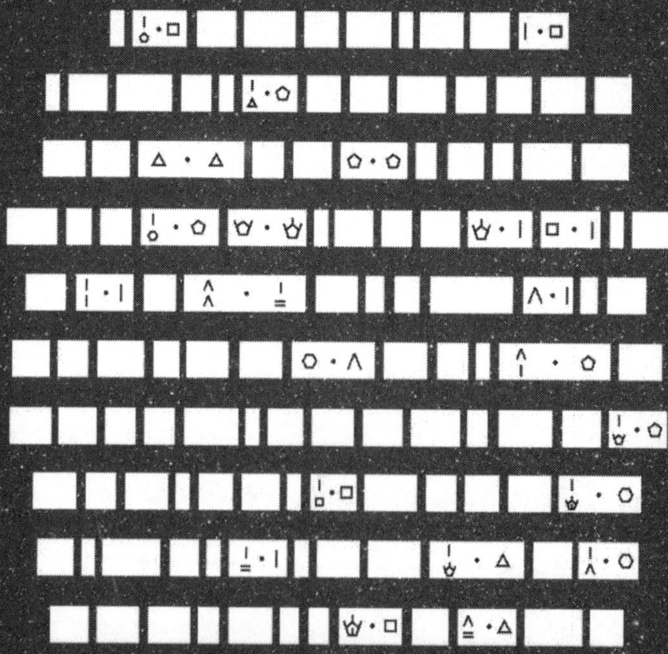

CHAPTER SEVEN

n 3 ^ O 7 I

Back in the library, the common room was a mess; books and shredded papers scattered all over the place, and on the side, Lee was giving Kara and Vi a hard time for causing a chaos that he will be forced to clean. Like a responsible servant, the magical broom reconciled between the two, and when they were about to shake hands, Gray and Icarus burst out of the lime carpet, spooking the three to flee disorderly.

Without saying a word, Gray held **I**carus's hand and walked him to the centre of the room. He rested his palms on Icarus's shoulder, giving him a serious stare.

"There is a possibility of a second door, **but** let us hope we are incorrect," Gray said ambiguously, focusing on Icarus's eyes, who stood there bluntly, thinking transparently with his brows cur**ved** up:

'*What door! Is there **more** to do?*'

"We want you to c**lo**se your eyes, and focus on Apollo's voice," Gray instructed, slightly tightening his grip on Icarus's shoulders.

The Mingan curved a displeased and confused grin. The same man whom made sure to cut all ties with that Olympian is **now** asking for her back!

"I don't know how!" an honest Icarus replied

"Just - - try. Close **you**r eyes and we will help," Gray insisted with a quick nod

Icarus closed his eyes as ordered, thus zoned out, trying to remember Apollo's voice. After moments of deep concentration, they both heard the echo of Apollo's voice sobbing:

'*Comeback please*'

Gray gave Icarus a sharp slap. It was a violent method to dispatch the link, but also effective.

"What the hell? Icarus cursed in a rebuking manner, moving his jaw to the sides.

"We had to cut the link," Gray justified his action with a dull shrug, gently pushing Icarus's shoulder to sit on the couch.

CHAPTER SEVEN

Gray walked back and forth between his desk and Icarus whilst stroking his nape tightly. He paused before Icarus, who barely sat down; one arm crossed while scratching his chin and cheek with a free hand. His silent penetrating stares made his apprentice insecurely uncomfortable.

"This is the only explanation we can think of," he murmured, painting an incredulous expression, one t**ha**t made Icarus question himself as if he had an incurable illness.

Gray star**te**d walking back and forth again, sharing his stressfulness with **I**carus, and before receiving an annoyed comment from the Mingan, he stopped and glanced up to the ceiling. He saw Kara peeking from her box, puzzled. It seemed that even for one who knew Gray for long, seeing the man in black thinking that hard was an unusual scene.

"Kara, come here love," he called for her with his arms thrown in the air. Kara wa**st**ed no time to fall right into his arms.

"Can **you** please get your brother something to drink," he requested with a smile while putting her down.

"I'm her '*what*' now?" asked Icarus with one brow lifted

"Brother - - and we forbid any other relationship between you two," a serious Gray replied, turning round Icarus.

Exchanging awkward stares, Gray sighed, then faked a pleasant grin, brushing his palms together like a salesman who is up to a scam.

"Look, we think - - you - - might have - - fallen__" Gray said, exaggerating the **mo**vements of his lips and the time between each word. But when Icarus reeled a hand to rush him, he continued quickly,

"__in love with Apollo!"

An impassive Icarus looked at Gray dully, waiting for a punch line or a ridiculous laugh. But Gray didn't. He stood still with a poker face, waiting for the Mingan to react.

Icarus smiled, tilting his head to the side when he figured out that Gray was serious. He exploded with laughter while Gray painted an annoyed feature on his face. One saw it as a dilemma, while the other as a joke.

The Mingan continued laughing hysterically, slapping his thighs and rolling on the couch. His loud laughter covered Gray's low words whilst calling for him,

"Okay shut up! This is serious," a fed-up Gray shouted loudly

"Serious!" replied Icarus with his brows frowned

"This is madness," he added with an insulting tone **while** reeling an index closer to his head. Their argument and jeering continued under the stares of a dull Kar**a**, who just walked back carrying the drink with both hands.

"We're not saying it's you, **but** the thing she did," choleric, Gray claimed, raising his voice over Icarus's.

"Oh! Mister all-knowing just **for**got Mingans are immune to magic?" a heated Icarus yelled back with a mocking tone while standing up.

"This is not magic, you featherless chicken," a disgruntled Gray interrupted with a penetrating voice

"If only you cared enough to give us the time to explain," he added with a suppressed high pitch, pointing to the bottle Kara placed on the table before **I**carus.

"Okay, spill whatever lunacy you have," a stubborn Icarus huffed with an acerbic tone, dropping his back on the couch.

"Good. Well - - this is more like - - an expression of gratitude. Think about it, the woman gave you the closest thing to immortality," Gray explained with a modulated voice, gluing his palms together.

"What? Gratitude, for this!" an offended Icarus interjected, placing a hand on his chest and bickered with squint eyes:

"This is more of a curse than a gift"

"Oh, shut up," Gray chided. He couldn't keep it **down** and calm after being lied to by his apprentice. His upper eyes glowed red as he replied with a degrading tone:

"All of us here know you really - - really enjoy this taste of power"

- Kara, who **was** the only plus one at this violent party, shook her head no in a surprised manner. The little creature knew it was best to stay out of it. -

Walking all over the place, an irritated Gray ranted out loud:

"The flying, the continuous increase of speed and strength, the heightened senses - - Should we continue__" He lowered his voice, giving Icarus a serious stare, one for him to stop being obstinate,

"__And let's say - - it is as you claim. That you don't feel grateful. Even so, your vassal does. Or have you forgotten. You still don't have full control over your own body"

CHAPTER SEVEN

Gray's argument silenced Icarus, pushing him to **re**flect instead of disputing things he knew nothing about. He gazed, swallowing the reality of those words, for he was having nightmares about **lo**sing control since he knew Apoll**o** could take over any moment. **The** Mingan was jumbled.

''Hey!" Gray called, but his voice didn't reach his troubled disciple.

Icarus's squeezed fists loosened, shaking nervously. The Mingan questi**one**d his own body, and at the same time, piling all his ideas about Apollo. He remembered that **w**h**e**n Gray threatened her life, the thought of killing her disturbed him, **wh**ile the idea of him being with her comforted him. He couldn't announce it audibly. In**st**ead, he gave Gray an admitting gaze of '*you're right.*'

"Hey!" Gray forced Icarus off his agape state with a loud call and a hard knock on the desk,

"Kara, leave us"

A quick Kara jumped off the couch, and on her way, she left the cup she forgot to put on the table, placing it before Icarus then patted his knee gently with a concerned look

"Thank **you** little one," Icarus said faintly

Gray waited for Kara to climb up to her hanged room while taking a seat. The masked man seemed wary of what to say to his disciple while in a fragile state, so it was best to first remind him that he wasn't alone.

"Remember, you will always have us on your side," a confident Gray assured with a dignified tone, at the same time two moon lanterns clattered above him.

"We want you to trust us, and this is why we think it's the right time for you to know this," he said slowly, resting his left palm on the desk.

"Hmm, so - - about the journeys we took inside our memory, they're not moral experiences to teach you a lesson - - I mean they were partly__" an unassertive Gray stuttered, forcing a suspicious stare on Icarus's face. So he decided to be straightforward,

"__Well, the real purpose was to secretly help your mind cultivate, thus maintain the balance between vassal and soul," he admitted, leaning back with both hands on his chest.

"Why in secret!" A confused Icarus perplexed, placing the empty cup on the table. Gray's words confused the Mingan even more. You can't ask someone to trust <u>y</u>ou then tell him **<u>you</u>** were playing with his mind behind his back.

Icarus rested both arms on his thighs, giving his full attention to G**<u>ray</u>**, who brushed his te**<u>et</u>**h with his tongue, as if he were fishing for a piece of meat that it was stuck between his teeth. He was just nervous because of Icarus's piercing glance as he waited for a convincing reason behind Gray's manipulation.

"If **<u>you</u>** knew, you wouldn't agree__" Gray clarified candidly, adjusting his posture, resting both arms on his knees,

"__And **<u>eve</u>**n if you did, you would be overprotective, which would disrupt the process,"

"And why do you think it is okay to tell me now?" Icarus asked in a pessimistic tone, Giving Gray a dead stare.

"Because by now, you trust us enough to know__" Gray answered, crossing his arms while discreetly creating an executioner's axe of solid smoke behind the Mingan,

"__we really - - mean you no harm"

Gray's claim was no lie, even with his extreme methods; he was always ready to pull Icarus to safety before any lethal danger. But he didn't want him to know that for the sake of his training. Not to forget the fact that he saved his life in the first place. Considering all that inside his head, a firm Icarus leaned forward, pouring himself a cup of sweet rum.

"We believe you, you can put this **<u>thing</u>** down," said a fixed Icarus, highlighting that he knew an axe was pointed at his head, likewise, the reality that Gray manifested it in a way to be noticed, to make sure that the Mingan trusted him completely.

"What now?" Icarus asked, drinking the tumbler in one go, hoping to ease down his nerves.

A pleasant Gray suppressed a grin. Without saying a word, he left his chair, heading for his room whilst gesturing Icarus to stay in his place, as if there was anywhere for him to go.

"We know the perfect book for that love curse you have," Gray joked with a sly grin, stepping inside his room. It took him less than ten seconds to walk out with a book. It **<u>had</u>** a black cover with a white circle on the back. Gray jiggled the book while looking at Icarus like one showing food to his hungry pet.

"Ac**co**rding to our experience, feelings - - can be manipulated as well, with the right tools of course," Gray claim**ed**, walking towards Icarus.

"So think of this as__" he added, placing the book in front of Icarus, thus continued in a playful tone **and** a malicious grin,

"__dropping two birds with one **st**one"

Gray smiled, tapping the book with his pointy claw. Meanwhile, Icarus, who didn't know the proverb, looked at the book awkwardly.

'*This is not a s**to**ne! And what birds?*'

"Meaning **what**?" Icarus perplexed, grabbing the book with a hand while examining **it**s soothing texture with the other. While sensing its cover, then its papers, he noticed that it was blank.

"There is neither a title nor a text inside!" He whispered low, closing and opening the book repeatedly as if the words would magically appear. Gray took his time enjoying Icarus's dull face before answering.

"Don't mind that. First, we deal with your love problem__" Gray clarified, taking the book off Icarus's hand while lifting a finger,

"__then teach you how it's done," he added, raising another finger.

"Ah, I see - - and it's gratitude, not LOVE," a frowned Icarus sighed, then corrected Gray with a **de**fe**n**s**i**ve tone.

"Whatever," Gray deadpanned, opening the book and without delay, he immediately got sucked inside.

Icarus squeezed his eyes shut. Waiting for the book to teleport him next, but felt nothing. He slowly opened one eye, then the other, to see that he wasn't. Baffled, he knocked on the book cover.

"Did he just leave m__"

Icarus got sucked inside before finishing his sentence,

"Swish!"

2022 – Los Angeles, California, a white pigeon with a black spot on its chest was resting on a rusty bar, until its tranquillity was disturbed by a hot wind from the bleak mountain on the back. The bird flapped it wings before flying away, leaving behind a huge sign that said '*Hollywood*'.

Wings spread like an eagle, and sharp cries like a crow. The pigeon flew over the crowded dry roads, heading to the city. The hot weather didn't diminish the agility of the inhabitants. Everyone looked like they were in a hurry, from the few walkers to the army of drivers.

(19-5) (2-7) * (10-2) * (4-6) * (8-5) * (9-2) * (1-1) (5-6)

The pigeon locked its vision on a roofless tour bus then swooped towards it, while transf**or**ming into a man-like figure.

Icarus fell upside d**ow**n o**n** one of the bus seats, exactly on the one next to Gray; **the** masked man was wearing sparkly orange glasses shaped like a star over his mask whilst holding a cheap camera with both hands.

"Snatching me off guard wasn't amusing enough for you? You had to drop me like a bag of wheat on this - - what is this!" Annoyed, Icarus complained, adjusting his posture to sit straight while probing his surroundings.

"A bus - - and this - - you c**all** amusing, is a part of your training, to keep you p**o**in**t**y," Gray deadpanned while taking pictures right and left.

"Clicks!"

Several minutes passed, and the **co**up**l**e were still on tour; one enjoying himself while the other tried his best to suppress his annoyance and boredom.

While zooming through the camera, Gray chuckled, looking at a cafeteria sign that said '*Angelic Café*'

"Ha, a city of angels bustling with demons," he derided with low voice

"Did you say something?" Blunt, Icarus asked. He heard the words, but the meaning was what he missed.

"We said - - time to go," replied Gray, standing up and leaving the camera behind. Icarus looked at the lance, thence to Gray, who already hopped off the bus. He tried to grab the camera but his hand ghosted through. The Mingan jumped after his mentor to land facing the entrance of Angelic Café.

He stood behind Gray, looking up and reading the sign.

"Shall we," said Gray with a pleasant tone as he walked into the cafeteria, followed by a curious disciple.

The first thing Icarus noticed was the aroma of a sour yet pleasant coffee. It was strong enough to make him miss the *'Free Wifi'* words written in white on the floor as he walked over it.

Modern technology used to be the first to capture Icarus's attention, but not this time. He locked his eyes on the long serving counter ahead; made of polished old wood, or maybe it was painted to appear as such. Icarus couldn't tell, but he liked how it was slightly similar to his hometown's popina. Likewise, it was pleasant to see the several pots of sunflowers on the side of each cashier, with their petals facing up towards the colour**ful** spectra of the

chandelier's crystals, instead of the faint sunlight that broke through the dark windows.

Icarus and Gray walked past the long lines of customers to one of the serving counters. The masked man rested his elbow on the **f**lat wood, looking at a tall, pulchritudinous **you**ngster wearing a scarlet apron over his tight white shirt, smiling genuinely while serving a customer what she **or**dered.

"Meet Aiden," Gray introduced the cashier to Icarus who stood straight with his arms crossed, looking at Aiden with his head slightly tilted to the back.

"Why is he wearing a mask? These people too!" Icarus asked

"Same as always, some wealthy humans wanted to be wealthier," Gray replied simply, and Icarus seemed to understand what he meant perfectly.

The Mingan locked his sight on his next task again. He **had** an impression that Aiden's soft and kind eyes didn't match his giant carcass. Icarus freed an inner chuckle.

"I'm already **feeling s**omething off about him. What's his deal?" He asked

Gray scrutinized Aiden and his clothes with a side smirk, as if he were gathering a scornful answer from the way Aiden behaved, but didn't.

"Mm! Let's see. Very kind, smart, loyal__" Gray turned round Icarus with a provocative grin,

"__but madly in love with a whore; does it ring any bells?" An insolent Gray answered with a derisive tone, giving his apprentice two harmless punches on the chest,

"Maybe **a** sexy Mingan we know!"

Ica**rus**'s reply to that **t**ease was simply a brief glare. It seemed that he was adapting to Gray's provocative behaviour.

After t**r**eati**n**g another customer, Aiden check**ed** the vintage clock hanged on the side wall while handing an intimidated ginger her change.

"Hey JJ," Aiden called for his co-worker who was serving a table with a low wave, then pointed to his wrist watch.

JJ raised a finger, asking for one minute. After spreading a full hand of sugar-bags among several tables, he paced to Aiden, taking charge of his booth.

"I got this. What can I get you miss?" JJ said to Aiden then asked the next customer in line with a smile while Aiden walked away to the staff room.

Ten minutes later, he walked out with his boring clothes, rushing out **t**hro**u**gh the back exit. Gray tapped Icarus's side, driving his attention from the TV to Aiden while leaving. He didn't have to say nothing, he just walked through the wall behind them and Icarus followed.

They caught up with Aiden, hopping in his **black** mini-cooper. While walking towards him, Gray smacked Icarus's chest, preventing him from approaching the car.

"Not you," Gray said before he transformed to smoke then rapidly permeated into the car and transformed back on the front passenger seat.

"Brum-rum-rum!"

Aiden started the car, thus checked all his papers before he departed.

"Why?" argued Icarus aggrievedly

Gray waited until Aiden rolled the window down so he could get his elbow out, making himself comfortable.

"We notice that your wings are getting stiffed, so - - flying lessons for you," replied Gray with a sly smile. He waved like a child while Aiden made his way out of the parking lot.

An easygoing Icarus ran a few steps before flying slowly above the car. Gray got his hand out as if he forgot to say something, so Icarus swayed slightly to his side, but remained on the car's tail.

"One more thing, dodge the vehicles instead of ghosting through, and no flying above," he shouted with his head up like a wolf howling out of the window.

CHAPTER SEVEN

The masked man raised his arm higher, intending to snap his fingers. The Mingan knew s**o**me**t**h**i**ng was coming, and the m**o**me**n**t Gray snapped his fingers, two co**ll**ars manifest**ed** around I**ca**rus's wrists, instantly pulling Icarus down to the ground; from the way his face and chest shovel**le**d a long trail on the hard concrete, it was obvious that the extra weight was insanely heavy.

"What in Zeus - -" lost, Icarus groaned wanly while pulling his hands and body up from the hot road. He didn't se**em** hurt or even bothered by the collars' weight, except for getting caught off guard.

"Good luck," Gray shouted, waving as Aiden accelerated ahead.

Icarus took a deep breath followed by a long puff, tightening his muscles until his veins throbbed. He placed each fist on the opposite side of his chest, forming an X.

"Challenge accepted," he smirked, spreading his wings wide.

"Woof!"

With one push from his right foot, Icarus darted after Gray and Aiden, easily dodging the slow cars while getting used to the new acce**ss**ories. It took him no ti**me** to catch up with them.

"Hey, **you** know - - I always thought that mask of yours fits perfectly. I mean those nine-eyed piglets are the slowest," a snide Icarus teased Gray, who washed the smile off his face while looking at the Mingan dodging a truck by running on its side before smoothly reeling back to Gray's side.

"Show-off - - Okay, how about this," a wicked Gray grinned, raising his relaxed hand, and a dozen cars up front floated at the same time, making a cautious Icarus slew down.

"You wouldn't!" Wide-eyed, Icarus said with his eyes locked on Gray's evil grin, knowing what was going to happen next.

Gray clutched a fist as a sign for some of the floating cars to spin faster than the rest; they rotated rapidly to the point where their metallic frames squeaked sharply, thus dashed towards Icarus one after the other, while crushing into the other cars on the way.

"Clatters!"

"Shit!" Icarus gasped, pausing in mid-air.

The cars arrowed towards him as if they were racing to see which one crushes bird-man first; the agile Mingan managed to dodge some of the cars but barely, one bumped h**is** arm, and another his leg. Luckily, nothing he couldn't wit**h**st**a**nd.

Seeing the rest of **the** cars spinning, getting ready to charge his way, Icarus thought of **an** idea. It was a simple one,

'Fly fast behind Aiden's car and use it as a shield, for Gray won't hit his own ride'

And so he did. Icarus rested his hands on the car's trunk while keeping his wings slightly folded to match the width of the vehicle.

Gray turned around, giving his apprentice a thumb up whilst smiling widely. Icarus smiled back proudly, enjoying several seconds of safety until he saw a car ghost through Gray and Aiden, heading his way. The Mingan's grin washed off while his eyes jumped. The car slammed him far away like a baseball batter hitting the ball up the ally.

Twenty minutes later, on the front gate of an apartment complex. Gray was sitting on the crooked sidewalk when he saw Icarus clumsily flying his way, thus crashed onto a tall tree across the street, falling down while breaking every branch in the way.

Gray enjoyed the view from a distance while Icarus fought his pain to stand up; his clothes were torn and so was his body, covered in bruises and stains of blood. He looked left and right before lim**p**ing **a**cross whi**l**e dragging his broken left wing. On the other side, Gray tried to hide his amused express**ion**s.

"You used the bracelet to find the place!" Gray guessed, standing up with his arms crossed. Icarus stayed sil**e**nt for a **mo**men**t**, using his hand to press his bleeding nose.

"Yes," Icarus answered with a nasal voice, what forced a quick chuckle blow out of Gray.

"Smart," said Gray, while suppressing his laughter. However, he then felt bad seeing his disciple in that state, so he snapped his finger and Icarus was healed in an instant.

The first thing Icarus did was shooting the blood out of his nostrils in a plebeian way. At that moment, a disgusted Gray regretted aiding him. After stretching his arms, he pulled his wings back inside.

"Thank you," said Icarus while moving his facial muscles and rubbing his jaw, painting ridiculous features that bothered Gray.

"Don't - -" Gray said in a dead tone, walking away and into the complex.

CHAPTER SEVEN

A dull Icarus followed his master to the compound, curiously inspecting the place, glancing at the sage bushes first, showing a lack of care and water. He turned round the three joint buildings of a caramel facade, shaped like a U, each **ha**d two-storey. **T**h**e** building in the middle had one apartment on each floor, while the ones on the sides had three each.

Finally, they reached Aiden's apartment. H**is** door had an engraved writing, and from the hand writing, it was obviously written by a kid. It said '*I love,*' exactly on the left of the door's number, which was twelve.

"Erini Se Sas," said Icarus low as usual before ghosting through the door after Gray.

The apartment was small that you could see almost everything from the front door. The lights were faint that the olive walls looked slightly moss instead. However, the furniture seemed neat and expensive giving how simple structured the apartment was; a living room on the right, the kitchen up front, where Aiden was washing the dishes. Two open doors on the left, one to the bathroom and the other to the bedroom.

While walking slowly away from the door, Icarus got spooked by a woman shout:

"Suck my d**k"

He turned round the long white sofa with a long neck, peeking to assess. A young woman stood straight before the TV screen, holding a game controller with one hand while ad**just**ing the puffed white headsets she was wearing with the other. Icarus shifted his vision from the girl to the screen until Gray's back blocked the way.

"And now - - meet the whore of Babylon," Gray insulted in an abasing tone, pointing at the girl with his middle finger.

A suspicious Icarus lifted a brow, walking past Gray and closer to the girl. He sized her up thence looked back at Gray, smiling barely.

"Why do I have a feeling that you hate this one!" Icarus inquired while scrutinizing her angry expression as she played the game.

"You'll see. Anyway, there is someone we have to visit," Gray replied, walking back to the door and ignoring Icarus's puzzled stares. He walked through it, then back halfway and added:

"And Hey - - Keep an eye on him, not the TV"

"Tsk!" Icarus rolled his eyes away, hiding his annoyed face. He ambled closer to the kitchen, but turned back round the TV the moment Gray left.

"Babe, **you** want a sandwich?" Aiden asked loudly from the kitchen, but got ignored, so he called again and again, still, no reply. Looking at her headsets, He thought that was **the** reason she didn't respond; however, a sharp Icarus noticed that her body reacted to his voice, meaning she heard him yet chose to not answer.

"I will make you one anyway," a blunt Aiden smiled, drumming his hands on the counter be**for**e grabbing the bread. He prepared a sandwich for his gir**l**fr**i**end, making sure it was perfect. He even removed the overcoo**ke**d edge**s** and sliced it in half before placing it on a flat plate. A cheerful Aiden rushed his steps to his partner.

"Babe," Aiden said, stretching the word as if he were waking someone up. He tapped her shoulder gently, handing her the plate. Instead **of** grabbing the plate off his hand, she pointed at the table on the side with her eyes fixed on the game.

"Ah yes - - sorry," Aiden apologized, placing the plate on the table while leaning closer to kiss her cheek, but she shrugged to avoid it. Icarus curved a sneering smirk, seeing the stiff and embarrassed face Aiden made.

"What an obsequious servile," Icarus whispered in a mortified tone

Aiden walked back to the kitchen whilst rubbing his nape.

"Shit!" the girl cursed again, slamming the controller on the couch. She removed her headsets before throwing her back on the sofa then grabbed the sandwich, placing the plate on her chest.

"So - - how was your audition?" Aiden asked, walking behind the kitchen counter whilst pulling two pieces of bread to make another sandwich for him.

His partner took her time to answer. She first took a bite, moving her big lips in and out while munching, then replied with her mouth full from a second bite,

"It was a No-No for me. And the director was an asshole. He kept staring at my tits the entire time," she complained apathetically, pushing the scraps of bread off her oversized boy shirt. Well, obviously Aiden's.

"And don't let me start with that lame role," boastful, she added, crossing her legs, after placing a pillow on her lap to use it as a small table.

"Careful with the grease," hesitantly, Aiden said low while squinting his left eye.

_ (8-3) * (5-4) * (8-13) (9-10) (9-11) * (13-10) * (3-2)

CHAPTER SEVEN

"What was that? Ahem," she carelessly replied with a croaky voice, then used her fist to repeatedly slam her chest **wh**ile trying t**o** swallow the morsel stuck in her throat.

A worried Aiden rushed to her with a cup of water in one hand and a **sa**ndwi**c**h in the other.

"Here babe, d**ri**nk," he said, giving her the cup while sitting next to her.

She aggressively took the water off his hand and drank it all in one go, squeezing her eyes shut whilst hardly pushing the staffed food down.

"Ah!"

She wiped her mouth with the back of her hand like a cave woman, and instead of a thank you, she gave Aiden an angry glare.

"Took you long enough, I almost died," she exasperated with a heavy sigh, faking an unnecessary cough.

"But Sousan - - I got it here the moment you choked!" A faint Aiden replied cowardly, and even so, Sousan didn't believe that he dared talking back.

Brows frowned and arms crossed, glowering at him with wider eyes while waiting for an answer to a question she didn't ask. Aiden had no response but to force a faint smile as an uncalled for apology.

"Clanks!"

Sousan slammed the cup on the table. The plastic cup survived but not the glassy surfa**ce** of the table. The impact drew a round crack, **fi**lling most of the table.

"Are you saying I'm exaggerating?" she bickered with a rude tone, creasing her forehead whilst shoving her face in Aiden's breathing space.

"No **love**! Sorry - - my bad," he apologized with a pitiful smile then implored obsequiously:

"Please don't be mad at me"

"This joke is pathetically annoying," an abhorrent Icarus grumbled, crossing his arms while taking a few steps back away from the couple.

"That old hag, does he think that I am the same as this submissive snail!" Icarus grunted, tightening his fists, while forced to continue on observing Sousan bullying Aiden from a distant.

"Give me that," said a grumpy Sousan, taking Aiden's sandwich off his hand. He didn't have the courage to tell her that was his, so he forced a beam and tried to change the subject.

"You know - - Lepou told me his peeps are working on a new movie and they need extras **for** hire," he said reluctantly, and at the same time, c**ar**efull**y** placing a napkin on the pillow.

"What do you say we go together?" an enthusiastic Aiden suggested with a wide smi**l**e. But So**us**an glared a**t** him once again, taking the napkin off the pillow to wipe her messy mouth. At least this time she didn't use her slovenly hand.

"Is this **a** joke? Cause if it was, I'm not laughing," brooding, she replied, rolling her eyes while pushing Aiden's hand off her thigh before standing up.

"I didn't pay for all those expensive acting classes to be an extra," she chastised while rushing her steps to the bedroom. In the mean time, a dull Aiden glanced for a **moment** then followed her with a jumbled face.

"I meant - - like hanging out together, maybe a date after," he tried to clarify, but she carelessly ignored him.

Icarus, who was in the kitchen, used his two stretched thumbs and forefingers to make a rectangle, just like an empty screen, one that followed Aiden like a cinematic scene until he got the bedroom door slammed on his face.

Icarus curved a pleasant grin, for he was more irritated by how Aiden was acting like a wimp than how toxic his girlfriend was.

"Babe, please - - can we talk." Aiden begged with his forehead on the door, and as he was about to place a hand on the doorknob, the phone rang. He ignored it for seconds, but the continuous ringing was too annoying to ignore. He headed towards it with his eyes fixed on the door, hoping that Sousan might open to see who was calling. On his way, he even thought of faking that he was talking to one of her family member to drag her out.

Aiden stood before the ringing phone for a moment while observing the bedroom door. But no luck, so he picked up.

"Hello!" he answered, slowly sauntering back to the door.

"Yes, hello, this is doctor Canon from Dignity Health Medical Centre, is this mister Aiden Vovk," replied a female doctor; short, curly golden hair matching her yellow eyes and olive skin. She leaned over the opposite side of a reception counter to pick some papers while pulling the phone along from its short wire.

Hearing the hospital name concerned Aiden, for it was where his sick mother resides. He orbited back and away from the bedroom.

CHAPTER SEVEN

"Yes! Is my Mother okay? Did she wake up?" Aiden quizzed in an anxious tone, grabbing his keys from the table on his side.

"Snick!"

She remained silent **for** seconds, then sighed audibly before announcing the reason behind the call:

"**I**'m really sorry, but - - there was nothing we **can** do"

Her words stupefied Aiden. His arm dropped and so did the phone, causing it to end the call while the doctor was still **ta**lking.

Aiden gazed at his hand holding the **ke**ys as it started to shake, followed by the other hand. Baffled, he walked to the front door with ponderous steps, and instead of leaving, he stopped before it, scared, looking at the doorknob vibrating and so did his hand while reaching for it. His breathing slew for a brief mo**me**nt then turned to rapid pants. Aiden used the bottom of his palms to cover his glossy eyes while clutching knots of his hair. The big man leaned his **back** against the door, for his legs weakened, sliding down slowly until he cocooned his body on the floor, sobbing quietly like a canine-cub whilst hiding his head between his muscular arms.

Icarus, who was watching him from far didn't know the reason behind Aiden's sudden break down. He approached him slowly.

"What happened to **you** big boy?" a concerned Icarus wondered, leaning his body down before Aiden as his sobs got louder.

Meanwhile, back in the hospital, Doctor Canon walked into a room not far from the reception bureau. She first turned off the TV that was on a figure skating competition, thence headed to the bed where a pale old lady was laying with her hand on her chest. The doctor pulled the white cover all the way up, covering the old woman's face, thus **asked** the nurse who was in the room to transfer her to the morgue.

As they pushed her bed out of the room, Gray walked out right behind them, moving cautiously as if they could see him.

"Farwell little one," he said low, looking at the nurse pushing the stretcher across the hall and into the elevator. He waited for the door to close before vanishing into mist and instantly appeared behind Icarus who was sitting next to Aiden.

The **M**ing**a**n spoo**ke**d when glimpsing a figure behind him, but when he saw it was his men**to**r, he released a relieved sigh. But that didn't spare Gray a smack on the knee for showing up without warning.

"His mother died. Get up," Gray said inexpressively, tapping Icarus's should**er** to stand. The Mingan was **su**rprised at first. He closed his eyes briefly then gave Gray a pity look followed by a down smile. His head shake said '*why?*' He didn't like the idea of choosing people who lost their mothers just like he did. Was it intentionally?

"Come," Gray said, walking to the living room. He peeked outside through the dark purple curtains until Icarus followed.

"What do **you** think of him so far?" Gray said, thrusting his hands in his pocket while looking at an old lady staggering to her apartment with the help of a **you**ngster wearing a black hood with a pink eastern dragon on the **back**.

"What - - you have nothing?" Gray queried, turning round Icarus who remained silent with a face that said '*you won't like my answer,*' but since Gray insisted, there was no running from it.

"I really don't want to say this about one - - who just lost his mother, but__" Icarus replied empathetically. He paused to fake a cough then continued talking while mingling his words with him clearing his throat,

"__unless you're telling me - - this man is bewitched, I see him as an obsequious and submissive weakling, and I have no respect for his kind"

Gray glanced up to the ceiling, humming low, thus started drumming his lips.

"His kind! Mm! His - - kind you say!" he commented

He started humming again after focusing only on those two words but stopped when he caught Sousan sneaking out of the room towards the bathroom.

"That was very interesting coming from you. Anyway, giving his state - - and your dilemma, we can confidently say that you and Aiden are the same," he stated, slowly walking past Icarus who interjected argumentatively:

"Seriously! I'm nothing like him. Just admit it, he was a bad choice"

Gray sighed, looking at Sousan as she noticed Aiden crying. Confused and ba**ff**led, she approached him with quiet steps.

"What's going on?" She asked with a faint voice

Gray pointed his palm towards her, slightly curving his fingers to manifest a dozen dark swords, all floating and pointed her way. A puzzled Icarus placed his h**and** on Gray's shoulder, thinking he was up to no good, but Gray was just expressing his desires openly.

He lowered his hand and all **the** swords vanished.

"The conditions may be different, but - - you both are facing the same problem," Gray ex**p**l**ain**ed. However, a stubborn Icarus was willing to interrupt and argue again, so his Master prevented him by one tense smack on the chest

"Just shut up and listen. Aiden here is of **a** very delicate heart, and he has this excessive need to always express love. Call it a curse," scolding, Gray clarified while revealing the truth about Aiden's condition. He stood behind Sousan, who tried gently to stop Aiden from crying.

"Unfortunately, on the day his mother **fel**l into a coma, he me**t** this harlot," added Gray, pointing his middle finger at Sousan.

"Are you saying it could have been anyone?!" **I**carus asked

"Yes, no jokes. Even if it were a featherless chicken like you," a sly Gray affirmed with a grin

"Or a nine eyes pig like you," and Icarus was quick to respond, but Gray took his comeback lightly,

"Yes, probably," he deadpanned, reeling his index to speed time a day forward.

Aiden walked to the front door in his black suit, adjusting his cravat, while followed by Sousan who was in a sweat pants and one of Aiden's football shirts.

"Is there anything I can do or say to change your mind?" Crestfallen, Aiden asked in an imploring manner, resting his hands on her shoulders,

"I really need someone to be with me through this"

Sousan tightened his tie, then gave him a quick kiss on the cheek.

"Sorry sweetie, but you know how I **feel** about these things," she replied with a down smile while handing him his car keys. From Icarus's understanding, she steered away when most needed. The Mingan looked at Gray, thus gave him a faint sign, as if he were giving him the green light to stab her with those swords he manifested earlier.

"I understand," faint, Aiden said, giving her a quick hug before grabbing his keys and walk out.

"Let us speed thing up a **little**," said Gray, reeling his index again to move time forward several hours ahead.

The door opened, and Aiden stepped in with a cinerary urn in hand.

_ (26-8) * (3-7) * (5-3) * (13-9) * (11-7) (11-12) * (1-2) * (7-10) * (33-7)

"Babe!" Sorrowfully, he called, putting the keys on the key hanger.

Aiden found no response, so he called again while ambling to the table. He gently placed the jar on it while keeping an eye on the bedroom's closed door. A closed door meant that she was there, and the clank he heard seconds after confirmed it.

Aiden walked towards the bedroom, thinking she might be taking a nap and just woke up. When he reached **for** the doorknob, Sousan opened the door. Wearing a black loosen and short bathrobe.

"Hey! You're back, already!" wide-eyed, she said with a fake smile, standing at the door whilst keeping a stretched hand on the frame, as if she were talking to a stranger.

Icarus focused his hearing for seconds, then looked at Gray, s**ur**pris**e**d.

"Did she - -" he gasped low and Gray nodded yes with a grin before Icarus finished his sentence.

"I'll be damned! And why do you look **pleas**ed about this!?" asked Icarus with a disappointed and confused headshake.

"You'll see," Gray replied simply, maintaining his easygoing smile.

"You're early!" said Sousan, lifting her brows the highest possible. She was obviously hiding something; anyone could see it, but Aiden, who was blinded by love.

"They had an opening so - - **mo**m got - - c**re**mated first," he wailed faintly, thus noticed her unusual outfit.

"Why do you have this on!" He asked whilst trying to get into the bedroom, but Sousan stopped him, placing her hand on his chest.

"This! Isn't Obvious - - you silly," a seductive Sousan cooed amorously while sliding her hand d**own** from his chest to his stomach.

"But first, I'm starving, so can you get this Lil-Cat something to eat!" she purred, thus coyly bit her lip while putting her hand on her neck, expelling the wistful expressions off Aiden's face with a sly grin. He approached her to give her a kiss, but a faint clunk coming from the bedroom interrupted.

"What - -" Aiden perplexed with a low voice, trying to peek inside, but Sousan was on the way. She placed both hands on his cheeks to kiss him, but he insisted on inspecting the noise.

"Now watch - - and learn," Gray smirked, walking towards Aiden. Black fog started steaming off his clothes, leaving a dark and gri**my** trail.

CHAPTER SEVEN

"With the right push, even emotions can be twisted," **a** wicked Gray added whimsically, stretching his arms down, thus wiggled his fingers.

He rested his chin on Aiden's right shoulder then hissed:

"Off the **way**"

Aiden spoke the words whispered to him by Gray. It looked more as if Gray spoke through him. The gentle Aiden dared to push Sousan and barge in. He **found** a shirtless man locking his belt; tall, skinny and covered with colourful tattoos, he didn't have a gangster vibe, **but** he seemed as if he wanted to look like one.

"Who the F**k are you?" A malicious Gray whispered again, controlling Aiden's words.

Appalled, the outsider wore his shirt rapidly while stepping back behind the bed. He waited **for** Aiden to step farther from the door so he could make a run for it.

"**I**'m sorry dude - - I just - - **I** had no idea," he stuttered

Before he got the chance to escape, a glowering Aiden grabbed him and pushed him outside the bedroom. The power gap between the t**wo** was vast, but that did**n't** stop the weasel from trying to intimidate Aiden with his salty words.

"Hey chill bro, don't make me mess you up - - you hear me, chill before you get cut," he threatened, puffing his chest and bouncing his upper like a box clown while walking back slowly.

Gray walked out of the room, following Aiden. He looked at the man heading to the jar that held the remains of Aiden's mother.

"Both of you stop, Jake, just leave," shouted Sousan with a quivered voice, pulling Aiden's arm.

Aiden complied but Gray wasn't willing to let her have it her way this time, so he decided to push him further.

"That should do it," Gray grinned, looking at the fake gangster's foot, then echoed the word '*Fall!*'

Both Icarus and the man stumbled, but unlike Icarus who ghosted through the table, Jake bumped it hard, causing the urn to drop.

"Crash!"

The jar broke, and the ashes dusted out.

"What the F**K is that." Jake groused, jolting his foot to shake the remnant off.

"Is that - -" shocked, Sousan said low, placing her hand on her mouth thence looked at Aiden who froze in his place. His vision etched inexpressively on what was left of his mother, **be**ing sca**tter**ed by the foot of some douchebag.

A **satisf**ied Gray grinned wide, showing his perfectly sharp fangs, thus whispered with a penetrating voice:

"Now"

Jake felt a strange chill on his back, as if his body was asking him to turn back, **and** when he did, he found Aiden right behind him, furious. He seemed like a completely different person. Not only his presence. Jake noticed parts of Aiden's brown beard turning bright red. Exactly like the light-bulb's filament when ignited with low electricity. Jake thought it was him being high on rocks, so he squeezed his eyes shut while taking a step back, but when he opened his eyes, he glimpsed Aiden's pupils narrowed like a predator.

Aiden took one **more** step closer to his scraggy adversary, giving him a vindictive glare that caused him to piss himself.

"What the f**k are you? Stay away from me!" bug-eyed, Jake shuddered with a quivered voice, running away with his eyes fixed on Aiden who followed with steady steps, enjo**ying** the looks of fear on Jake's face.

"What is wrong with you," Sousan shouted, pulling him back to give Jake the chance to run away. She stood before him as if he were at fault, forgetting that she was caught cheating minutes ago. That was how much confident she was with Aiden being a ring on her finger; however, she didn't know there was a malicious creature behind his back this time, meddling with his thoughts.

"She cheated on you," Gray hissed in Aiden's left ear like a demon, causing his head to twitch. He then swayed to the right ear while his black smoke coiled and infiltrated Aiden's head,

"And if it weren't for her, maybe - - you would've had the chance to be with your mother - - on her last moments. You heard what the doctor said, your mother woke up before she passed away. She called for you, and this whore took that moment," he hissed again but louder

"Geez, we were high as f**k. Plus - - you came in before anything happened," Sousan continued yelling, trying to clarify what she did, but her voice was fading inside Aiden's head as the sound of his breathing kept increasing. All he could hear was his own pants followed by beastly shrieks. Gray took a step back, then tapped his back.

CHAPTER SEVEN

"Shut the F**k up!" glowering, Aiden shrieked h**is** lungs out, flashing his eyes scarlet! Sousan's eyes rolled up before she fainted instantly.

A surprised Icarus was caught between **the** two. See if Sousan's life was at risk, or wary about Aiden's unknown nature.

"Is she dead?" a worried Icarus rushed **to** check on Sousan first, pushing Gray off his **way**.

"The whore is fine, this champion's aura was **to**o much for her to handle - - that's all," Gray grinned, explaining what happened to Sousan.

Gray's words weren't enough. Icarus focused on her chest to make sure she was breathing, and she did. He then stood straight facing Aiden, who was still glaring down at Sousan, as if all the love he felt turned to **hate**. But that wasn't the reason behind Icarus disturbance. It was that Aiden's aura was similar to a fierce monster he encountered before; the Minotaur.

"Who is this man?" A cautious Icarus inquired in a fixed tone, sizing him up with a belligerent look.

"Don't worry about it, time for us to leave," Gray responded, pulling Aiden's book out of thin air. However, Icarus didn't feel like leaving without getting an answer first, but Gray **ignore**d him.

"Very well," Gray said then snapped a finger.

Icarus took a step back, but didn't see the giant hand of black fog Gray manif**est**ed **b**ehind him. One smack was enough to toss Icarus straight toward Gray who had the book open and ready to suck the Mingan in.

"It's nice to see you again kid. Don't worry about your uncle, he just doesn't know you - - yet," Gray spoke to Aiden, smiling before teleporting himself,

"Swish!"

Six months after, Aiden walked from his kitchen to the living room with a big bowl of popcorn. He dropped his back on the sofa while grabbing the TV remote; the screen was paused on a classic movie.

The moment Aiden pressed play the door knocked. He checked his hand watch spontaneously, wondering who would visit on this late hour. The knocking continued non-stop.

"Coming, coming," annoyed, Aiden whisper shouted, rushing his steps to the door. He first peeked through the door's peephole, but the flinching light outside prevented him a clear look. All he saw was a pink dragon on the visitor's back. It was suspicious, but that didn't stop him from opening the door, **and** when he did - - the hooded visitor turned around removing her hoodie. It was Uniss; hair cut short and a tattoo on her neck.

"Hi," she **gre**e**t**ed with a wide fake smile

Aiden gave her an annoyed stare then shut the door on **her** face, walking back to the living room as if nothing happened.

"I really need your help," Uniss kept talking out loud while knocking on the door. Aiden jumped back on the couch, ignoring her completely, but his annoyed features said otherwise.

"Go away, I want nothing to do with you people," he shouted back, grabbing the remote. He increased the TV's volume to mute her voice.

Uniss stopped knocking on the door then spoke up with a serious tone:

"It's **about** Kara - - she's missing. Please, you know I can't lose her too"

Her words switched Aiden's annoyed and creased face to a concerned one.

"She's the only family I've got left - - Please Aiden," Uniss begged, resting her **for**ehead on the door to hear the door's lock click.

"Come in," Aiden invited her without opening the door

Uniss sighed while painting a relieved smile. She rubbed her glossy eyes then opened the door, and before she stepped inside, she whispered low:

"Erini Se Sas"

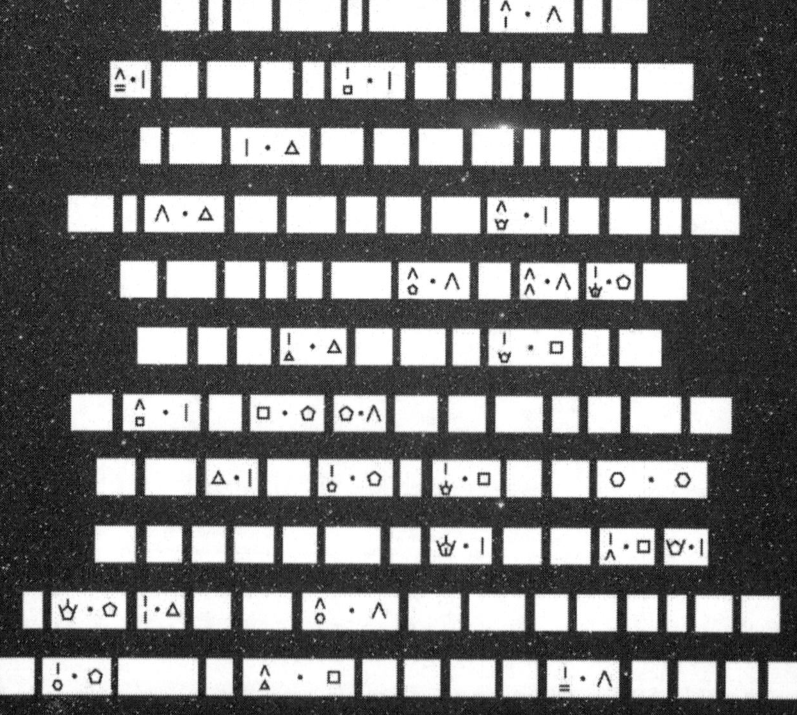

CHAPTER EIGHT
HEARTS OF BLUE FIRE

The library was quiet in the absence of the two, but not completely silent. On Gray's desk, a cheerful Kara was enjoying her alone time.

"Eek eek!"

She sat on an ice-motif covered book wagging her tail with her legs dangling down the edge, holding a banana in each hand that she used as puppets. The bananas had eyes made of emerald and brown pins, and mouths drawn by a red marker, one looking like a man and the other one like a woman.

She looked at Lee, sweeping the floor while heading to the third section.

"Wesh! - - Wesh!"

With her eyes focused, Kara waited keenly for the broom to be gone. She then stared at her leopard bananas, deliberately driving their tips closer to each other while twisting her lips into a kiss.

"Swish!"

A stun**n**e**d** Kirada turned quickly towards the **fi**rst section, rattled by an ambiguous presence. She quickly hid the bananas behind her back.

"You always treat me like a nobody. We don't need a puppet you said, well guess what? **I** f**king feel like one now. Damn it, one **can**'t really **belong** in here, and you're making it even harder"

Kara heard **I**carus's far complains coming from the first section. She panicked, turning around her tail while looking for a place in **where** to hide her inappropriate toys. She ended up placing the girl-banana under a scarlet book, but there was no space for she-banana's lover.

"Hey! What is this thing?" She heard the voice of a perplexed Icarus, getting closer.

"Boom!"

A loud bam mixed with an anguished gasp from Icarus stunned a nervous Kara. She hopped off the desk to see Icarus thrown out of the first section, reeling his arm as if he were unwillingly swimming in mid-air to end up landing before her feet.

"Shit! Agh!" He groaned

CHAPTER EIGHT

Pained, Icarus rubbed his jaw while standing hardly, and behind him, a man appeared out of the first section, wearing a black armour that covered him from head **to** toe, followed by Gray, wearing a wicked grin.

"This is Pixie. He will be helping you with combat training," said Gray, drumming his fingers against the hard armour as he walked past Pixie.

"Clang!"

Pixie punched his own palm after **a** fist-slam against his chest, as a way to show hostility.

"Tpixaieg acrcucht Ticaarusg," he said in a sharp and unpleasant voice, pointing a finger in Icarus's face then gave him a thumb down, hinting that he will beat him down.

"Aficghtt," an aggressive Pixie grunted

Icarus looked at him with one brow up, grasping the angry vibes but couldn't understand a word.

"What did he say?" he **ask**ed, baffled, cracking his muscles.

"Tpixi-bug afi-shit! What was that?" Icarus puzzled, using a finger to draw a **question** mark in the air whilst looking at Gray with a side eye

"Tpixaig Aficghtt," groaned Pixie, objecting to the mistake Icarus did while mimicking him.

The two were ready for a fight, but Gray meddled with a chuckling clarification, while noticing Kara acting overly innocent,

"This is Pixie language __ and you, what were you doing?" he asked with a suspicious tone.

He beckoned her, leaning a knee down before turning to Pixie, while Kara hesitantly approached him with her hand behind her back.

"Pixie, go feed your friend," he ordered with a fixed tone

"Wait! You're letting him go, after he sucker-punched me?" Scowling, Icarus argued aggrievedly, bumping his fists together, hinting that he wants payback, but Gray ignored him completely.

"Pixie, just go," he repeated in a serious tone

"And you, that punch was for us, not him," Gray added, grabbing Kara's arm to find out what she had behind her back.

A provocative Pixie laughed weirdly, giving Icarus a middle finger while hiding it from Gray with the other hand. He then walked away through the long corridor.

"What is it with eve**r**yo**n**e here and flipping others off?" Icarus grumped with a squint and tense cheeks.

"And what do you mean '*for you*'?" He turned his attention **to** Gray, who fought Kara to show him what she had hidden. **I**c**a**rus approached the little creature and pulled her up without exposing her secret.

"Hey!" Gray protested.

Icarus walked away without saying a word. He placed Kara on the entrance of **the** third section, giving her a gentle push.

"You can go little **one**," he said, looking at Kara rushing to the last bookshelf to hide her boy-bana**na** behind the books.

Icarus **took** his time walking back to the couch, painting a satisfied smile.

"Now **that** we have your attention, what do you mean '*for you*'? Was that some sort of punishment?" A curious Icarus Asked while opening the box of pizza.

"Well, we were offended," said Gray with a critical tone as he walked back to his desk. He sat down, organizing the books Kara misplaced to find the banana she left there. He glanced at its weird decoration for a moment - - then placed it back where he found it with a deadpan face.

"We took you in - - and protected you, yet there you are, saying you don't fit in here. We're not good enough for you?" Gray said, highlighting that Icarus sounded ungrateful while saying those words. The masked man rested his crossed arms on the desk, waiting for a satisfying response from Icarus, who stuttered in confusion. He did not expect that a cold person like Gray could be sensitive.

"Well - - you know - - I **me**ant I am human, and you are__" a hesitant Icarus spoke low at first, carefully avoiding any insolent commentary, until he decided not to,

"__I don't really know what you are! I thought you were a mage at first. But now, I'm not sure if I even have category to place you in!" Icarus kept on spilling excuses instead of a direct apology:

"Not to forget Kara, the cleaners, that Soul-Aymen weirdo - - and now that iron head. The last two obviously hate me"

Gray listened to him silently as he blubbered, giving him the chance to speak his mind.

_ (9-5) * (12-2) * (11-2) * (23-5) * (3-12) * (10-5) (1-5) (4-10) * (8-1)

CHAPTER EIGHT

"Is there anything ordinary **in** this place?" a beefing Icarus whinged with a down grin.

Gray freed a flat and long sigh while resting a palm on his **mask**.

"Define ordinary," he asked with a relaxed tone, resting his chin on a relaxed fist, simply waiting for a straight answer.

"What do you mean?" Quizzical, Icarus asked low

"Define ordinary," calm, Gray repeated with a slower and higher pitch.

"Ordinary is - - no**r**ma**l**," replied Icarus with a blunt look on his face. He bit his lower lip softly, taking a moment to think.

"To fit inside **the** usual standards - - I think," he added with a dim smile, thinking he was winning an argument.

"Standards! Like - - a **s**pecifi**c** place and time?" hinted Gray, somewhat nodding his head, and so did Icarus a**g**ree**i**ng while reaching for a slice of pizza.

"Thus, according to this place - - and time, you are the abnormal," Gray grinned, casually lifting his shoulder to a half-shrug.

Icarus forced a wide and sulking smile on his face, exchanging awkward stares with a glazed Gray.

"Ha Ha!" he laughed dully, throwing the slice of pizza back in the box and slammed the cover shut.

"You know what, you validated my point," he agreed pessimistically, leaning back while spreading his legs halfway.

Gray stared at him for moments, thence looked at the lowest drawer on his left. He tapped his finger on its handle, thinking if he should open it or not. It took him a while but decided to do so, and when he did, he swiftly snatched a lapis book out.

"Finish your food," he said, gently placing the book on the desk, thus do**ub**tfully tapping a claw on its h**a**rd cover before noticing Icarus locking an eye on the book.

"Go on, why you looking at us?" he admonished, rushing Icarus to finish what was on the box instead of curiously gazing at the book and him.

Icarus lowered his eyes while opening the box. He grabbed the two slices left and placed one on the other. It took him a few bites to finish.

"So, what now?" asked Icarus with his mouth full, wiping a hand on his pants while standing.

(13-8) (8-3) * (1-5) * (10-4) * (12-4) (26-1) (26-7) * (3-14)

"There is - - a napk**in** on your__" Gray fr**ow**ned, shaking his head disappointed, but Icarus continued rubbing his hand on his clothes.

"__never mind. Hey, take off your shirt," **a** direct Gray ordered Icarus while leaving his desk.

Shame-free, without asking, Icarus did as told. He threw his shirt on the couch before rotating his arms as a warm-up.

"Do you know how to increase your body tem**p**e**r**ature?" Gray asked, **s**ta**n**ding closer to Icarus **who** jiggled his loo**se**ned hand right and left as if he were getting ready to fight, but in the Mingan's mind, he thought Gray was about to apply some sort of spell on his body or something of such.

"Of course, it's a basic breathing technique," Icarus answered with a breathy voice while stretching his arms up,

"But only to a limited extent"

"Exactly. We will help you break those limits," said Gray, handing the book to Icarus,

"And step by step, you may turn into a freak like us"

"Hey, I didn't say you guys are freaks," Icarus argued

"You didn't have to," Gray interjected, offering the book for Icarus to grab.

Icarus looked at Gray's slight smile, thence at the book.

He postponed patching things with his mentor for later. Focused, he tilted his head left and righ**t**, then released a strong puff and s**i**gnalled Gray before grabbing the book, but Gray teleported him before he touched it,

"Swish!"

1916 – Ukraine. Aghast, Icarus found himself s**cr**a**mbli**n**g** inside a heavy body of water. He sensed an unusual **c**oldn**ess** snatching the heat out of his body, but that was not the problem. The real dilemma was that he couldn't see anything. It was pitch black darkness.

"*Night - - No, it's not. There is no source of light*," he thought while trying to swim haphazardly.

'*Or is it one of Gray's tricks?*' He mused pensively, not knowing if he were moving towards the surface or the depth of this unknown place.

The Mingan stopped his frenzied navigation. He relaxed his muscles while slowly reaching for his eyes. He used a thumb and a forefinger to sense them, to find a seal of his own skin. His eyes were glued shut as if his eyelid fused together. But even in such a state, Icarus managed to stay calm. He remained

_ (3-8) * (8-1) (1-8) * (7-9) (1-4) (25-6) * (8-5) * (24-7)

motionless until he noticed his body slight**ly** floating towards his left. **It** was a brilliant move to use the air inside to detect the surface's direction. Icarus tightened his muscles while cocooning his body, then stretched it fully **at** once, supp**o**rti**n**g is with a slow flap from his wings.

"Bubbles!"

Gratitude to his wings, Icarus bolted towards the surface faster than a swordfish. He used his arms to cover his head, knowing that if the water were that much chilly, surely there will be a solid cover of ice waiting for him up ahead.

Finally, Icarus bro**k**e through the hard surface and up to a freedom, spinning fast to expel most of the water **off** his body.

"Crash!"

The Mingan relaxed his exaggerated panting with steady deep breaths, and while regaining his body temperature, his eyelids detached, allowing him to see again.

Icarus first noticed mountains of white and stained with splashes of cedar rocks coiling most of the area, while a white group of trees covered the rest, and down at the snowy shore of **t**he l**ake**, he glimpsed Gray with his hand raised and fingers wiggling a hello to Icarus.

The Mingan swayed down smoothly, hiding his wings right before landing on the thick snow.

"We apologize for that. We were having some difficulties with these specific memories," said Gray simply.

"**D**iffic**u**ltie**s**, huh! No need to lie. You're still mad at me but I'm not. And I don't mind your extreme methods when it comes to training, but don't you think it's useless?" asked Icarus, approaching Gray while pointing his finger back at the lake.

"Physical training should be in the real world, not a memory," he argued with a shivering tone while rubbing his hands against his arms for warmth.

"To the contrary. This is about skill, and mind training is best for skills, likewise, faster," Gray clarified, stopping Icarus from using his hands to warm himself with a quick smack on the chest.

"Stop this and use the heating technique. You said you know how," he instructed, crossing his arms in observing mode.

"Of course I do, I call it Oven. But I don't believe it will work with this level of coldness," **a** negative Ic**ar**u**s** said pessimistically then shook his body getting ready. He closed his eyes, focusing on his breathing. **The** Mingan started absorbing small amounts of air through his nose, causing his chest to slightly pu**mp** with each one taken, and a**f**t**e**r getting his full, he puffed a long breath through his mouth, freeing a body of **va**pour. He repeated the same process, and on the fourth time, Icarus's skin smoked out with steam.

"I feel it - - it's warm!" Amazed, Icarus said with a smile while trying to maintain his concentration.

"Not just warmth, I feel hot," he stated with a cheerful smile.

"Your vessel is evolving - - fully, not just speed and strength," said Gray while snapping his stiff f**i**ng**er**s.

The masked man beckoned Icarus silently before walking north, thrusting his hands in his pockets, and un**like** Icarus **who** had his feet sink all the way down with every step taken, Gray walked as if the bottom of his feet barely touched the snow.

_ (14-6) * (2-3) * (6-5) (4-13) (12-5) * (14-8) * (5-4) (2-5) * (3-10)

CHAPTER EIGHT

"We want you to be ready for a**n**yth**ing**, cold, heat, **hu**nger - - everything," Gray stated, entering the woods, followed by a slow and observant student.

"My Oven technique is more than enough now," Icarus gloated, noticing that he was falling back because of his curious na**tur**e, so he rushed his feet to walk with Gray side by side.

W**he**n he caught up, G**r**ay slapped the side of his arm.

"What do you mean enough? You're still way behind," he reprimanded Icarus, putting his arm back inside his pocket.

"Think of all possibilities. What if you had **to** apply it while fighting? Or use it to break your speed limit and agility?" Gray hinted, showing Icarus that he was too quick to be full of himself.

Icarus painted a concerned expression, realizing Gray's words, at the same time, curious,

"True," he agreed, looking at the faint steam he had in his hand, reducing to nothingness.

"Look kid, when we say '*we want you ready,*' we do not mean in this realm alone, but all nine," Gray added in a serious tone, freeing a hand out of his pocket.

He approached the nearest tree, and with a relaxed grip, he gave its trunk a quick finger-flick, causing a small pile of snow to drop right on his open palm. Gray squeezed the snow into a ball.

"You see this - - it is considered a hot beverage in Jötunheimr. In fact, this cold snow can burn the **skin** of a frost giant," he claimed, dropping the ball down and causing a tortoiseshell to fly out of a hollow beneath the tree.

"So tell me, young Mingan, what if you clash with frost giants? There is no **sun** in their realm you know," Gray queried, observing the butterfly flying up his way. He snatched it.

"At your level, you will be squashed," he warned with a deep voice, whilst squeezing his grip to crush the butterfly.

Icarus stared at the butterfly being dropped dead **from** Gray's grip, putting himself in the same situation.

"I understand, and I will do my best to improve this technique to its limits," he acknowledged Gray's lesson with a serious stare.

After a five minutes' walk, the two met the end of the woods at a steep slope of dark rocks, and at the bottom, a small village of fewer than fifty **s**hac**k**s. They were all similar in shape, likewise, the white snowy roofs, coloured in different shades of brown, but mostly burnt-um**be**r.

"Take us down," said **Gr**ay, lifting his arms **to** the sides, just enough to expose his armpits. Icarus stood behind Gr**ay**, thus placed h**is** hands under his arms. He blew **out** his wings and flew his mentor down in the count of seconds.

"Thank you," said G**r**ay when his apprentice placed him gently next t**o** the first house.

Icarus turned round the faint sun, fading behind the mountain, turning the sk**y** slightly d**a**rker than usua**l** when sunset. However, a group of children didn't mind the dark. **T**he**y** were playing in a yard cantered by a dry oak tree.

One of the boys ran to the tree, and while he was attempting to climb, he paused when he saw the door of the house facing him opening.

"**She**'s out. Hey, come, she's out," he shouted with a grin, **call**ing for his fri**e**n**d**s.

The kids gathered around the tree, staring with excitement at the opened door while exchanging giggles and humorous thrusts, except for one girl, she stayed behind.

Gray sighed, walking to the side of the tree, throwing annoyed stares at the kids before him.

"Icarus, the next time you think that you do not belong, **we** wa**nt** you to remember this," said Gray in a flat tone

"This person can't resist the sun's spectra, nor can she properly breathe the air outside," he added, fixed on the door that caught the attention of everyone around, and so did Icarus curiously.

A bronze scuba helmet appeared out of that door, worn by a little girl in an ivory dress. Her arm coiled a thin flask half her size, one connected to her helmet with a rubber tube. So many thoughts roamed Icarus's head.

"Why is she wearing that thing? Wait, her dress - - Isn't she cold?" he gasped, hesitant to ask another question to an answerless Gray, for he seemed too focused on what will happen next.

The scuba kid placed one of her bare feet outside, rubbing it against the thick snow.

"Narnia, be careful, and stay with your sister - - don't stray away," said a woman from inside, holding a wooden spoon.

Narnia turned to the woman with her hand adjusting the oversized helmet.

_ (13-1) * (20-12) (20-13) * (5-3) * (3-9) * (2-7) * (13-12) (14-1)

"I will Mama, and Spasybi for the candy uncle," she said in a cheerful tone, her spoken words slightly echoed inside her helmet.

"You're welcome, Pryntsesa," a man replied with a throaty voice, without showing himself.

Narnia leaped outside, thrusting her feet in the snow. She hardly waved to the kids, for she had to adjust her helmet every two seconds.

"So she's the book - - owner! A girl!" Icarus commented incredulously, looking at Gray with his brows down.

Gray crossed his arms while placing his right hand on his chin then painted the most honest smile Icarus ever saw on his face.

"The most beautiful girl in this world," he smiled, walking closer to Narnia.

All the kids started shouting in a singsong tone, while trying to flee Narnia, who ran after them around the yard.

"**Ice freak** - - **dirty fask**"

Peeved, Icarus glared at the kids insulting the little girl.

"These little bastards," he grunted, clutching his hands into fists. And when he turned to his mentor, he caught him snapping a finger to stop time.

"You look mad. How about showing you something to wash that expression off?" Gray smirked, walking towards Narnia, who had her arms stretched, reaching for a boy up front.

"You - - step aside," Gray whispered low, placing a hand on the kid she was chasing. The boy walked away with a blank face, as if he were an android.

Gray beckoned Icarus to stand by his side, facing Narnia.

"Are you ready?" queried Gray with a grin, swaying his hand around Narnia's helmet to turn it from bronze to transparent.

The first glance widened Icarus's eyes. He painted a surprised smile followed by a spontaneous chuckled.

"She looks - - magical!" Amazed, Icarus complimented Narnia's pure and innocent beauty, but what really captivated him was her warm and innocent smile. Although they insulted

her, called her **names** and some even threw snowballs at her, she still had that wide smile patched on her soft, round face, free of hatred.

"Thank you," Icarus said low, trying to press a loosened lock of hair behind her ear, forgetting that he's incapable of doing so. He retreated his hand slowly;

however, Gray place his han**d** on Icarus's shoulder then nodded, hinting that he should try.

Icarus reac**he**d for the lock of hair again and succeeded. He pressed her messy hair behind her ear and while doing **so**, he couldn't pr**even**t himself from poking her fluffy cheeks.

"As a Mingan who can read people - - **and** met a **l**oa**d**, I dare to say, this lovely girl is the purest human being I have ever seen," Icarus stated with a **smile** then straightened his stand, allowing Gray to snap his finger and reset time.

The two sauntered to the side, watching Narnia play with the other kids, or at least that's what **she** thought.

Icarus closed his eyes, using his breathing technique to warm his body after starting to feel the cold again. This time, he tried to breathe while talking.

"Can't she - - feel - - the cold?" Icarus asked, maintaining the correct amounts of breaths taken.

"We don't know," answered Gray, looking heavenward, thence towards

_ (4-11) * (4-8) * (10-4) * (7-16) (1-5) * (6-8) * (3-2) (6-11)

Narnia approached by the **g**irl that wasn't inter**es**ted in playing with her the entire time.

"Time to go home," said the girl with a cold tone, grabbing Narnia's hand tightly.

"Caught you," Narnia chuckled, wrapping her arms around the girl's waist. But the feeling wasn't mutual. Narnia was propelled away and down with a vigorous push.

The other kids started laughing scornfully at both of them.

"The Dirty Fask hugged you. Eww! **No**w you're dirty too," a boy laughed loudly, pressing the snow with both hands to make a solid snow-ball. The rest of the children started singing after him:

"Dirty Fask, Dirty Fask, Dirty Fask"

The girl seemed ashamed. She tightened the woollen collar roll of her coat all the way up, covering half of her face out. She glared at the blunt Narnia who stood up, shaking the snow off her lower back.

"You see what you did, I told you not to touch me. Agh, I **hate** you," the girl snarled, rushing her steps towards Narnia's house, and before reaching the door, the boy tossed the heavy snow-ball straight to the back of her head.

"Pok!"

She fell down on her face but got up quickly, slowly running inside the house while keeping a hand on the back of her head.

"I'm sorry, Olena, come back," shouted Narnia with a sad voice, running after the girl under an enfilade assault of snowballs. When she finally reached the door, it was shut on her face.

"Olena, open - - I'm sorry," Narnia apologized repeatedly while knocking on the door, until her mother opened the door and let her in.

Icarus's forehead creased, looking at the kids laughing proudly for bullying their friend.

"Kids can be real jerks. This is why I never attempted to have one," he **gru**nte**d**, trying to smack a kid who ran past him, but his hand went through instead.

"What about the other girl? Is she her sister?" Chagrined, Icarus asked, then turned to Gray, who walked to the boy who missed Icarus's slap, also the one who targeted Olena's head.

"Twins, she's **her** twin **sister**," answered Gray, smacking the boy's **hea**d and making him turn on his friend. One push lead to a**no**the**r**, the two boys started a fight, and Gray gave Icarus thumbs up as a mission accomplished.

Icarus was laughing on the inside. He suppressed a smile of satisfaction, then inquired p**en**si**v**el**y**,

"What now? Does this mean - - it's okay to not belong?" He quizzed, while enjoy**ing** the fight as more of those wicked kids got involved.

While **l**aughing at a boy for getting kicked in **th**e balls, Gra**y** took a few steps back for a better view.

"**Who** said we're done here!" He smirked cunningly, looking at an old man who ran towards the fight, forcing the kids to break apart. Gray's sly smile faded, turning to a faint glare of annoyance towards the old man.

Seeing his mentor more occupied with a kids' fight more than what's really important, Icarus shoved his face into Gray's space, lowering his head while looking at Gray with a brow lifted and wide impatient eyes,

"So! Are we at least done with this imaginary scene?" he said in an unsure tone

"Who said this is imaginary?" Ambiguous, Gray replied simply

Gray walked towards Narnia's house without adding any calcification, leaving a puzzled Icarus behind.

"Also, we will stay the night. We continue tomorrow," he said with a high-pitch, looking at the kids being scolded by their parents on his right.

When the masked man reached the door of Narnia's house, he orbited to face Icarus who was on his tail with his palm up.

"You stay here," he ordered in a fixed tone

"Why!" a baffled Icarus argued, slowly pushing Gray's palm off his unclad chest.

"To train obviously, grow your - - oven," blithe, Gray replied rapidly with a strict tone.

"And we forbid you to sleep," he added while walking backwards and vanishing through the door. Icarus waited for him to fade inside the house, to safely flip him off.

"We saw that. You're inside our mind you idiot," Gray castigated him from inside, but Icarus didn't seem to care.

CHAPTER EIGHT

The Mingan walked to the side then s**at** down under the house's window with his legs crossed, and without delay, he **st**a**r**ted practicing his technique forthwith. However, he **was** slightly distracted since he could hear the loud argument Na**rn**ia's family was having.

"I don't want her to play with me any**m**or**e**," he heard Olena sobbing first, then her mother consoli**dat**ing h**e**r:

"Dochka, she's your sister, and you know how much she loves you"

And right after, a faint confirmation came from a sad Narnia:

"I love you Olena"

Hearing her voice painted a sad smile on the Mingan's face, one hidden by the rising steam that his skin freed.

"Off to bed now," the mother ordered them with a soft voice. She closed a door and walked to the room where Icarus was sitting.

"I'm sorry you had to witness that, Brate," she said with a sigh

"Don't worry a**bo**ut it," a man with croaky voice replied, making Icarus's eyelids quiver as his brows fell down with suspicion. That voice was familiar to his ear.

"But you know, you can live in a castle if you wish, yet you chose this - - nowhere!" said the man again with a disappointed tone

"I already told you I want her to live a normal life__" she whispered but the man whisper-shout over her words,

"__but she's not normal, Olena could be too," he highlighted with a clear voice.

"We - - are not normal," he added slowly

Icarus's suspicion rose to a point he lost focus. He tried to stand up and peek through the window to see who the mysterious guest was.

"Focus - - on your training," Gray spoke inside Icarus's head, preventing him from standing up or eavesdropping.

"I am," replied a dishonest Icarus, giving his head a sharp shake to the left and back, thus reset to breathing.

Early on the next morning, a drowsy Icarus fought hard to keep his heavy eyelids separated. The Mingan was used to staying awake for days, but with that cold and maintain a technique that hard was a different story.

"Clang!"

Icarus heard a noise behind the house. He didn't bother to **sta**nd, for he could **si**mply lean all **the** way to the side to peek from behind the wall, and when he did, he saw Gray walking halfway up the steep slope, heading to the woods. Icarus was more lazy than curious, so he adjusted his cadaver back, thinking if his **me**ntor needed him he would've called for him. He gathered a pile of snow to place on his lap, and some on his shoulder, then back to training.

Gray walked through the woods, and back to the lake. He stared at the lake from left to right, seeing a **wh**ite bunny with red eyes on the **o**ther side, staring back at him. The man in black walked to the edge of the lake, taking some time to enjoy a chilly beauty. Afterwards, he bent both knees down, placing his left elbow against the lower part of his thigh, thus rubbed a palm on the lake's solid surface.

"This is for your own good," he whispered, easily thrusting his claw in the ice as if the frosty surface was a bar of butter. He took small inhales through his nose followed by a rapid exhale, one that puffed like a hot breath through the fissures of his pressed teeth: a moment after, his pierced claw glowed red, and from that point, the lake's surface beamed in a flash, melting the ice to a thinner cover.

"That will do," he said low, shrinking his long nail out of the ice then tapped it gently, causing a shallow crack to extend wide through the lake.

Back in the village, and after the shouts of several roo**ster**s, the people started roaming around. One walked past a sleepy Icarus. The bearded passerby woke the Mingan up with a loud hello tossed to the neighbour.

Slightly jumbled, Icarus yawned, rubbing his eyes to notice that his eyes were welling, and while the confused Mingan was wiping his cheeks dry, Gray stepped out of Narnia's house through the wall on his apprentice's side.

"Well done," he said, stretching his arms up, then massaged his shoulder and neck.

"Where were you?" Icarus asked after he facepalmed, drowsily standing to stretch after an exhausting night.

Hiding his hands in his pockets, a blunt Gray answered with a question:

"What do you mean?"

"Lock!"

The door opened, interrupting the two, and out of it walked Olena, zipping her coat with one hand while grabbing a torn straw bag in the other.

_ (2-4) * (1-12) (4-14) * (2-1) (19-11) * (8-6) (8-13)

"I mean the woods!" Icarus resumed his question, looking at Olena running away with small steps because of her tight coat, while placing the fol**de**d bag under her armpit.

"Don't worry about it," **re**plied Gray, sauntering towards the oak tree.

He stopped under the low branches, then u**sed** his right to call for Icarus.

"Sit here," he ordered with a tap of his foot **to** point a spot two feet apart from the tree. Icarus sat down obediently, not minding the muddy snow.

"Now, stage two," Gray smirked, taking his hands off his pockets then gave it a slight shake.

He leaned down facing his clueless apprentice, whilst placing the back of his hands on the snow. Gray started raising both hands slowly, evoking from the ground around Icarus four walls of rough ice, growing taller to a height controlled by Gray's hands. Icarus knew the ice was extremely thick, for he could barely see through, but thank**fu**lly, the upper side was still open.

"Smack!"

Gray clapped his ha**nd**, mani**fe**sting a roof of ice in an instant.

"Hey!" Icarus protested, impatiently punching the ice above his head. He slid his hand against the wall that stood between him and his mentor.

"At least open a window so I can breathe," a peeved Icarus spoke with a high-pitch so he can be heard, punching the wall again with the soft side of his fist.

"Bam!"

Gray didn't bother shouting back. Instead, he replied telepathically:

"No. If you want to breathe, you need to melt this ice prison with whatever air you have inside"

"Hey, wait! There isn't enough air to melt all of this, and what if I run out of air?" A belligerent Icarus debated frantically while front kicking the wall, knowing it won't work.

"Well - - obviously you will die," stolid, Gray responded in an apathetic tone

Hearing that forced a side grin on Icarus's face, he was sure Gray wouldn't risk his life.

"That must be a joke! I can't die inside a memory," he said incredulously, forcing a breathy chuckle out with a trivial of doubt.

"Not your carcass - - but your brain will. Don't worry, we already made a copy of all your memories, so - - even if you die, it will still be you - - but not you," a deadpan Gray clar**i**fie**d** briefly then added in a provocative tone while walking away:

"Good luck"

Agape, Icarus processed the words, seeing Gray's wavy figure fading away.

"Come back," bug-eyed, Icarus shouted loud then used his hand to quickly block his mouth. While holding his breath, he looked in all directions, thinking of what to do.

He began examining the chilly walls. The sun's spectra caught Icarus's eye as it invaded his cage. He gently rubbed a hand on the illumin**ate**d spot, sensing the sun's apricity, thus observed t**he** drops of wate**r** sliding down his shivering fingers. He prostrated hurriedly, placing his palms against that same bright ice.

"Pants!"

The Mingan started applying Oven while trying to **con**centrate all of it on one h**and**. His face and body turned reddish then **s**l**o**w**l**y paled except for his hand.

After minutes of deep concentration, the tips of his fingers glowed a brighter red, as if his hand were harnessing lava beneath its skin.

"I got it, you bastard," Icarus grinned as his hands started to melt the ice and sink in.

Determined, Icarus wasn't ready to give up, even with the slow process. It took him several hours to pierce a hole through the wall; finally, a source of air.

A fatigued Mingan shoved his face close to the melted cave, taking a pining breath, and while gaining respiration, he glimpsed Gray through the hole. Icarus smiled, then spoke through the gap like a speaker.

"Ha! I did it, you hear me you sadist bastard," a cheerful Icarus laughed out loud, falling on his back to continue breathing at ease.

Gray sat on the east side intentionally, to show Icarus that he did believe in his skills. He knew his apprentice was smart enough to figure it out. However, he had a look on his face, one that prevented Icarus of his satisfaction.

One of Olena's friends ran out of the woods and down to the village in a rush, as if he were being chased.

"Auntie, Auntie," haunted, he screamed harshly while running straight to Narnia's house.

"Knocks!"

CHAPTER EIGHT

The boy drummed the door vigorously while shouting.

"Auntie - - hurry - - Auntie!"

He ran to the side window, thence back to the door. Icarus stood hunched. Baffled, hearing the **no**ises ou**t**side. He peeked through the cold chasm to see Gray in the same place.

"What's happening?" A wary Icarus asked, pushing some ice scraps off the way.

Gr**ay** stare**d** at him without saying a word, thence turned round to Narnia's mother stepping out of her **home**.

She ran urgently towards the woods, followed by the boy.

Gray looked back at Icarus, who glimpsed a slight image of the woman running.

"Some**one** is about to die," Gray spoke telepathically. His tone **was** dead and so was his expression.

"What do you mean? Let me out," Icarus demanded, throwing a sharp punch against the wall. He felt a rage but didn't know its source. On the other hand, his mentor was cold as the ice cage he was trapped in. He replied with a faint smile and a shrug.

"Who is it?" An irritated Icarus asked, but no reply. He knew the only way was to free himself on his own.

The Mingan suppressed his ire then restarted the Oven technique, and gratitude to the fresh air he received, he didn't need to be conservative.

"Click!"

The door behind him opened, interrupting his focus. He rotated a neck first, then his entire body when recognizing the shape of that big head. It was Narnia's de**for**med image stepping out of the house. She ran towards the woods, ghosting Icarus's imploring screams.

"No No, No - - Come back, please, no! Pryntsesa, come back," his shouts faded slowly with her going out of sight.

A sudden headache agonized Icarus, one quickly turned into a sharp pain, and while squeezing his head with both hands, he saw a faint reflection of his face on the crystal wall, turning to Gray's mask then vanished alongside the pain when he blinked.

A confused Icarus turned back slowly. He glanced at Gray with his welled eyes. He shook his head no faintly, while his partner nodded his head yes,

_ (12-1) * (8-2) (8-1) * (10-1) * (12-11) * (4-4) (4-5) * (9-6) * (25-1)

confirming the de**s**pairing thought Icarus had, and forcing Icarus's purple lips to qui**ver** until he pressed them tight.

"No," Icarus said faintly with a **we**a**k** tone and wretched voice, feeling a drop on his cheek.

"No," he repeated with a pai**ne**d whisper. His eyes glistened, turning his vision glossy. The Mingan squeezed his eyes shut as a weak attempt to fight back his tears.

'*Why does it feel painful?*'

A confused Icarus rubbed his eyes then rested his forehead on the cold wall, roaming in thoughts with quivered whispers:

'*I don't remember being this emotional*'

He gently tapped his head on the wall,

'*But why - - do I feel this - - loss?*'

"P**lu**ks!"

He started tapping his head harder. And harder until the slow taps turned to head-blows that caused his forehead to bleed. He stared at Gray again while the blood streamed between his eyes and down to his runny nose, shaking his head no.

"I swear I didn't mean to - - forgive me," crestfallen, he wept with a nasal voice.

Seeing him sobbing and begging, an upset Gray looked away while standing, and without warning, he turned to a body of black fog, arising, then da**she**d towards the woods.

When Gray disappeared out of sight, Icarus's appalled face creased, slowly turning black and angry.

"Pants!"

Icarus breathed rapidly, turning his hands carmine-red in seconds. He placed them on the gap he pierced, melting the ice faster than before.

At the same time, deep in the woods, ran the little Narnia, following her mother. She held her air-flask tightly to keep it safe, while the sharp rocks and broken bra**nch**es cut her bare small feet, but that didn't stop her or even slow her down. She continued, leaving behind a trail of bloody footprints.

"Olena!"

Hearing the screams of her mother motiv**ate**d the little girl to dash faster towards the **l**ake.

CHAPTER EIGHT

Her mother, alongside some kids stood on the shore, calling with dreadful and fearsome shouts **a**t Olena. Narnia turned round the lake's midst while wiping the foggy glass of **her** helmet, just enough to see her sister trapped in the lake; her lower body sank through the thin ice while her upper body strived to stay up. Olena**'s** arms kept reaching for solid ice to end up breaking every piece she landed a hand on.

After a phase of hesitation, her mother stepped cautiously onto the ice to **save** her child. The first step was safe, and the moment **she** forced a smile to ease Olena's fear, her leg plugged in on the second step.

"Aagh!" pained, she shrieked loudly while taking her leg out. Her skin was steaming like a cube of ice that was splashed with boiling water. While trying to retreat back to the shore, her left arm sank in halfway, and the same thing happened again. The kids and several villagers who got there rushed to help her out then jolted their bodies away, confused about what was going on with her leg and arm.

"Please, anyone," she wailed, begging for someone to help her daughter, but no one there dared to.

While she cried heartily, Narnia ran past her and onto the lake. Her agape mother gazed at the brave girl silently, she knew it was her daughter, but couldn't believe it. After a moment of thought loss, she came back to her senses.

"NARN - -" she **scream**ed but her voice gasped at the end.

"Cough!"

She recklessly tried to follow, but one of the men pulled her back and kept holding her tight.

Narnia moved forward, ignoring her mother's cries, and the cuts all over her legs, for one of her legs thrust inside every few steps taken. What kept the courageous girl going without hesitation was the aghast looks on her sister's face, a sobbing stare that said '*please help.*'

The crowds turned from scared and concerned to hyped and hopeful. Everyone started encouraging Narnia to keep going while preparing a long rope to pull out the two.

"You can do it. Keep going, just a few steps more," they cheered loudly.

Narnia kept raising their cheers and hopes with every step closer to her sister, but those hopes shattered a moment after. Olena was betrayed by her own strength. **She** couldn't hold anymore. Her hands loosened, causing her cadaver to slowly skid down the bar of ice then sank in.

She slowly blinked her **ey**es on the sun's faint lights while **drowning**. Her last vi**ew** wasn't as bad as she **th**ought, which made her surrender and let go. Her weak vision followed the last bubble she freed, wobbling up to the surface.

"Splash!"

Before shutting her eyes off, she glimpsed a figure swimming her way; however, her eyelids were too heavy.

Moments after, Olena felt a heavy pressure coiling her head, to notice a few seconds more that she was able to breathe.

"What!" lost, she whispered, narrowly opening her eyes, to see a snow-white hair through a round window, swaying like waves of white snakes. She recognized that unique hair colour instantly. It was Narnia's.

Olena felt her sister's strong embrace around her waist. She remembered how she always pushed her away every time she hugged her, but this time she couldn't. She also glimpsed strings of blood rising from the bottom, so she looked down to see a small pair of bleeding feet hardly **k**icki**n**g the water.

Narnia swam her sister like a football tackler, pushing Olena under a rooftop of ice after failing to go up while holding another person. However, Narnia got used to the density of the water. She made it halfway to the shore, and giving her speed, she was confident that she could save her sister, she even had a flashy thought of the two of them getting closer after this, but, Narnia released her last bubble.

Olena was always pushing Narnia away out of shame, but this time, the roles had changed. It was Narnia's turn to push her sister away, out of love. And even in such a dark moment, Olena received a warming smile inside that frozen body of water.

"Narnia!" Olena quivered, seeing Narnia parting away.

"Come back," faint, Olena's scream came out as a shaken whisper.

"Please forgive me, I will play with you all the time," she begged, throwing a desperate hand upfront, miserably reaching for her younger sister.

"Please come back. I will never push you away again," she sobbed, trying to swim towards her.

Narnia used a finger to poke her chest twice then pointed it at Olena before placing both hands upon her heart.

CHAPTER EIGHT

Tears **ra**n down Olena's blue cheeks.

"I love you too, always **will**," she cried with a croaky throat, hardly moving her hands.

"Woosh!"

A rope of dark smoke grabbed Olena's leg. And like a black whip, it pulled her towards **th**e shore and up like a f**is**h.

While she was thrown out onto her mother's arm, Icarus swooped from the sky and **di**v**e**d inside the lake.

The Mingan swam down, searching for Narnia inside a body of darkness, until a strong beam from the depths of the lake dashed his way, forcing his arm to block his eyes. He peeked carefully as the light slightly faded.

It was her. Narnia was wrapped in a blue glow. Her legs joined together then fused, elong**at**ing while her feet flattened, turning into an almost transparent caudal-fins, while her legs rounded into a long fishtail.

"Bubbles!"

Icarus used a hand to block his mouth after running out of breath. He kicked his feet, heading to the surface with his eyes fixed on Narnia, who eventually transformed into a complete mermaid, looking more beautiful and pure in that form.

She gave him a wave before diving deep into a low dark pit.

Icarus burst out, spreading his wings wide. He quickly vaporized the water off his skin, keeping an eye on the chattered surface of the lake, thence round to Narnia's mother and Olena crying their hearts out. He attempted to dive again, but Gray's voice interrupted:

"It's time,"

Icarus_jolted his sight right and left to glimpse Gray's coat b**e**hi**n**d one of the trees in the west. He gave Olena and her mother a last stare of pity then flew to Gray.

While approaching his mentor, he started seeing that all the trees behind Gray were dead; an entire field. Even the ground underneath was lifeless, bleak. What happened?

A Puzzled Icarus walked past Gray, gazing at the circle of death before him. Before getting the chance to ask, his shoulder was grabbed by Gray to force him back inside the book he was holding in his right,

"Swish!"

Icarus was thrown from the library's roof onto the couch, while Gray fell from one of the moon lanterns, dropping on one knee **but** stood up quickly.

"Are you okay?" Worried, Icarus asked, **pl**acing his hand on Gray's shoulder, and when he did, he felt a faint quiver.

"You look - - sick," he said, try**in**g to face Gray, who gently pushed Icarus's hand away to take a step closer to his desk.

"We are fine," a weak Gray replied, barely standing.

"You saw her. She fo**un**d where she belon**ged**. Lived happily ever after," said a reluctant Gray while sharply coughing after every sentence.

He tottered left, but Icarus grabbed him before he fell.

"Easy big guy!" said Icarus, moving him to the couch

"Something is off about you," he hinted, gently placing him on the couch.

"Nothing is 'off' kid. Anyway, **Narnia** is you, and the library is your lake," Gray explained the objective behind the journey,

"Lesson received"

He undid the first buttons of his shirt then rubbed his chest, taking a deep breath, while Icarus tried to help by adjusting his posture straight whilst giving him a disillusioned stare.

"You can be honest with me," a concerned Icarus said low, gently placing his palm on Gray's chest to monitor his heartbeats.

"Trust me. Or at least tell me if this is new. Is it because of me?" he quizzed for the truth for he knew something seemed strange.

"Actually, those feelings I experienced inside, that was not me - - was it?" He asked calmly, but received no answer.

"Come on, just trust me and speak," he sighed but annoyingly shouted the last word.

Kara was alarmed by Icarus's shout. She peeked from up her cubical room. She read the atmosphere, knowing it was best to not interrupt, however, that didn't stop her from curiously eavesdropping.

"Correct," replied Gray while panting. He rested his left hand on the couch while placing the other on his mask.

"It wasn't you, it was ours - - it was mine," he admitted with a throaty voice, pulling the mask an inch off his face. It was the first time Gray referred to himself as a singular.

_ (2-10) * (13-6) * (3-7) (8-5) (8-8) * (5-6)

CHAPTER EIGHT

Icarus saw the **fe**atures of Gray's nose, mouth and chin **changing**, **ex**cept for the half covered behind the mask, but Icarus knew, his mentor's face changed entirely.

"Sobs!"

Tears ran down the ma**ster's** cheeks, as if the mask were there to hide his face, powers, intents, **li**kewise, emotions.

"What you saw there - - was an illusion I made," Gray said with a completely different voice. Icarus stood there agape, full of confusion.

"She loved mermaids most - - we used to read **her** fairytales about **Si**rens, Merrows, Aicaya and all kinds of mermaids. Some were real stories, but she didn't know that," Gray smiled sadly, telling Icarus about Narnia's fantasies.

"So I chose - - mermaid - - for her," he snivelled, tapping the upper edge of his mask against his forehead **with**out revealing his face.

"But - - the truth is - - it wasn't for her, it was for me. To bury the guilt," Gray continued while slowly sliding a quivered hand down Icarus's face.

"I only wanted to scare her mother, that's all. For her own good. I swear. A spell was placed on Olena, one to pull her to safety before she dies. But - - but Pryntsesa wasn't supposed to be there," Gray whimpered, looking down thence up at Icarus.

"Why was she there?" He asked a pointless question out of guilt.

Icarus shook his head no, confused and speechless. But Gray nodded his head continuously while putting on a weak smile.

"Yes, Yes, Yes - - I KILLED **HER**!" he screamed indignantly then dropped his mask down.

"It was me, I killed her," he shouted on Icarus's face, mindless of his weak state.

Kara tried to look at Gray's face from above but one of the floating lanterns blocked the way while Icarus took a small step back, shocked and stupefied.

"You! It was you all along!" flabbergasted, he whispered.

"Ahem!" Gray cleared his throat then threw both hands towards the Mingan.

"Sleep," he ordered with a clear and flat tone

Icarus's eyes closed instantly when hearing the word. He fainted straight into Gray's open arms.

(1-12) (1-11) * (22-6) * (5-3) (1-4) * (12-6) * (8-9) * (8-12) (4-5)

"We do trust you son, but - - it's not time yet," Gray said, hugging Icarus kindly while trying to rub his tears dry

"We never **me**an**t** to cause you any harm, you know that. You and Kara - - are our dearest - - you will always be," a calm Gray whispered low in the ear of a sleeping Icarus.

While patting his apprentice's head, the lanterns roaming near the first section **fa**ded off one by one, leading the first section into pitch black darkness; next, followed slow heavy steps, closer to the common room.

"Eek eek!" A frightened Kara squeaked loudly before **she** rushed inside her hanged room.

The s**te**ps stopped at the line separating the dark floor from the bright one, as if that person preferred to remain hidden from the light.

"So many memories to pick, yet you chose that one!" said the man inside the darkness with a harsh voice.

Gray smirked faintly, running his hand through Icarus's hair.

"Mm! Maybe I missed seeing **her** face," he smiled sadly, hardly standing up to place Icarus's sleeping body onto the couch.

"I'm counting on you. But this time, erase everything," he said, looking down at Icarus.

"Are you sure!" the mysterious man sighed.

"Yes please," replied Gray, wearing his mask before he turned around then walked past the man until he faded into darkness.

TO BE CONTINUED

Note

All illustrations used in this work are either permitted by the creator or self-made by the author
Please, do not use any of the illustrations without permission

Credit to the artists:

Mochiibon: Icarus – Oscar
Manako: Flaco
Genko: Chaker
Kai: Yaashva
Chamu chamu: Oscar's wife – Icarus's mother (angel version)
Chano hana: Oscar's date
Hachio: Uniss – Icarus's mother (adult version)
Emomen: Aiden
Kashiwa moshi nagita: Narnia

Thank you

What did you think of The Bizarre Journey of Gray Truema?

Dear reader;

Thank you for reading **The bizarre journey of Gray Trueman**. I know you could have chosen any number of books, but you chose this one, and for that I am honestly grateful.

I'd like to hear from you and hope that you could take some time to post a **review** on **Amazon**. I Personally read all reviews and take every detail seriously. Your feedback will help this author to greatly improve his writing craft for future projects.

Dear reader, I wish you all the best in life, and thank you again for reading **The bizarre journey of Gray Trueman.**

___ *M.F Aidoudi*